REDHEADED REDEMPTION

REDHEADS BOOK 2

REBECCA ROYCE

Redheaded Redemption (Redheads #2)

E-book ISBN 978-1951349-72-1

Print ISBN 978-1-951349-75-2

Copyright @ 2021 by Rebecca Royce

Cover art by Lucy Smoke at Smokin' Hot Designs

Content Editing: Virginia Nelson

Copy Editing: Jennifer Jones at Bookends Editing

Final Proof Editing: Meghan Leigh Daigle of Bookish Dreams Editing

Formatting: CBR-Services

Published by Rebecca Royce

www.rebeccaroyce.com

To Jennie Wilson, for being my friend since the day I stepped foot in Austin.

AUTHOR'S NOTE AND TRIGGER WARNING

In the whole of my career, I haven't written a lot of trigger warnings for my books. There is a lot of controversy about them, which I won't go into here. But this is a strange year in which I find myself writing, and people have enough pain. I don't want anyone stumbling upon this book, reading it, and having the love story make anything harder for them. Because of this, I'm going to suggest if you're a person who gets triggered by reading dark content—like a past history of rape—then you shouldn't read this book. Skip it. Go no further. Return it. Don't read it. The heroine has been through some stuff. The hero is not responsible for the pain in her past, and what happens to her happened off screen. However, she will recount her experiences. If you can't read that kind of content, please don't read this book.

This is a standalone novel in a series of standalone novels. You do not *have* to read Hope's story. Layla and Bridget have not been through the kind of experiences Hope has been through. You can read Layla in *Redhead on the Run*, skip

Redheaded Redemption, and pick back up just fine with Bridget in *Real Men Love Redheads*.

I thank you for your understanding.

Also, I made up a country in this book. It is not meant to be representative of any real country, but rather a compilation of many actual places and entirely unique on its own. Please don't place political meanings where there are none or assume I'm really talking about an actual place.

Like I've said before in other books—it's fiction, y'all.

Best to all of you,
RR

Promise me you'll always remember: You're braver than you believe, and stronger than you seem, and smarter than you think.

—A.A. Milne

CHAPTER 1

MY NEPHEW WAS THE CUTEST KID EVER BORN. HE WAS. I mean, maybe every proud auntie feels that way, but they were all wrong because I was right. As I sat in the car driving me across town in five o'clock traffic, I grinned at the newest photos Layla had sent me of Noah. At two months old already, his cheeks only became more pinchable. I should fly out to Washington State to see him again soon. I'd been there when he was born. Bridget too. We were triplets—Bridget, Layla, and me—so it seemed only right that we were all there when the first of us to have a child gave birth to their baby.

I didn't know if Layla's husband, Zeke, particularly appreciated Bridget and me hanging around for the whole thing, but he kept quiet if it bothered him. He understood Layla, which meant that he didn't interfere when she needed us. Or when we needed her.

We were a package deal in some ways. Always had been. Only when we tried to deny that truth did we get ourselves into trouble.

After minutes of stops and starts in gridlock traffic, we finally arrived downtown at the new, hip, fine dining restaurant Hyperion. Ever since celebrity vlogger and all-around annoying human being Amanda Hill called the chef, Max Broadley, as delicious-looking as anything on the menu, everyone wanted to see him. Well, not me. I was going because my good friend Kylie wanted to see him, and it was her turn to pick the restaurant.

So although I lived on the Upper West Side, I headed downtown to sate her curiosity. That was what friends did, after all, and if I was nothing else, I was a good friend.

It would have been faster for me to take the subway. At this point, I could hoof it there in less time, but I wasn't *allowed* to do that.

Blah, blah, blah, I should be more careful about my safety. Apparently.

I sighed. It wasn't that I didn't know there was danger in the world. There certainly was. My sister Layla had been kidnapped for two days by the Russian mob. Those were the worst days of my life, and I could only imagine how frightening the experience was for Layla. I thanked the universe and any deities listening for her safe return all the time, but it was over. The newest worry was that my father and brother Justin were in Russia, working for a different mob over there and pissing off the original one again.

I didn't believe they intended to harm us. If Dad had gone to Russia, it was to fix things, I was sure of it. Bridget and Layla disagreed with me, but I liked to keep a hopeful mind. I couldn't walk dark paths for too long. It was too…hard.

Finally, we arrived at our destination. Yes, we were in the Financial District, practically on Wall Street. The place was hopping. While the restaurant was certainly a boutique establishment, it gave off the appearance of trying to be considered upscale. Fancy drapes hanging in tall windows could be seen from the outside.

I got out of the car followed by my security guards, two of whom were provided by the same company that drove me. Michael Li, the owner of the security company, used to work for my father and I'd known him since I was sixteen. Since he started a business of his own, Zeke, Layla's husband, hired him to take care of all of us. One of his men—Luke—would stay outside, and Theo—the other one—would find a discreet place inside to stand guard while I ate.

"Hope," Kylie squealed. "You're here. I thought you might be late and we'd miss our reservation."

We air kissed each other's cheeks. It looked pretentious, but it saved our makeup. I didn't know why people had started doing it, but that was why I'd picked up the habit. Truthfully, I was a little bit pretentious, but I'd accepted it about myself.

"You know me—I'm never late. I'm allergic to lateness, although it was a close call. You look gorgeous."

Kylie was always the lady in black. She pulled it off too. Tonight, she wore a long black skirt and a mock sleeveless shirt that showed off all her curves. Before she started her own fashion line, she'd been a plus size model. She turned heads wherever we went because she was so gorgeous. Her long black hair and dark eyes added to the look.

I'd dressed more simply for our meal. I wore gray khakis with a white collared shirt. I'd rolled the sleeves and unbuttoned the collar, so it showed off just a bit of cleavage. At twenty-four, I wanted to feel sexy, although it wasn't a look I cultivated most of the time. Normally, I went for a professional and serious appearance.

Layla was gorgeous, so much so that people used to follow her around to figure out how to dress and what to wear. Bridget managed to always look like the girl next door. I was sort of Hope in the middle, never quite sure how to dress, so I was trying something new. I'd even cut my hair. It was short, and I embraced my curls. Well, I used a lot of mousse to tame them, but I wasn't trying to straighten them anymore.

All in all, I wanted the look to work. I wanted this to be how I presented myself to the world. It needed to work because I had to have something working in my life, since everything else was getting a little blah around the corners.

We went inside. Kylie had made the reservation, so we were quickly seated. No one waited by the door because it was a solely reservation based establishment. You either had a table waiting or you didn't.

The waiter poured us water and handed us a menu.

I scanned through it. Truthfully, I loved food. Adored it. Eating was my favorite thing to do in the world. I would eat all the time if I could. Their menu aesthetically appealed to me. Someone took the time to make it appealing to the eye and easy to read with nice font and lace covered corners. *Very nice touches*.

"Will you be ordering wine tonight?"

Kylie eyed me. "I will. How about you, Hope?" I could hear the unspoken question in her voice. She wanted me to drink with her, but she knew I didn't usually do so in public, not even in restaurants. From past experiences, I knew when I let my guard down, my world exploded. Because of that, I only indulged with a trusted friend or loved one at home. When I was out, I stuck to water. Maybe an occasional seltzer if I felt sassy.

"I'm going to stick with water, thanks, but, Kylie, you should order something."

She rolled her eyes at me. As much as I liked Kylie, she didn't understand why I chose not to drink in public, as I'd never explained and I didn't intend to tonight.

4

"I'll take a bottle of this." She pointed at the menu. "Thanks."

The waiter smiled, and I smiled back at him before he left to put in our drink order.

"Once upon a time, you knew wine better than anyone else. Your sister owns a vineyard. I know you're not an alcoholic, so is it medical? What happened to you?"

I sighed. "Is it really that important that I drink? I'm not stopping you. You know, we're having fun. We always do. I just…don't do it all that often anymore." I set down my menu. I could always order fast. Tonight, I'd have tuna tartare and the oyster stew the place was supposed to be famous for. I absolutely couldn't wait.

"So, tell me about Gordon." If I got her talking about her boyfriend, she'd get off the drinking subject.

"Well…"

The maître d' who seated us returned to our table. The tall, thin man in his black suit blinked fast before saying, "Excuse me, Ms. Radford?"

I stared at him. Him recognizing me was highly unusual. Maybe Layla got interrupted at dinner years ago, but it never transferred to me. Not really. "Yes?"

"I have to ask you to leave." He cleared his throat several times.

I opened and closed my mouth. I must have misheard him. He couldn't have just said what I thought he did. That was…impossible. "Excuse me?"

"You have to leave." This time, another voice spoke, so I turned to look. *Why, it must be the chef himself.* I only saw pictures of him previously, but in person, he was such a presence, it seemed all the other people in the room disappeared.

"Why? What did she do?" Kyrie sounded downright

hysterical. I didn't answer her, too busy staring at Max Broadley.

He was tall, dark haired, with an arrogant expression on his face that radiated confidence and not giving a shit about the world. His gray eyes stabbed all the way into my soul, and I actually rubbed my chest as if they'd injured me.

"Chef, hello." I put on my best manners. The nannies had done their jobs. I knew how to behave in public. "Is something wrong? I was just admiring your beautiful place."

Flattery frequently got me where I needed to go. I knew how to make people feel good about themselves to the point that they didn't even notice me doing it.

"Yes, there's something wrong. We reserve the right to not serve whomever we want, and I don't want to serve you, so get your ass out of my restaurant before I physically haul you out."

I gasped. My security arrived at the table. Theo looked between us. "Everything okay, Ms. Hope?"

I shook my head. "No, I guess I'm being thrown out."

This had never happened to me in my entire life. *I couldn't... That was... I didn't?* "Why are you doing this?"

He turned without answering me and left me stunned with no answers. In a daze, I grabbed my purse off the side of the chair and exited without another word. I didn't want to make any more of a scene.

Kylie took my arm and waited until we were outside to speak again. "What just happened? What did you do to Max Broadley?"

I didn't have a clue, but as I glared at the restaurant, I vowed to find out. No one threw me out of places. Like it or not, I was Hope Radford. That name came with a lot of things that sucked. My father was a fugitive from the law. My sister had been hurt. My mother killed herself when I was a baby.

I'd... No, I wouldn't think about the last one. I wouldn't even let myself think it.

Regardless, I was a socialite who used my influence to raise money for causes very rich people cared about. I got things done, I made things better. I'd be damned if one temporarily trendy chef took the chance to humiliate me.

"I'm going to find out."

Kylie hugged me. "What an asshole."

I didn't say anything, but I agreed.

I MADE it home in half the time it took to get there. After toeing off my heels, I stormed to my computer. As quickly as I could, I typed his name into my search engine.

A lot of things popped up, mostly articles about his restaurant. I scanned page after page until I stopped at one that caught my attention.

Broadley's restaurant closes after rumors of trashy food is spurred by Redhead.

What? That didn't sound like Layla. She wouldn't say things like that. Did he think I was Layla? Is that why he'd thrown me out? Because he thought I was Layla?

I spotted a video, so rather than read the article, I clicked on it, hoping for answers. The link proved to be Amanda Hill's most popular video. Why had I never seen it before? Millions of views on the one video, even more than the one she'd posted when Layla ran away from her first wedding, and that had gone viral.

What had...? I gasped.

It wasn't Layla. No, it was me. I saw myself wearing a red dress I hadn't worn for years. Sparkly. I could never pull off that kind of dress now, but five years ago, it was briefly in fashion. Layla had bought it for me. I paired it with red heels, and my hair, which had been long at the time, was pulled back in a messy bun.

Five years ago. I caught my breath. Oh *fuck.*

In the shot, I knelt on the sidewalk puking into a gutter. *Gross.* I mean…really bad. I could practically feel the burn of bile in my throat, but I couldn't remember the moment captured on film. Not a second of it. Months of that year were just gone. What had my psychiatrist called it? Major depressive disorder and anxiety. Sure, it was all those things, but also so much more.

It was just that I couldn't let myself remember.

A man with a camera filmed me puking. "Hope," he shouted at me. "Why are you puking?"

I could see the background. The name of the restaurant was Hayley's. My stomach clenched. What had I said?

Fuck me, what had I said?

"Well, the food inside Hayley's is trash. I ate there, and now I'm puking."

I groaned and closed my eyes. *No. No. No.* Why had I said that? I didn't even have to search hard to find the answer. I hadn't wanted anyone to know the real reason I was puking at the time. I was pregnant. If the date was right, I would be for four more days before I lost the baby. That would have been the end of that time for me.

I'd gone to the hospital with the miscarriage, and someone had noticed I wasn't okay in ways that had nothing to do with losing the baby. Help had come after that, because I was rich, and things like that happened for people like me. They'd tested me for all kinds of things, and somehow, even though unprotected sex had gotten me pregnant, I hadn't picked up anything else from the night I never let myself think about. I was free of any infections or permanent issues, even the baby gone like none of it ever happened. The whole experience was a giant, permanent blur in my consciousness.

The time that happened, yet…didn't.

I wiped at my eyes. I didn't want to cry about it. I'd said something terrible, and if I was reading the situation correctly, Max lost his first restaurant afterward. I scanned through comments on the article. People made fun of him. They called his restaurant trash, despite the likely high ratings prior to my visit, which spurred me to eat there in the first place.

Who had I even been there with?

I wiped at my eyes again.

I'd done a bad thing. It took him five years to open shop someplace else, and I understood why he'd thrown me out. I was lucky he hadn't done worse, like publicly call out my bad behavior. He likely assumed I returned to eat his food, bash it, and ruin his life again.

I got off the chair and paced the room. This wasn't okay. I'd ruined this man's life. He'd obviously recovered it since then, but his ability to spring back after a disaster didn't negate what had happened to him…because of me. I couldn't imagine what it must have been like to have worked so hard to open a restaurant, have it succeed spectacularly, and then have someone like me come along and destroy years of his effort.

I had to make it right, somehow. I had to…figure it out.

I just didn't know how.

I sent a text to Bridget. It would be early for her in Hong Kong, just after eight in the morning, but I needed her.

I fucked up.

She was fast to answer me. *What did you do, love?*

I wasn't ready to tell her the whole story just yet. Hell, I didn't know if I'd ever be ready to tell anyone. That was a

9

thing. I could get stronger, I could get help, but—short of confessing the whole nightmare to a few doctors and a psychologist—I'd never told another living soul what happened to me.

I wasn't sure I ever would.

Why? Because I couldn't stand the thought of what people would think after they knew what I did. For years, everyone claimed Layla was the most like our mom—the one likely to fall apart, to go to dark places. I never understood why. Layla was strong, even if she didn't see it. Things had gone askew, but she'd run—literally—toward the life she wanted. I was the one most like Mom, silently breaking while pretending I wasn't.

No, that had been who I was before, not who I am now.

I'd done something—I'd sought help privately, while she never did. I survived, so no one ever had to know.

I texted my sister back, decided. *How about if we don't say what I fucked up? How about if I just ask you what to do if I've done something wrong? If I ask you, what do I do about it?*

I knew the answer; I just wanted to see her say it. I regularly checked in with my sisters because they kept me balanced. Sometimes sane, even if they didn't know to what extent they helped me.

Her answer came back pretty quickly. *You know what to do. You make it right if you can. If you can't, you say you're sorry, you mean it, and you don't forget what you did so you don't do it again.*

I nodded. All of that was exactly what I thought. No shortcuts when it came to making amends. I was going to do the work until I somehow made this up to a complete stranger, one who hated me because I'd destroyed his life.

I hit the button and played the video again. And again. I'd

made him into a joke, and he didn't seem like the kind of man who would ever want to be a joke. Those intense gray eyes, the way he held himself. Max took himself very seriously, and he'd absolutely enjoyed throwing me out of Hyperion today.

I couldn't say I blamed him.

I TRIED to work through the morning. There was a lot to do. Muffy—yes, that was her real name—expected to hear from me with at least a partial proposal for the Save the Slomestikan Children fundraiser we planned to host next month. She was anxious to get it done. Well, *she* was anxious to get her face out there on all the PR we were about to release. I was excited for the actual fundraiser.

I loved that I could raise money to help others and get paid for it.

It might not have been my personal cause, but I became invested in every cause I helped to raise money for and took it to heart like it were my own.

Still, I couldn't help looking at the clock every two minutes. I called my friend Danny and asked him what time Max usually arrived to open his restaurant. Danny was the person who knew everything that was happening in Manhattan all of the time. So, as my walking source of information, he'd told me Max arrived at noon. I intended to arrive at one o'clock so I didn't pounce on Max the second he opened his restaurant. It was noon. I had another hour to get through before I descended on Hyperion and got Max to talk to me.

Even if he ousted me from the building at the same time.

I gave up trying to work around twelve-ten. At some

point, it was fruitless, so I went to check myself in the mirror. I worked from home most of the time. Technically, I had an office, but it really was just a space for a business card. I was never there.

Love you, I sent to Layla. She might or might not answer. The baby had her up a lot. When she wasn't helping Zeke get their vineyard set up or nursing the baby, she was frequently asleep. I couldn't blame her. How did she function with so little rest? I wasn't sure I ever could.

I dressed simply and for the purpose of apology. I didn't need to look fancy. In fact, that would be super inappropriate. I wanted to look simple, so my jeans worked. I put on a purple V-neck T-shirt and a denim jacket. Sneakers completed my look, along with a dab of lip gloss, then I left the house.

"Where are we off to?" Theo asked as he caught up to me. Most of the time, he sat in a car outside of my apartment.

"Back to Hyperion."

He side-eyed me. "Really?"

Theo was fifty-five years old, fit like a twenty-year-old, and I was pretty sure had a military background no one asked about. Aside from his two daughters, aged twenty and twenty-one, he sometimes also parented me. Since I had my own father to deal with, when he was around to be dealt with, I really didn't need it or appreciate the pseudo-parenting, considering how much freedom I already surrendered by doing what Zeke and Michael wanted from me.

"I have something to do."

He nodded and opened the door. I got inside. I didn't think he was technically required to do that, but he did every time. It was nice of him, which made my mean thoughts seem even more petty. He jumped up front with Luke, and away we went. With no traffic, the drive passed much faster, and I was at Hyperion before I knew it. I blinked. Funny, when I *wanted* to go somewhere, it took forever. When I dreaded arrival, time zoomed by.

I got out of the car and steeled my shoulders.

I wasn't sure what to do. Should I go around back and knock on the door to the kitchen or try to go through the front? It was probably locked. They weren't open for lunch.

Decision made, I walked to the side of the building, where I saw a door that had to lead to the kitchen. I mustered all my courage and knocked. After a few seconds, a man opened the door. He was tall, all in white, which looked like a uniform, and he absolutely wasn't Max. The stranger was maybe twenty years old, with a piercing in his nose.

"Yeah?" he said.

I swallowed. "Hello. I'm hoping that I can see Mr. Broadley. Please." I added on the last word as a final thought. Politeness would get me where I needed to be faster than being rude. Sometimes, as a woman, I had to be outright rude to get anyone to follow directions. It went beyond being a squeaky wheel. If I wasn't just mean all the time, I got nowhere.

That said, this wasn't that case. *Flies and honey.* I needed to apologize. The trick would be even getting far enough to see Max, past his gatekeepers.

"Hey, Anna, there's a woman here to see the boss. Can you deal with it?"

I smiled. "It would be a lot easier if you let me speak to Max directly."

"Yeah…that's not how this works."

Of course not.

CHAPTER 2

ANNA TURNED OUT TO BE A STUNNING BLACK WOMAN WITH dreads that fell past her shoulders. Her deep red lipstick seemed striking against her identical all white outfit.

She looked me up and down. "It's you."

I didn't pretend to misunderstand her. "It's me. Can I please speak to Max?"

She leaned on the door. "No, you can't. Haven't you done enough to Chef? You aren't getting anywhere near him."

I swallowed. "Well, he can't stay inside all day and all night. I'll stand here. Right here. Or better yet, I will put myself in the corner over there so that I can watch both the front door and this one. I will live on that corner. Eat there. Sleep there. Go to the bathroom there. Until I can speak to him."

She lifted her eyebrows with a slight smile. "That's quite a statement."

"Well, I'm really quite a person. See if I won't. Test me." In that moment, I meant it. I completely and one hundred percent committed to live on the street corner until I got to see Max and make my apology.

"What the fuck is going on here? We have meals to prep for and…" Max's voice trailed off to a sudden stop as he recognized me and must have realized the problem. He glared at me, and I might have been halved into two separate pieces from the forceful slice of his gaze. That was okay. I'd been hated before. This was the first time I'd earned it, so my guilt made it feel much worse.

Guilt ate at me, it took over my insides, infested my brain. Others might be able to forgive themselves, see their actions as some sort of lesson learned, but that wasn't me.

"Chef," the young man who answered the door interrupted. "I can't find any peaches. The guy I talked to said sorry, he loved the whisky you sent, but they're held up in customs and we ain't going to get any peaches today."

"Fuck me sideways. So much for the cobbler. Fine. We'll change to something else. Ask Dante to come up with an alternative for the third dessert."

Well, if they wanted to make cobbler, there *were* other options. "Aren't there other kinds of cobblers? I've eaten apple. Blueberry…" I immediately stopped talking. It wasn't the time or place for me to make suggestions.

Max stepped outside, shooing Anna and the unnamed guy back inside before he closed the door. "What the fuck do you think you're doing here? I thought I made myself very clear. You aren't welcome."

I nodded. "Well, I'm not inside." Okay, I had to stop. I should launch into my apology. "Mr. Broadley, um, Max. Last night I… That is to say that… I am so very sorry about what happened with your restaurant Hayley, and I'd like to apologize and see if there is anything I can do to make it up to you."

He laughed, which surprised me, but then abruptly stopped. "Oh, you're not kidding. Are you out of your fucking mind? You can't make this up to me. Not ever. You destroyed the life of a stranger because you could. Because you're some kind of sick, bored rich girl with nothing better to do. Let me be very clear—you're not welcome here. The whole world might be in love with you, but I see you as the nothing you are. Stay away from me now and always. In case you're wondering, this whole space, I don't want to see you in it. Ever."

Max's gesture barred me from the whole street. I shook my head. "I'm not trying to stalk you. I just needed to come and say I was sorry. I don't know how to make you believe me, but I truly am sorry." I stepped back. "I'll leave you alone now. Good luck."

I turned my back and walked away, but I felt his eyes bore into me the whole way back to my car.

Theo raised a fatherly eyebrow from where he stood at the end of the street, but he didn't interfere. "Get what you needed?"

No, but that was an impossibility in this case. Max Broadley was the first man to stir an awakening inside of me in five years. Those gray eyes... How could anyone have such an intense gaze? He hated me, and I couldn't blame him.

But that was such a Hope thing to do—want what I couldn't have.

Inside the car, I pulled up the privacy divider between Theo, Luke, and myself. Calling in favors from family in the State Department was best done alone. If, on some nebulous future date, anyone ever testified about my actions, they could say they didn't know.

Although if they wanted to make a federal case out of what I was going to ask for, then it was a slow day in American justice. Not to mention, Darrel, whom I was about to call, could always say no.

I dialed his number. Years ago, when I'd needed him, he failed me, despite being a cousin of my mother and some of the only members of her family we had left. If he didn't come through now, I would write him off, and so help me, he'd better not try to come to any more parties that I threw, ever.

It rang twice before he answered. "Hope?" His voice was growly, rough, like he'd smoked a million cigarettes over the years. I'd heard him give speeches that commanded the attention of the world and also seen him disappear into the shadows like he wasn't there.

"Hello, cousin." I crossed my legs, trying to get more comfortable. "How are you?"

"I'm well, but I doubt this is a social call. I never hear from you anymore, and I can't say I blame you. So what can I do for you today, cousin?"

I swallowed. "Peaches."

"What?" He cleared his throat. "*Peaches?*"

"I realize this might not be what you specifically do, but I want to get a shipment of peaches to a friend of mine who owns a restaurant. He needs them today, and apparently, there is an import problem."

He was silent, and I thought for a moment he would deny me. "Text me the address. I'll get it delivered."

"Thank you." I meant it. "That's a big help."

"Getting food through customs? That's easy. Listen, Hope…"

I knew what he was about to say, and I didn't want to hear it. "Thanks." I hung up. Quickly, I texted him the address. I'd never be able to fix things with Max, a near stranger, who was out there thinking I was a ruiner of lives. I sat back and closed my eyes. I counted to ten. And then I did it again. As many times as it took.

When I got home, I locked my door four times. That

wasn't too bad. Four, I could manage. If it got to six, I was in trouble, but four was still reasonable. I had my own thresholds for how far out of control I could get. Four still worked. It did.

~

THE SUN CAME UP, as it always did, after another bad night. I made plans to go out for tapas with my group of friends that night. I used to love going with Layla once a week before she moved to Washington state. Tapas with other people just wasn't the same as with her.

Love you too.

I smiled at Layla's text. Okay, she was averaging twenty-four hours to return a text. That wasn't too bad. I shook my head. I had to live vicariously through her. The chances I would ever have kids were small. I was too fucked up to maintain a relationship, let alone a baby. Who would want to go through life on the crazy train with me?

I dressed up in a pair of black pants, since I intended to stop by my office to pick up my mail. Snail mail drove me crazy. *Couldn't we just do everything online by now? Did I really need a catalog of stuff I was never going to order?*

Well, actually, I might order something. If it was really cool.

I grabbed my keys, locked up behind me, and headed to Midtown. Usually, I met with new clients at my office, but most of my existing clients were happy to talk to me on the phone. Muffy preferred to meet there still, and I didn't mind. She was a character, and there were fewer and fewer of them in my life.

My father's notoriety could have sunk me. It did the opposite. Sure, I was a bit of a spectacle when people first met me, but they quickly discovered I knew the right people and I was good at raising money for their charity of choice.

I stepped into the car, smiling at my security. They were such nice people, but sometimes I didn't feel like talking to them, and it was like I hated the idea of being rude. It was hard to see people every day, particularly if you hadn't hired them. They would risk their lives for me because Michael paid them and Zeke paid him to see to my protection.

Did other people really live their lives without being under constant surveillance?

We made it to my office, and I headed inside. The air conditioning was cold, and I wished that I'd remembered my sweater. I never did. That was okay. I was there to get my mail and leave, it wasn't like I had to sit and work in the chill air.

I bent to pick the mail up from where it fell all over the floor of my office when they'd pushed it through the mail slot. I gave it a cursory look as I picked it up. Bills and magazines, as predicted. I yawned. Some things could be counted on, and bills were certainly one of those things.

A masculine voice said, "Sir, you're going to have to stop right there while I ask Ms. Radford if she wants to see you."

"Oh," a deep, angry voice answered him. "She'll talk to me. Now."

I peeked my head around the door to confirm my instant suspicion and discovered Max. What was he doing at my office? I leaned against the doorframe into the hallway where both Theo and Luke stopped him from approaching me. The men eyed each other like they were making silent assessments I wasn't privy to. Their body language tipped me off. I was really good at telling when someone was about to get violent. Or was thinking about it. None of them were there yet, but they were close.

My survival skills were pretty darn honed these days.

"He can come in." I motioned toward my office. "Come on, Max. You're welcome."

I stepped out of the way, proud because I managed to keep my cool.

Theo stepped out of the way, and Max stormed into my office. When he would have closed the door, I shook my head. "Stays open. Thanks."

I didn't like to be closed in with people I didn't know. If he fought me about it, well, I had two security people in the hallway who would ensure the door remained open. Fortunately, he didn't. He just spun around to look at my office itself.

"You don't have any furniture."

Not true. I had a desk. "I'm almost never here. When I am, this is all I need. How can I help you, Max? I don't believe you can bar me from being everywhere in Manhattan. I have every right to be in my own office."

A muscle ticked in his jaw. "I spent all night and hours into this morning trying to figure out how those peaches suddenly, magically made it to the restaurant on time. It finally dawned on me that it had to be you. It was, wasn't it, Hope? After Dano told me that we couldn't get them, you did whatever rich person thing and got those fucking peaches delivered."

He seemed awfully upset for a man who'd gotten what he wanted—the peaches arrived in time, after all. "Were they rotten? In bad shape? Bruised?"

He blinked. "No, they were fine."

"Then what is the problem?" I picked up some papers from my desk to give myself something to do with my hands. What were they? No clue, but it didn't really matter because I used them as a prop.

Max shook his head, some of his brown hair falling in front of his eyes. He brushed it away. His dark locks looked thick and soft.

"I never asked you to do that."

The conversation circled back, but it still didn't make sense. "No, but I had a way to help you, so I did."

"You wanted to *help* me? Why would you do that? Don't you get off on ruining lives?" He sneered at me, and it wasn't a good look for him. I didn't know Max, but there were ways to tell when people behaved in a way natural to them or not. It was like the muscles on his face didn't really work in that direction.

Max was a smiler. Just not at me, which was fine. "Maybe I've turned over a new leaf?"

"That's what you want to say? That you've turned over a new leaf."

I sighed. "You sought me out, Max, not the other way around. What is it you want me to say? I've apologized. You've said there is no making it right. I get that, and I agree because I can't undo my past actions. But I could get you the peaches, so I did."

He took a long deep breath like he was counting to ten. I'd certainly done that enough myself over the years.

"Do you know how hard it is to run a restaurant?"

I shook my head as I sat down on the edge of the desk. He was right—I really should get more furniture. It would be nice to have something more comfortable for things like the lecture I was currently sitting through.

He was waiting for an answer. "I don't, actually."

"There are a million things that go on beyond cooking and serving food. The financials are miserable. I have investors to answer to—a highbrow problem, considering how lucky I was to find any after what happened with

21

Hayley's. Nationwide, sixty percent of restaurants don't make it past their first year. The odds against success are higher here."

I nodded. Most things were harder in Manhattan. "You have a hit. My guess would be you're going to make it."

"Yes, but my point is, I can't have you fucking with my life again, Hope. Maybe you meant to do a good thing, and yes, I needed the peaches. So thank you for that. It did make desert one hundred times easier. But whatever this is? Whatever game you're playing, it needs to stop."

Now that I could answer. "It's not a game."

"Just stop. Stay out of my life. You can't make things better for me. That's not a possibility. If you actually want to make things right, leave me alone."

I swallowed. "Listen, maybe you're right—maybe leaving you alone would've been smarter, but I don't agree that it is. I don't want to make things harder for you, but I believe that I can make at least small reparations for my actions. And you can't stop me from trying to make little things, like peaches, better."

This time when he spoke, he pointed at me. "You're not welcome in my restaurant, so you're never going to know what I need again."

Unfortunately, he was likely right—it wasn't like I could magically predict what Max needed for the dang restaurant. Drat. He had a point. He turned to leave, and I took a long look at his tight ass. Fuck. There was something wrong with me. That man hated me. The first guy I was sexually attracted to in five years, and he didn't even want me to get him any more fruit.

Max stopped, turning around. "Do all rich heiresses have this much security? Someone want to steal your designer bags?"

Now that was low, and he hadn't gone to that level before. I'd take abuse where it was earned, but not in that way. "No, actually. But see, twenty-one months ago, my sister was kidnapped at gunpoint in Paris by Russian mobsters. They held her for two days and shaved her head. Then that security you're pointing to—the one on the left specifically, with the dark hair? He was part of the group that got her out, also at gunpoint. Now, my father, who is a fugitive from the law, is hiding in Russia with my brother. The Russians could show up at any point to kill me."

I deliberately told him the story like I was recounting a funny anecdote and not recounting the worst memory of my life or the new situation that made me constantly on edge and under surveillance. He'd obviously searched for me on the Internet to get my office address, so it surprised me that he might not know. Maybe Max had a singular ability to focus on small things or maybe he hadn't looked hard enough when he'd searched?

All of that information was pretty quickly accessed about me. I knew it was, because I occasionally looked to see what people were saying. I had a reputation to uphold, which was why my clients came to me to begin with. The socialite with the bad past who could get attention to their causes. The full circle of my life.

His mouth fell open. "Really?"

"Yep." I smiled. "So you see, I've had kind of a shit life. I'm not an heiress. My father is broke, and he's hiding from the FBI. I earn a ton of money. I made my famous-being-famous self rather wealthy based on my skills. The same sheer determination to not end up a cautionary tale means that if I want to send you some hard to get fruit, I'm going to, and there isn't a thing you can do about it."

This time, he stormed from my office.

I forced myself to not stare at his ass again. I had to learn to control myself. If my sex drive was back online, I could get in trouble if I weren't careful.

Control was, after all, how I got through every day.

It was why the world worked for me.

~

I SAT LISTENING to my friends gab over tapas. I drank my seltzer while watching them enjoy their sangrias, but my mind kept traveling back to Max. What was I going to do about the fact that I couldn't figure out how to help him again?

"So I finally got to eat at Hyperion last night." Kylie smiled. "You know Hope and I got thrown out of there a few days ago."

As if they didn't know? It was on social media, as I could have predicted. So far, I'd had no blowback from the incident. "How was it?"

"So good. The best food ever." Kylie winked at me like we shared the same joke. None of it was funny, but sometimes I lived on another planet from the rest of them. That was fine. Story of my life.

"It was," my friend Jessie piped in. "The best lobster risotto I've ever eaten."

I sighed. Yes, this could get worse. I loved nothing more than food. Truly. It was the single biggest joy in my life outside of my nephew and my sisters. I supposed I'd put my brother-in-law in there too. He was pretty cool.

"Hope, are you listening?" Kylie touched my knee.

No, I really wasn't. I got to my feet. "Sorry, ladies. I think I'm not feeling well tonight. I'm going to go. Enjoy the food. See you later."

I turned and walked-slash-ran from the restaurant before any of them could stop me. I hustled to the car, directing them back to Hyperion. Max had said that I couldn't go inside or be in his alley. Nothing said I had to obey his orders, after all.

I just had to wait for the garbage to go out.

It didn't take long. Dano, the nose ringed guy, came out a few minutes after I arrived. I jumped out of the car.

"Hey, Dano."

The shocked man turned to stare at me, his mouth falling open. "You again?"

"Yes, right, me again." I rushed over. "I know I'm not supposed to be here. I get it. I'm going. Here." I handed him a hundred dollars with my business card. "That's for you texting me, at the number on that card, anytime the restaurant needs something it can't get. Okay? Like the peaches. I'll get it for you. Can you do that? Hundred dollars every time you do."

He stared at the money and then back at me. "You're serious?"

"As cancer and a heart attack. Yes, it'll be our secret. I'll never tell Max who told me. Can we do this? Our little secret."

Dano shrugged. "It doesn't seem like a bad thing."

"It's not. Your chef is just being stubborn. I want to help."

He was quiet. "He is stubborn, but I heard you're why his last restaurant failed. I think he called you a meddling nuisance."

"Well, that was nicer than he had to be. Look, have you ever screwed up so badly that you didn't think you'd ever make it better? That's what I did. But I want to try. This is a small thing."

Dano pocketed the money and my card. That was when I

knew he was going to do it. "I've fu—screwed up a lot. So, yes, I get it. I do. I'll help."

I'd never felt so relieved in my life. "Thank you."

I rushed back to the car. Max couldn't catch me, or he'd ban me from the whole street.

I leaned back in my seat. The smell from Hyperion had been fantastic. My stomach grumbled. I'd never get to eat his food, and that was a huge bummer.

When I got dropped at home, I tried to only lock the door once. But my head wouldn't clear until I'd gone three more times. I was stuck at four. As long as it was four, I wasn't calling the doctor. I took a long breath.

This night called for romantic comedies and ice cream. Who needed dinner when I could skip right to dessert?

My phone dinged. It was Bridget. *Something is going on with you. You still haven't told me what you did.*

I texted back fast. *I don't want to. How are you?*

I've had five bad dates in the last three weeks. I swear I've done something karmically to only meet terrible men.

That was probably true. Bridget's dating life often seemed almost unreal. She was beautiful and smart, not to mention she absolutely wanted to find a true partner for life. I was never looking, not lately, and Layla was off the market. It seemed ridiculous that Bridget couldn't find someone, since she tended to massively succeed at everything she tried to accomplish.

Hang in there. Somewhere in Hong Kong is a man worthy of you.

I could practically see her eye roll from across the world.

CHAPTER 3

MUFFY LIKED TO MEET AT MY OFFICE AND THEN GO TO lunch. It was how we did business. She had placed more money than most people would ever see into an account so that I could throw her choice cause a party. That meant she could do whatever she wanted in terms of meetings. Today, she brought her son with her and his nanny, Berta, as well. Timothy was five years old, cute with his chubby cheeks, blue eyes, and bright smile. He had the blondest hair I'd ever seen. It was practically white, and he looked just like Muffy's husband, who was never with her and I had never seen, other than when I'd searched for them online in the beginning of our business relationship.

We'd never known each other before this all started. It wasn't like my father had a social life or was ever seen in public. My sisters and I had created personas—sometimes on purpose in my case, sometimes not in theirs—which grew to the point where the public called us The Redheads. Why not make that work for us? Layla had run from it because that was what she needed, and Bridget didn't care one way or another about it. But I'd managed to get the attention of people like Muffy, and that was helping me to A, save the world, and B, support myself very well in the meantime. Sure, maybe I wasn't actually saving the world, but I did believe I helped.

That had to mean something.

For now, as we sat in Tatty's, the lunch place where I liked to take Muffy because she enjoyed the wine list, I half listened to my client, instead sort of focusing on her son. He played quietly with his mother's phone while his nanny ignored him. He was really, really cute. I loved kids, always had, even if I was fairly certain that I had no business raising them.

I was a mess. Hands down. And I wasn't going to leave children to survive in the wake of my mess like my mother did. Besides, it wasn't like I had a slew of men lining up to have babies with me. I wasn't going to become a parent unless I had a partner to share the experience with me. Single parenting with my already uphill battle of issues was out of the question. I wasn't strong enough for those challenges. I admired those who did so much, but I knew I wasn't up for that task.

It would have to be the right person too. I wasn't going to maybe leave behind a bunch of kids with someone as inept at parenting as my father had been. Nope, I needed to cut off that train of thought immediately. It wasn't helpful.

Muffy treated Tim like an accessory. In truth, she was more concerned with her purse than her son, not that it was any of my business. It really, truly, wasn't. She was my client. What I thought of her parenting didn't matter. Besides, what did I know about raising kids?

She liked to talk, and I could usually manage to take breaks from paying attention for periods of time. I cued back in right as I needed to. "Yes, we can find someplace unique. Tell me what kind of venue you are thinking about?"

Now that I'd finally nailed her down on a date—Muffy was flighty—I could work on where we were going to host the charity night. In the next month, I'd booked out the Metropolitan Museum of Art and the roof of Chelsea Piers. There were lots of subtler places, but Muffy wouldn't want subtle. I could just about guarantee it.

"What is the newest, hottest venue?"

The waiter chose that moment to set down my tuna tartare in front of me. I stared down at it. This was just what I'd intended to order the other night at Max's place. I hadn't gotten to eat it there.

Max's place…

I stared at Muffy and smiled. "Well, you know lunch is the new dinner, when it comes to charity events."

Her mouth fell open. "Really?"

"Really." I nodded. I was totally lying, but if I could pull this off, everyone would be happy. "It's cheaper, and it shows the person who is throwing the event cares more about giving the money to the cause than the venue. Just a thought. It might not be traditional or what you're looking for, but…"

She nodded fast. "I'm in."

"Then I just might be able to suggest the absolute perfect place." I took a bite of my tuna. It wasn't fantastic. Next time, I'd order something else.

Max wasn't done with me. Not yet. I was determined to do something to help him, whether he liked it or not.

～

I KNOCKED on the backdoor of Hyperion again. This time, Anna answered. She lifted her eyebrow by way of greeting, and I lifted both of mine back.

"I'll get him." She stepped away from the door and motioned for me to follow her. "Don't stand on the street. It looks funny to have people at the door. This is a classy place."

It looked funny? It was two in the afternoon. No one was there to eat yet. Still, I wasn't going to argue with her, so I followed her inside where she stopped me with one look. "Stand here."

Okay. I'd never been in the back of a restaurant before. Visible in the distance were two offices, and beyond that, an active kitchen. Ten people busily prepared food, and although it was quiet, two people spoke in low voices as they chopped.

My phone dinged, so I looked down at it. My secret accomplice had texted me. I smirked. He had no idea I was there, but they needed green onions. Why were green onions short? I could do a whole study on the food that could suddenly go scarce and still not understand it. How did these things work?

I sent a quick message to my cousin, who responded he'd take care of it for me. That was right. I was the provider of missing food. I was the source for it. Smirking, I shook my head. The things that happened in life could be really downright weird. Who would have ever thought I'd be doing this?

"What now?" Max leaned against the wall, looking far too sexy for so early in the afternoon. How was it his whole body screamed sex when he was doing nothing but leaning against the wall? He once again sported a chef's uniform.

I smiled, even though I knew he wouldn't return the effort. It was just polite. Our nannies taught us to use our manners, especially in difficult situations. "I have a proposition for you."

"Sex won't replace my restaurant, no matter how good you think you are at it, so if that is the proposition, you should leave right now."

I sucked in a breath. Ouch. Okay. "I'm not...I'm not offering you that."

If only he understood how absolutely I would never, ever offer sex to anyone. It was completely off the plate.

Anna walked by and hit him hard, right in the arm. "Not funny."

He winced. "Sorry." Max walked toward me. "Sometimes other people don't appreciate my sense of humor."

"Because it's not funny, Chef," Anna called over her shoulder as she disappeared into one of the offices.

"I..." I cleared my throat to give myself a moment. "I raise money for a living. For people's charities, for the causes they care about." Or as Bridget might have said, the rich's pet projects, but I wasn't going to disparage my career in front of Max. Especially not if he was going to start accusing me of offering him sex. "I need a place to hold our latest event. The payout for the venue would be significant." I grabbed my business card out of my purse and wrote down a number. I intended to pay ten thousand dollars an hour to cook and use his space. That was well more than the going rate for a place like his. Muffy wouldn't mind. She wouldn't even know, honestly. At the end of the day, she'd get the press she needed and her cause would raise millions. If I could throw thirty grand at Max in the process, I would. I'd give her back ten thousand, from my fee, so I wouldn't be stealing from her.

It would all work out.

If he would just say yes.

He stared at the number and then handed me back the

card. "We're booked every night but Sundays and Mondays for dinner. I'm not asking the staff to work the nights that they're off."

"Not night. Lunch. It's the new thing." Or it would be because I'd be making it the new thing. Everyone would want to have lunch now. "Eleven to one."

I might even make it brunch if I had to. I'd tell Muffy that the trend was shifting again. She was sweet but not too bright.

He scowled at me and then ran a hand through those dark locks that I couldn't stop staring at. I forced my attention back to his face. That wasn't better. Why did he have to be so handsome? He was older. My internet search told me nearly forty. Maybe that was what I liked. There was something chiseled about him that said he'd lived life and it hadn't bowed him. It was amazing, really, how little information there was about him on the Internet. He was clearly a person who valued his privacy.

I didn't know what that was like.

"Anna," he called over his shoulder. "I want to tell this woman no because I want to hate her, but this could be for Eric."

She came out of her office and stared at me for a second before she looked back at him. "Do it. I don't think she's the monster you think she is, by the way."

"Oh." I hadn't expected that. "Thank you."

"I didn't say you weren't a monster. I just said you weren't the monster he thinks you are. There are lots of areas of monster to get through in that direction." She held her hand over her head. "You were pretty much up here." She moved her hand to her waist. "And I'm saying maybe you're there."

I nodded. Well, that still sucked. Not that I'd expected to make friends. "Gotcha."

"We'll do it." He nodded. From his own pocket, he pulled a card. "Email me the contract. We'll do it."

Happiness flooded through some of my discomfort. "Great. I'll do that."

"Yep. But this doesn't mean anything in terms of whatever you're doing here. You should just stop."

Yes, I heard him. "I'll take care of all of that tonight."

He turned to leave and then stopped. "I looked up what happened to your sister. That was fucked up."

Well, that was one way to put it. "Seriously fucked up."

It was time for me to leave. Probably past time. "Your green onions are on their way."

He hit the wall. "Who is telling her? I'll double whatever she's paying you to stop."

"No, he won't," I called back as I exited. Anna walked to the door to close it behind me. I caught her gaze. "Who's Eric?"

She scowled, and I was pretty sure she wasn't going to answer. "His sous chef before I took it over. They came up together in the military. Best friends. He's my fiancé." She looked away. "He's sick. Needs an operation. Insurance won't pay."

I almost told her I could raise money for Eric. I'd find a rich socialite in search of a cause. We could make Eric that cause. But as I stared at her proud gaze looking back at me, I knew that was too far. Anna didn't want to be charity, even though she needed help. That also meant I couldn't randomly offer to pay either. But I could book Max to cook at Hyperion for three hours. That was working to raise the money, and it came down to her not wanting anything she hadn't earned.

I'd learned to read people when I was a child. It helped when I wanted the nannies to give us what we wanted and my father's temper to cool when it would have gotten out of hand. I was the reason he hadn't added *child abuser* to his list of faults.

Well…not physically.

And it all made sense. It explained why Max would say yes.

"You don't wear a ring." I pointed to my left ring finger that was also without jewelry.

She shrugged. "Hard to cook with it."

Max poked his head out the door. "What's the cause?"

Took me a second to realize he meant the luncheon and not Eric, who I'd never met but spent the last minutes thinking about. "Mrs. Muffy DelMonte wants to feed the starving migrants in Slomestikan."

I expected a comment, but instead, he just nodded his head. "Tough situation there."

It was. I'd certainly raised money for worse causes.

FOUR TIMES. That was how many I locked and unlocked the door before I could leave it alone. I was really on the edge for needing to seek some help. My therapist and psychiatrist understood my personal limits. I wasn't sure they agreed with them, but everyone understood I would call if I hit six lock-unlock events or if I couldn't sleep for three nights in a row. Also, a whole slew of other things, but those were the bordering events.

I leaned my head up against the door. "Pull it together. Nothing is wrong. You did something bad. You can't fix it, but you can try to make it right. That's the best anyone can do." I put my hand on the door. "Taking personal responsibility. You're not a terrible person." I hit the door with my open hand. It burned. "You should find a way to get a pet. It would be nice to come home to some kind of pet."

Stepping from the door, I went to my kitchen and poured myself some cereal. That was all I could manage tonight. If I'd been Bridget, I would have found something funny to say back to him when he'd made the sex joke or stared him down so he exploded into ash right in front of her.

If I'd been Layla, he wouldn't have said it. By now, he'd have understood, because she wore her heart on her sleeve, that she never meant to hurt him. All would be forgiven.

But I was Hope. Absolutely hopeless Hope, so lost in her string of self-worth issues and secrets that I could barely stand myself.

"Enough."

I sat down at my table and ate my cereal. I would not think about the smells coming from Max's kitchen that I'd distinctly ignored when I was there. What had that been? Something with garlic.

Nope, I wasn't thinking about it. Not at all. No.

Later that night, lying in my bed, I was just about asleep when my phone dinged.

Do they even eat?

Did who even eat? I had no idea who had just texted me. *Sorry. Who is this?*

Max Broadley. Have you forgotten me already? You're harassing me with your helpfulness.

I rolled my eyes. *How did you get this number?* I didn't give out my personal one on the website. I had a business cell phone number public.

His texts were fast. *You handed me your card.*

That was right. I'd written on the special cards printed with my private line. It was more like a social card, for people I either wanted to be friends with or friendly acquaintances I could invite to things like Muffy's events. It was sort of awful, but we all did it. I used person A, they used person B. Such was life.

You gave it back. In like three seconds, if I remembered correctly. In fact, I was pretty sure I still had the card in the pocket of my pants.

I can always remember numbers. It's a gift and a curse. He paused before he texted back as I digested that information. Max Broadley. Rememberer of numbers. Restaurant owner. Veteran. *So do they eat?*

I rolled onto my stomach. *Everyone eats. If you don't eat, you die.*

Do they actually eat a reasonable amount of food, or should I just make finger foods for them to pick at?

I thought about it. I'd never had a chef or a caterer ask me that question before. Usually, they just handed me a menu. Depending on my client, I either chose the food or asked them to do it. *The second. They'll never notice because it's lunch that you didn't do a whole sit down.*

The phone rang, and I answered. He didn't say hello and neither did I. We just had a few moments of silence on the line before he spoke. "I hate texting."

It wasn't my favorite thing either. "I don't blame you."

"I was thinking of eggs. Specialty eggs. And maybe some finger foods. With gluten free, dairy free options."

Rolling onto my back, I stared at the ceiling. "Shouldn't you be cooking?" It was only ten o'clock. His restaurant would be open a lot later than that.

"Anna's got it." His voice was low. I liked the sound. "Do you like the menu?"

"I do. I was just thinking how good your restaurant smelled tonight. Like garlic."

He was quiet. "You like garlic?"

"I like all food. It's my favorite thing in the world to do—to eat." I sighed. "And garlic is one of those great treats."

Max didn't answer right away. "Everything? Everyone has something they don't like to eat."

That was true. I absolutely detested pesto, but I wasn't going to tell him that because he'd probably figure out where I lived and have loads of foods that I loved delivered here—only they'd be covered in pesto. No, actually he wouldn't. That would require him to give a shit, and it was clear that other than disdain, Max didn't care at all about me. Why should he?

"What do you not like to eat?" There, I changed the subject. Turned his question back on him. People loved to talk about themselves. That was universally true. I never had to say a word about myself to anyone if I didn't want to. It was easy.

"I don't like chocolate."

I sat up. "What?"

"You heard me. I know it's sacrilege, but it's true. I don't like chocolate. I like all kinds of other desserts but not that. Now, your turn. You don't get off that easy. I want to know what *the* Hope Radford—who once found my cooking so disgusting, she puked on Fifth Avenue in front of cameras—doesn't like to eat."

I closed my eyes. I was on the phone with the most attractive man I'd ever seen, yet that moment would always be between us. One sentence, and I was sure I could make that whole thing go away. I could tell him the truth. Yet...I couldn't tell him, because I was sure I would die someday with this secret never having told to another soul. It was mine to live with, mine to endure. No amount of therapy had fixed that.

"I...I hate pesto." I was sure the next time I saw him, there would be pesto all over everything.

"A lot of people do. I don't cook it because it's not my favorite thing either. I don't hate it. My mother makes a good one, but I don't cook it in the restaurants, so it wasn't that."

I opened my eyes. "Wasn't what?"

"I've wondered all these years what you ordered that made you sick."

I couldn't remember anything about that night. "I really am sorry, Max." I couldn't help the hitch in my voice. I was alone in the dark. My defenses were down, and the persona I carried around was shed by this point at night. It was just me here, alone with myself. "If I could go back, I would..." Not get drunk with Shawn and black out from whatever he gave me so that I wouldn't get raped and pregnant. Not go out too soon after that when I should have stayed home. Not destroy my already shattered psyche so that I had to be hospitalized. Not mess up this man's life so that he lost his dream and hated me. "Never do that. I can't really explain it more. I am so sorry." It bore repeating the last part.

He was quiet. My answer would never be good enough, but it was all I could give him.

"Okay, Hope." He sighed. "I'll call if I have any other questions."

He hung up.

I rolled onto my pillow and buried my face in it. This was the trick I'd learned as a girl, so no one knew exactly how much I cried. If they'd really understood the amount of time I used to spend in tears, they'd probably have addressed it. I never wanted to be the one who had to have things examined too closely. We'd been rich but always moving. Turned out Dad stayed on the run a lot. So we'd shared a room, the three of us, and Justin had been in another one. Three bedrooms plus one for the nanny. Four. Never more than four. My sisters would worry. I couldn't have that.

So I learned to hide myself. Cry just enough they thought I was sensitive but not sick. Then after Shawn and his... No, I hated that word. I'd thought it once tonight. Wouldn't even think it again. Didn't want to. I didn't cry about that anymore. I forced it to stop. I stared at the ceiling.

My phone dinged.

I got the onions. There was such a long pause, I was about to put the phone down. *Thank you.*

It was like the best gift I'd ever been given. Those two words. *You're welcome.*

I didn't feel like crying anymore. Instead, I put on the television and found the mini-series for *Dune.* I loved it. Couldn't watch it enough. Late night TV was filled with science fiction and great for insomnia.

Still, I fell asleep with the TV on and only woke up to shut it off at three a.m. I rolled back over, found the colder side of my pillow, and drifted back into my dreams.

Only they weren't easy or happy.

No, it was me walking down a NYC sidewalk with the Brooklyn Bridge ahead of me. I was alone, no one there, and even though I knew I was being chased, I couldn't run. My feet would only take slow steps, one and then the next. My pursuer had no such problem. He or she ran at me and would catch me soon.

When whoever it was got to me, I woke up in a cold sweat, bringing my knees to my forehead. I didn't care what time it was, I needed someone in the dark. A pet. I had to get one. And soon.

I grabbed my phone. There was another text message from Max.

What about dessert? Small finger foods of cake?

I smiled. *Not chocolate.* I sent back the response before I thought about the time. Fuck. I hoped I didn't wake him.

His message came back fast. *Not sleeping either? Well, now I know who I won't wake up when I'm up.*

I loved the idea of Max texting me when he was up. With shaking fingers, I texted him back. *Anytime.*

Maybe I wasn't the only one who hated to be alone in the dark. I didn't suppose I could ever be friends with him. It was too rough between us, but maybe we could be those people who filled a need for each other. Text messages when it was way past the point of acceptable, even though we both hated texting.

40

CHAPTER 4

THE SAVE THE WHALES CHARITY EVENT WENT OFF WITHOUT a hitch, and my client ended up raising ten million dollars for her trouble. She was thrilled. It looked like she was getting her name on some kind of plaque, but that went beyond the scope of my know-how. I was the one who could throw the party and get the right people there. It wasn't really event planning. No one would ask me to plan their wedding or business dinner.

I could probably pull off a birthday party, if it were a who's who kind of a thing.

"Hope." A woman named Drea pulled me into a hug. I'd known her for years, but we'd only seen each other in these kinds of settings. "You look so gorgeous. Who made that dress?"

The way I answered this would determine how she treated me for the rest of the night. "It's vintage."

"Oh, I love it." She spun me around like I was her plaything, and I let her. As long as she showed up and wrote checks that kept me in business, I'd let her be as

41

condescending as she wanted. My feet were killing me in these heels. They pinched and I was going to regret wearing them later, but they matched the short black dress that I was getting attention for right now. "But then again, when do you Redheads not dress to impress?"

I smiled. "You know us."

Truth was these days, Layla wore jeans more than anything else, while Bridget was always found in business suits. I was the only one dressing fancy, and I didn't think I was altogether that good at it. I was still trying to figure myself out in that way.

I left Drea and headed toward the exit of the party. I never had to be at these things the whole time. It was getting louder, and people were getting drunker. I'd done my job, I'd gotten the right people there. My clients needed something from me they couldn't get enough of on their own—attention from strangers.

My phone dinged, and I looked down at it, surprised to see Max there. He hadn't texted me in two days. We were weeks from the party, and the details were ironed out. I'd become convinced our night of texting was a fluke. I'd sent over oranges they'd needed, but I hadn't heard any acknowledgement of them.

What is your favorite restaurant?

That was a random question, considering things. I thought about what I wanted to say in answer and almost texted, *Well, I've heard there's this hot new restaurant downtown called Hyperion, but even after you manage to get a reservation, there's no guarantee you'll get to eat there*. I quickly deleted that. No. Not sending that. As amusing as I might find it, we weren't there yet and might never be.

I like this fish place called Aqualina uptown. It's quiet but busy, and they make the best scallops I've ever eaten.

He'd asked; I'd answered. That was the way to handle it.

I'd made it into my car, and Luke had pulled us onto the street to go back home by the time he answered me. *That's a really good one.* I was getting ready to put my phone in my purse when he called. I picked it up.

"I make better scallops."

I lifted an eyebrow. "Really? That's remarkable. Of course, I have no way of knowing." I winced as the words flew out of my mouth. Oh well, in for a penny, in for a pound, as one of my nannies used to say. "You could just be lying."

He laughed. It was a low sound, and not one I'd heard him make before. It was smooth like velvet, and it moved right through me. I wished I could make him laugh again and again and again. I leaned back in my seat.

"That's true. I could be. What are you doing right now?"

I yawned. It wasn't even that late. Maybe I was just old at twenty-four. Worn out. "Going home. I just worked."

"How did whatever event you were throwing go?"

I watched the traffic move around us, the pedestrians on the street going about their lives. In the front seat, Theo and Luke spoke to each other in low tones. "The gathering I organized was very successful. My client was happy."

"And you? Were you happy? What were you saving tonight?"

I shook my head. People didn't really get it, and I couldn't blame them. My role made little sense to anyone who wasn't living in this echelon of BS. Most people hated it if they ever got the chance to touch it. My sisters couldn't get away fast enough.

"Whales." I didn't touch the happy question. I wasn't sure anyone was happy, not really. But I wasn't in the mood to deal with the subject of happiness at the moment. It was too much.

"Did you eat?"

I looked at the time on my phone. It was eight thirty. "No. Shouldn't you be working?"

"It's Monday. We're closed on Mondays. I'm here because I'm working on your menu, but I could stop. I could meet you at Aqualina right now and go over some of this stuff."

The truth was that menu was set. We had set it in the contract. So he didn't want to meet me for that reason, unless he wanted to renegotiate, and I doubted he'd be doing that with me. Muffy had her lawyers for that sort of thing. He probably wanted to meet to talk more about why I'd done what I'd done.

And I wasn't in the mood.

"It's been a long day. I don't think I can take being yelled at tonight, even if I deserve to be yelled at every night, so I'm going to say no, but thank you."

He was quiet for a second. "I didn't ask you to have dinner to yell at you. I'm just…hungry. I thought maybe you'd be interested in joining me after hearing that you were too. Sometimes I get tired of cooking for myself. I want to eat other people's food. We don't have to talk about anything except that. I'm having…a day."

I could certainly understand that feeling. "I'll meet you there."

"Great."

Things had taken a sudden left-hand turn I hadn't seen coming.

～

AQUALINA WAS BEAUTIFUL INSIDE, serene. On a Saturday, we'd never have been able to walk in without a reservation.

44

Monday, however, at nine in the evening, I stepped through the door and easily found a table.

The waiter smiled at me. I was there enough to be recognized, even if I wasn't a favored customer. I didn't come in nearly enough, but timing was key. I ordered a water and waited. Just as I'd started to wonder if he would stand me up, and that was really why he'd set this whole evening into motion, Max arrived.

He was gorgeous, dressed in a pair of dark jeans and a white collared shirt that clung to all of his muscles. He wore black shoes.

"Hi." He sat down without much preamble. "Sorry, that took a hot second. There was a subway delay. Anyway, looks like we aren't the only ones eating late."

I smiled at him. There was something sort of surreal about sitting across a table from him like this. "I like when the restaurants are a little quiet, even if it's better for them to be busy, from the business standpoint."

He nodded, shooting me a look I couldn't quite decipher before looking at his menu. "The scallops are your favorite thing here?"

"Yes." I didn't even need to look at the menu to know. It was always the scallops. If they ever took them off the menu, I was going to be full-on sad.

"I'll get that." He crossed his hands together and stared at me. "You look really pretty in that dress."

I'd almost forgotten I was dressed up. My cheeks heated up, and in that redheaded way, I was going to be very red any second. "Thanks. It was for an event." He already knew that. "So, um…"

"I wanted to say thank you. The operation Eric needs is just not covered by insurance. It might be a last shot in the dark. He's had these terrible tremors and seizures for the last

45

few years. We took fire on our last mission together. We both walked away a little dinged up, but some neurological damage occurred that doctors missed right after it happened. It's very serious, and we've been having a lot of trouble getting him help. This might save him. Thanks."

Well, that was incredibly unexpected. I swallowed. "Um…you don't have to thank me. You *never* have to thank me. If I can help your friend by doing the very little that I did, then even better."

I picked up my water as the waitress greeted us.

Her interruption gave me a second to make my pulse stop racing. Max was intimidating, and it was hard to make me feel that way. It was like he sucked all the air from the room and only left enough for just the two of us to be there. If I weren't careful, I could get pulled into his vortex and never return. *Wow. I am being dramatic.*

And it was actually possible to have my nipples harden just by staring at him. I'd never had that happen before. Was it obvious? Could he tell? I looked down as discreetly as I could while he ordered himself a glass of red wine and couldn't see the telltale nubs, which was a good thing. *Phew.*

"And you? Can I get you something? Oh, and I'm sorry, I never do this, but you're a Redhead aren't you? One of *them*?"

I forced myself back into the present and my mind off my breasts. "I'm good with water, and sometimes I'm called that. I think you probably followed Layla more." I turned to Max. "Should we order?"

He lifted his eyebrows slowly. "We'll wait a minute."

"Great." The waitress stepped away.

Amusement flooded his expression. "People do that. They call you the Redhead? Like it's some kind of title."

It was bizarre, I'd give him that. "I share the title with my

46

sisters. It was given to us, strangely, when we were teenagers. The three of us showed up together somewhere, and someone gave us the name. It stuck. Spread. Social media. Came with being part of a young, rich group of teenage elites. There was a moment in time when being all those things were made really popular online by badly behaving socialites getting photographed everywhere. We were swept up in it, and at some point, my father decided it could be good for business. To help promote his business by using us. So he hired a PR firm, and we were pushed even further down the Redhead hole." I took another long sip of my water to cool down. "We handled it various ways. It hit Layla the hardest because she let the title take her instead of taking it. Bridget doesn't care. She ignores the hype and lives her life. And…"

"You used it." He filled in the blank when I didn't know exactly what to say. "To do what you wanted."

"Essentially."

The waitress dropped off his drink and took our order. We made small talk until our food arrived, and then I took a bite, letting the flavors rush me through. If I'd been alone, I'd have closed my eyes and I might have even moaned, but my manners kept me from expressing my joy aloud in company. Instead, I just smiled and quietly chewed. Yep…that was fantastic.

"It's really good." Max took bigger bites than I did, cutting bigger pieces. I watched as he chewed and swallowed. Okay, I was really getting preoccupied. I looked back down and cut another bite, making sure to eat my salad too. It had a sweet dressing I loved.

"So where are you from?" I really knew nothing about him except that he had a friend who was sick and I'd ruined his life. Oh yes, he also suffered from insomnia and didn't like chocolate.

I knew a few small things.

"A little coastal town in Maine. On the southern coast. Almost no one lives there in the winter, but the number of residents more than doubles every summer when it becomes a theater haven, a real place for art and performance. Every September, it's empty again, save for a few people from places like here who drive up to see the leaves change. By Christmas, totally empty."

I'd lived a lot of places but nowhere that resembled what he described. We'd always lived in big cities, no matter the country. "Does everyone know everyone else?"

"They do. My mother was one of those artsy people who used to go up for the summer, but she fell in love with a local man and stayed. They say that her first two winters, she almost left him because the winter is hard, but my mother is pretty tough and she grew to love it. Had eight kids, so I guess she'd have to be tough."

I stared at him. "Eight?"

"Eight." His grin told me he was used to that kind of reaction. "Dad taught history and then eventually became the high school principal. Six boys and two girls. I'm number three of eight. Boy, girl, boy," he held up his hand to indicate himself. "Boy, boy, girl, boy, boy."

"That's amazing." I guessed we were considered a big family because there were four of us, but we'd never been what anyone would consider functional, so I didn't think of us that way. "Where is everyone now?"

He smiled, finishing his food then setting down his fork. "Everyone is still there except for me. They all left and came back. There's a strong history of military service in my father's family. My Dad served. All of us guys did, and one of my sisters. The younger one, Trina, she didn't, but that's not surprising. She's really the most like my mom out of all of us. She tried to make it here on Broadway, like my mom did, but ended up going back home two years ago. Married her high school sweetheart. Teaching theater in the summers now."

I was totally fascinated. "That is…amazing. All of you together. Really sticking it out. But you're here?"

"Someday, I'll go back. I have things to do first. I served the longest. They were all in and out when their obligations were over, but I liked it. I kept going back." He looked away. "Until I was done. And then I wanted to do this. I never cooked a thing until I joined. But I loved it. Was good at it. Went to culinary school when I came out and then this life." He waved his hand. "My father calls it fancy food. He doesn't know how I picked up a love of fancy food." Max's smile was warm, loving. "That's basically me in a nutshell."

All the big details and none of the small stuff, but it was a start. "There is almost nothing about you online, other than some photos that get a lot of attention. Very little is publicly known about you."

"Well, that's on purpose. It turned out that was a good thing because few people have connected me, Max Broadley, with Maxim B, which is what they were calling me with the first restaurant. It helped I'd kept mostly to myself. I don't want to be a celebrity. I just want people to like my food." I'd stopped eating to listen to him and then quickly caught up. As I was finishing, he asked the question I avoided at all costs. "How long can you do what you're doing?"

I smirked. "Eating? Hopefully forever. It's a great joy of life."

"No, I mean trading off your celebrity to fill parties with the right people?"

I sighed. It was a valid question. I had no discernible skills outside of knowing the right people. "I ask myself that a lot. What's next? I don't want to end up sad and pathetic." *Fuck me.* Why had I said that to him? "So I'll have to figure things out. I just don't know what is next yet."

I was running out of time to figure it out. "My father is a fugitive. It bought me enough notoriety that people continue to be fascinated when they should probably have let me go."

"Oh, I doubt that. Your sister got kidnapped. That had to add time too."

Anger pulsed through my veins. "I would never trade off what happened to Layla. That was the worst day of my life, and trust me, I've had bad ones. I am many awful things, which you have seen for yourself better than anyone, but I love my sisters. They matter more than anything. I'll never trade off their pain."

Something crossed his gaze, and I wished I could read him, because I really never had any idea what Max was thinking. It was so unusual for me.

"Fair enough." He leaned back. "Hard to make you out, and I've been trying. You never fit the labels you should fit, Hope."

Well, that was something at least. The waitress offered us dessert, which I would have declined, but he smiled a small, sexy, private smile. "Split something with me?"

I found myself nodding before I could overthink it. "Sure, I love dessert."

We ended up with crème brûlée, a real favorite of mine, and a non-chocolate selection.

"So where is Layla now?" The waitress refilled my water glass before she delivered the food. This one was chatty.

Most of the time, waitstaff left me alone after making sure they'd correctly identified me.

I smiled at her. "Living her life someplace where no one gets to see her without permission."

She didn't like my answer and frowned as she left us alone. I'd have to make sure I tipped her well so Bitchy Hope didn't become my next nickname.

"I see what you mean about protecting your sister. Mine would have done the exact same thing." He handed me a fork.

We ate in silence, and eventually, I laid down my fork, much fuller than I'd expected to be at dinner. "Well, this is better than the cereal I'd probably have poured myself or some meal I'd microwaved."

"This is New York. You can get the best food in the world delivered any time, day or night. I think you should be able to do better than those two options."

He was right. "That's true, except I tend to shut off the world once I close the door to my apartment. I can't bring myself to order food and have to open it back up."

Why did I say the things I said to him? That wasn't something I readily confessed.

"I get wanting your sacred space to stay sacred." He shook his head. "I thought I might be able to make you out after tonight. I thought I could get a handle on you. Ever since I met you, I've found you aren't at all who I thought you were for years."

I took a last drink of my water, finishing it. "And? What have you decided?"

"I'm not sure of you at all, Hope. Every time I think I've got you handled, you surprise me. And I have no business wanting to be around you, but I do. I was just thinking I'd like to do this again. That I could eat with you all over

Manhattan. That it would be fun figuring out what you like to eat."

I forced myself to stay calm or to at least to look like I was. "I'm always up for a good meal. I'd like to know you too. Maybe you'll see I'm only a quarter the monster that you think I am."

"Sure, you're totally monstrous. You and those brown eyes that show nothing about what you're really thinking except when you're really mad. I can't tell too much else about you yet."

I winked at him. "I'm not the only one at this table who is hard to read."

"Years of learning it in the military. Before then? You'd have thought I was an open book." He rose and held out his hand, which I took because I liked that he'd offered it. "I'll walk you home."

That was sweet but unnecessary. "I have my car. My driver will get me home fine."

"Ah, yes, those special forces guys that you have trailing around watching you."

I liked how his hand felt in mine, how his was so much bigger than my own. "How did you know that? What they were?"

"It takes one to know one. We can always spot each other. They've made me too, that I guarantee. Well then, I'll walk you to the car."

When he squeezed our linked fingers, I almost became a pool of mush on the floor. "Which branch did you serve?"

He side-eyed me. Maybe I'd said it wrong. "I was in the army."

I could imagine him in uniform, and it was a damned sexy thought. Those broad shoulders and big muscles. He must have been sexy as hell in uniform. "Where were you guys when you took the fire that hurt Eric?"

He shook his head. "Maybe another night, but maybe not ever."

With a look he shot Theo, Max opened the car door for me. Right before I would have gotten in, he stopped me. "I don't do relationships. I'm bad at them. Whatever is happening between us, we can be friends, right? However it turns out, that's enough?"

I squeezed his fingers one more time. "Do you always hold hands with your friends?"

He tilted his head just slightly. "Depends if the friend in question looks like you in that dress, but point made."

I didn't let go when he would have pulled his hand away. "Look, I'm in no condition for a relationship. To put it bluntly, I am not really in a good head space for one. So yes, I'd like to be friends, whatever that looks like. I won't pretend I'm not attracted to you. That would be lying. But I have no idea what to do with that."

This time when he took his hand back, I didn't try to stop him. He ran his fingers through his dark locks before he gave me a full-on grin. "I guess we figure it out. Maybe we end up in bed together, maybe we don't. As long as we both understand there is no such thing as romance in our lives."

I nodded. "Don't worry, Max. I don't believe in Prince Charming, and I think you know better than most that I'm not Cinderella. We can both be grownups if that is what we both end up wanting."

He stepped back. "I think we both want it."

I got into the car and left him there on the street, glad when Theo drove away. I had to breathe. Had to think. *What is happening here?*

My phone dinged, and I looked down, blinking twice at the person whose name showed up there. Justin? My brother?

I hadn't heard from him in a long time. Not since he left Layla penniless and alone in France.

Hope, I think... I think I'm in big trouble.

Thoughts of Max flew from my head. Yes, I bet Justin was in big fucking trouble.

CHAPTER 5

JUSTIN WAS ONLY A LITTLE BIT OLDER THAN US. MY MOTHER had four kids in two years and had really suffered through it, from what I understood. She was an artist, a redhead like her four children, and when she'd died in her bed from an accidental overdose, two-year-old Justin had tried to care for us for over a day until my father got home. Four traumatized babies, starving, crying, and clinging to each other.

I'd always heard it was an accidental overdose. That was the running story. Somehow, everyone else had figured out she killed herself except for me. I'd only learned that fact a little less than two years ago from Layla, when she'd had to be hospitalized after her ordeal. Bridget had already known.

I waited for Justin to answer me, pacing around my apartment. Four locks. I'd gotten in and kept it four, somehow. This was like a point of pride for me. Exactly how many times did I have to lock my door in a building with doormen and my own paid security outside?

I paced from one side of the apartment to the other side. I wished Justin would answer. It wasn't like we were close. We never had been, and our relationship certainly hadn't changed since he'd handed Layla a bad credit card and left her penniless after stealing from her in Paris, when we'd taken even a further downswing. He was a drug addict, and I had absolutely no idea how to help him recover.

But he'd reached out, and he was my family. That meant I had to pay attention. I had to help him.

Didn't I?

I sat down on the bed and my phone dinged, only it wasn't Justin. It was Max. *Tonight was fun.*

I couldn't help my smile. *It was.*

I copied the message that Justin sent me and texted it to Zeke. I wasn't sure what else to do. I supposed I could send it to Michael Li, but truth was, I didn't know how Justin was being handled.

Before I could overthink, I sent Max another message. It was easier to be distracted by him, simpler to focus on that than what was happening with Justin. Max was a person who never had to know about my brother and the things he'd done to my sister. How it tore me up inside. One of them hurting the other. Layla was fine now. Happily married. She had a baby that Justin didn't even know existed. How could that be?

Shouldn't our shared history bond us?

Those were the thoughts that pushed through my mind as I texted Max.

Obviously, what you said is true. I'm very attracted to you.

I threw myself back down on the bed and stared at my ceiling as the phone rang. I picked it up. "Don't make me regret saying that."

"I'm not. But what I want to say to you next, I want to say, not text like some seventeen-year-old kid who can't own his words, can't hear his own voice saying things."

I rolled onto my stomach. "You already had my attention. Now you really have it."

"I told you tonight, I don't do relationships, and that's not something I just say. I tend to get what I want. I work for it. Sheer force of will sometimes. If I wanted to be someone's boyfriend or husband or anything like that, I would be. I don't."

If only he knew how perfectly fine with me that was. "You get that I'm a little fucked up, right? I mean, I don't have to spell it out, do I? I'm not on a path to traditional normalcy. Stop assuming I'm looking to marry you and go live in Connecticut with two kids and a dog."

Although I really should get a pet. But not a dog. They needed too much attention. Maybe a goldfish.

"I don't get you at all, Hope, and I've known a lot of fucked up in my life. I don't know if you qualify or not. I just know I want to spread open your legs and put my mouth on you until you come on my tongue. I know that can't happen as long as you think you're in some kind of debt to me. I'm not taking you as long as things aren't equal between us. So I'll just say this. If we have sex, it all stops. You stop using your connections to help me out of some need to fix what can't be fixed." He was quiet for a second. "Or this stops right now."

The last thing he said was very final. I didn't think I'd get him to budge on that point if I wanted to. "They're two separate things. Me wanting your body" —if only he knew how rare a thing that actually was for me. He was like magic or something—"and me wanting to get onions for you when you can't."

"They're not to me." His voice was so low, it moved through me like a gust of wind that almost knocked me over, even though I lay on my bed. "What's it going to be, Hope?"

"I'll stop with the food." That was how badly I wanted him. It was like a desperate wanting, and I was terrified it would go away.

"Give me your address. I can be there soon."

No. If he came here, then he might see through the layers I still had separating him from my level of not being okay. "I'll come to you."

"I'll text you my address."

I swallowed. This was really happening. "Great. Max, is this officially a booty call?"

"This is me getting off the phone. I'll see you soon." He hung up, and I grinned. I'd never had an experience like this before. Mostly because I'd avoided it like the plague. I didn't do things that ended up with people asking me to come over for sex.

Nerves settled in my stomach. I had almost no experience with this, and what I did have was…bad. I got off the bed. I could say no. It would be easy enough. I'd text him back and just be pithy about changing my mind.

Only I didn't want to. No, I wanted to know what it was like to have sex with this man whose presence had woken me up inside in a way I'd thought wasn't possible.

Can I go through with this?

I could.

I still looked relatively put together from dinner and quickly adjusted my makeup. On my way out the door, my mother's painting caught my attention. I'd bought it in an auction my first year out of college. It was worth a fortune, and I'd never have been able to pay for it now. Then, however, I'd been living off my father without thinking about money and getting a paycheck for doing very little for his company. I'd wanted it with a focus I hadn't had since.

Funny, I'd never considered how I'd bought it right after I

got out of the hospital. I might not have been in the best frame of mind, but that didn't matter anymore. I had it.

My mother had painted the sun coming over the horizon, only the colors weren't bright. They weren't the golden touches of a new morning. No, they were blue, black, and dark purple. The sun itself seemed to be glaring at me.

She'd painted it toward the end of her life, and my father had sold it, and every other work she created, almost immediately afterward to pay the bills.

Then he'd gotten very rich.

The title of this one had been *September*. She would die in October. My birthday was in September. I sighed.

Before I could overthink it, I sent Justin a message. *There's nothing so bad we can't fix it.*

I had to believe that for myself too. There was nothing I couldn't get past. I promised myself, my future sunrises weren't going to look like *September*.

I grabbed my coat and headed outside to search for a future that might start because I had one night with a man that wouldn't end in a relationship. Tonight could be about sex, and maybe if I could figure out how to keep it just that, I could start to let go of the past.

It shouldn't embarrass me to tell Theo where I was going, but it did. I just gave him the address and then totally pretended I wasn't embarrassed to have given them the address of where I was going to have sex.

I just stayed silent and pretended I was cool. I was a twenty-four-year-old woman. I could have sex with whomever I wanted without being judged by the guards employed to keep me safe. I sighed. My life was a little bit fucked up.

I texted my sisters. *I'm going to have sex.*

It took a hot second for Bridget to answer me. *Congratulations?*

She didn't get it, and that was my fault, not hers. I put away my phone. The building was right in between Midtown West and Hell's Kitchen. It wasn't a neighborhood I frequented. His home was on the corner of 48th and 10th. It was pretty there, so I made a mental note to check it out more later.

The building looked like it was a converted…something. I couldn't describe it better because it seemed like all the apartments in the area had been turned from one thing into something else. The last apartment I visited in the area had been made from a converted schoolhouse. They'd left chalkboards hanging in the apartments to indicate the past of the structure. I sort of loved it.

But I didn't know what his had been in its previous life. Some kind of warehouse, maybe? I wasn't sure. My hands shook as I sent him a quick text that just said *here*. Of course, I could just turn around and run. I could. Theo might not even judge me. Luke wouldn't care. He'd drive home and never mention it again. What was wrong with me? Twenty-four-year-old women went and had sex all the time. It was the thing to do. And yes, I—

My train of thought stopped as Max opened the door. I'd sort of expected him to buzz me in. With buildings like this, if the doorman was off or even if there weren't one, then that was the way it worked. Mostly. But there he was. He'd come to open it up himself, and that was sort of…sweet.

I forgot I was nervous.

"Hi." I smiled at him and left my worries on the street behind me. This would be fine. It would.

Max threw a look over my shoulder at the car, where

Theo stood on the street, but then turned all of his attention toward me. "I was hoping you'd still be in that dress."

"Well, I aim to please." Not really, but it seemed like something a woman with any sense of how to behave in a situation like this would say. I even winked at him, which made him frown at me. I hadn't meant that. Was I already fucking up?

He lived on the second floor, so we took the stairs because he told me the elevator was crazy slow. That was okay. I always preferred to walk when I could, and it had the added benefit of showing me where the stairs were, something I also really liked to know. Oh boy. This might not go as well as I hoped. There was nothing like not being able to control my thoughts. Escape routes and strange frowns. I might be behaving a lot odder than even I realized.

Maybe.

His apartment was beautiful. I saw so many and I wasn't easily impressed, but his was gorgeous and I loved it. The twelve-foot-tall windows must've let in incredible light during the day. With the shades open, I could see the lights of Manhattan surrounding us. I sometimes forgot, because I was simply used to the spectacle, how extraordinary New York looked at night. I kept my own drapes closed all the time. I never looked at anything anymore.

He didn't have a lot of furniture. A table that was low to the floor in what must have been the living room. There wasn't much of a separation between that and the eating area and the kitchen. Very standard for apartments this size. His table seated two. Max must not get too many guests. I smiled at the thought. Maybe this was unusual for him too. He had one couch, and it was white. Honestly, I would never have pictured him in such a bright place.

"This is gorgeous."

He nodded. "I was lucky it was available when I was looking. The first time I lived in New York, I lived downtown. This time, I wanted some separation from the restaurant."

He must be renting the space. Coming and going. If he'd owned his apartment, he would've come back to it. That was just how it worked with real estate in the city. I would probably own my place until I died, even if it were a hundred years from now.

I turned to look at him. Now that I could see him standing there, I realized he fit the space. Everything was clean, orderly. His kitchen in the restaurant had looked this way too. He might be the kind of person who kept order in his life. Clean lines, bright lights. No *September* here, for certain.

The whirlwind of mess that was me wouldn't fit in his space. Not long term. "How am I doing? Acting weird?"

His grin surprised me. "How am I acting? Wondering the same thing."

"Well then, maybe we could just both acknowledge doing this kind of thing is a little bit off and move forward from there."

He stepped toward me, touching the side of my face. "We could just talk."

That was sweet and absolutely the right thing for him to have said, only it wasn't what I wanted. I'd love to talk to him anytime, but that wasn't why I was here. Of course, he had no way of knowing how much I had on the line.

Or how gorgeous he was, and how I felt alive just looking at him.

Maybe he did know. I wouldn't put it past him to be fully aware of how good-looking he was.

I shook my head. "Always happy to talk, but I'd like

to…" I let my voice fade off. What was the right word to use? *Have sex*? *Fuck*? I didn't know, so I left it unspoken.

He nodded once, stroking his finger over my cheek. "Me too. Want a drink?"

Yes, but the answer had to be the opposite. "No thank you, but I will take some water."

"Water it is." He strode to the kitchen, and I immediately felt bereft from the lack of his hand on my cheek. It was cold where it had been warm. "I also have seltzer. Want that? Or flat water?"

"Oh." I followed after him. "I love seltzer."

He poured some in a glass and then side-eyed me. "Ice?"

"Yes, please."

His fridge was one of those that made ice, and after making a little bit of a squeaking noise, it deposited two ice cubes into the glass with the smallest of splashes. He winced. "Should have put the ice in first."

He was cute. I didn't think I'd ever seen him flustered before. He handed it to me, and I took it. "Thanks."

The water was cold on my tongue, and I was glad for it. He picked up a drink off the counter. It was an amber liquid that I'd guess was whisky. I actually loved a good glass of whisky. He drank it straight. Well actually, he sipped it. I watched him for a second because that was what he seemed to be doing to me. It was an odd moment, and not one I was sure we'd ever repeat—two people obviously watching each other drink.

I set down my water. He wasn't aggressive, that much was obvious. A woman my age who wasn't fucked up would know what to do with a gentle man—of that, I was sure—so I stepped toward him. "Should I kiss you?"

Maybe I should have just done it, because talking about things wasn't sexy.

63

"I'd really love you to." He set down his drink and tugged me to him. Tight against his body, I waited for the anxiety that even thinking about being in a man's arms would have caused just a year ago, but none came. He was warm, and he smelled fantastic. Clean and spicy, which I guessed came from the whisky.

I reached up and kissed him. He leaned down to meet me halfway, which was good because I was significantly shorter than him. His lips were warm and moist. I could immediately taste the whisky on him and decided that the mixture of Max and that liquor was my favorite new thing.

He was warm. I wrapped my arms around his neck. He drew me even closer, picked me up suddenly, and placed me on the counter. I yelped, then laughed. He'd managed to surprise me. I waited for the panic, but it didn't happen.

I pulled back to regard him for a second. He was beautiful, and I'd bet he'd hate it if I said the word aloud. I stroked my fingers down the side of his cheek. He'd let a little bit of facial hair grow, and it scraped against my fingertips. He smiled, a slow, sexy grin, as I stroked my finger over him.

Eventually, he stopped me, bringing my hand to his mouth to kiss it. I shivered. Neither of us said a word. Were most people silent during sex? I had no idea. But in this case, I thought perhaps the less said the better.

He kissed me, this time with so much heat, I thought I might expire from it. How could such a thing happen from just the touching of our lips? It never had in the past. I'd been kissed plenty as a teenager.

I tugged at his shirt, and he shook his head. "Not so fast."

"Why?" I lifted an eyebrow. "Are we waiting for something?"

"Yes." He picked me up again. "For starters, I really like

the kissing part. I can tell you do too, so why rush through it? We have all night."

The idea both comforted and terrified me, but not so much that I wanted him to stop. Max carried me in his arms across the apartment to his bed. His bedroom was medium sized for a New York City apartment. That was all I noticed. Well, that and the sexy black sheets as he laid me down on them.

I caught my breath. It just became very, very real. "I don't do this."

I don't know what compelled me to be so honest, but there it was. I had to say it, and now he knew. Well, he knew as much as I would ever confess. Maybe he could get the gist —I wasn't the sexually experienced woman social media called me, if he followed such things.

He shook his head. "Neither do I. Can't remember exactly how long it has been for me. But you got under my skin, and I have to have you tonight."

Something about his words, about his tone, about his possessive attitude, spurred me forward and shed what remained of my anxiety. Right then, I didn't care what happened in the past. I only wanted now. "Have me."

Max kissed me again. I no longer felt compelled to rush him through it. Maybe it wasn't the finish line that I needed to reach as much as to go through for this journey. He didn't know the gift he gave me tonight. After this, there would be freedom from wondering what the first time since the incident would be like. I would know.

And so far, I loved it.

His mouth came down on my own as he held his much bigger body off my smaller one like he was doing a plank. I didn't know how long he could maintain the position—I'd never been great at it—but he didn't seem to have any trouble, so I decided not to worry about it. I kissed and kissed him. Time passed, and I was so hot that I squirmed beneath him. He was hard everywhere, and I wanted to rub against his strength until I got lost in it.

But I controlled myself. I didn't know if that was weird or something. What I needed for this to be was as normal as was humanly possible, considering *things*.

He kissed both my cheeks and then tugged his shirt over his head before he winked at me. "Put your hands over your head."

"Why?" Some of the good feelings I had fled. Why would he want me to do that? My heart rate kicked up a notch, and I wasn't sure how I felt about what he said.

He tilted his head. "So I can take off your clothes."

"Oh, yes. Sure." I did as he asked, and he pulled my dress over my head.

Max didn't look down at my chest or check out my body. Instead, his gaze stayed on my face. "Nothing you don't want to happen will happen. This can stop right here."

"I do want this." I smiled. "I was just confused, I guess."

He kissed my chin, and then my nose. "A little dominance in bed can be fun, but not if we don't talk about it first when we're both dressed. Nothing even remotely like that is going to happen tonight. Or ever."

When I spoke, the best I could manage was a small voice. "Okay, Max. Sounds good."

He shook his head. "Nope. We're not here yet." He tugged me to him. "I can't do one-night stands most of the time, and I'm feeling like you can't, either."

"What?" *Oh fuck.* I'd somehow screwed it up. "I mean… you're right—I don't. But I want to. I'm sorry if I gave you the impression that I don't."

He scooted next to me, tugging me to his side. "I scared

you. Casual sex is great for some people, and I'm glad for them. But I think for me, there has to be something else. There has to be the connection that says you know the other person, their limits, and that you know that they know you. We could have pushed through anyway, but why bother? At the end of the day, neither of us would have gotten what we needed tonight."

I wanted to cry, but I managed not to. He was right, and he didn't even know how much so. I wasn't doing this just because I wanted him. I needed to prove something, and maybe I wasn't...able to do it. He'd just wanted to take off my dress, yet panic had started to set in.

I picked up my dress from where he'd flung it. "I'll go home."

"Only if you want to." He turned my face by touching my chin until I looked at him. "I'd still like you to stay here tonight. I like having you in my space." His smirk was fast. "I can't believe I feel that way, but I do. Let's...spend some time together."

I lifted an eyebrow. "Like...friends?"

"Like friends who are half naked in a bed together. Hope, we may very well end up in bed together another time, just not tonight."

Oh, I doubted that very much, but it was late, and I didn't really want to go crawling back out to my car where they were sure to know something was wrong. I hated that I even worried about it, but my life had always been about hiding the truth from prying eyes.

"What kind of television do you watch in bed?"

He kissed my cheek. "Whatever you want. As you know, I almost never sleep."

Yet another thing we had in common.

CHAPTER 6

IT SHOULD HAVE BEEN AWKWARD TO LIE IN HIS BED AND watch late night nothingness on television, but it wasn't. Actually, it was kind of nice. I was usually alone in bed, staring at the ceiling or zoning out on the TV in the hopes that I might eventually turn off my brain and go to bed. At least here, I had company. Max was actually very nice, which only made the fact that I'd basically screwed up his life even worse. Not that I should feel better about it if he were a monster, but still. These were the sorts of thoughts that raced through my mind as we stared at someone demonstrating a product that promised to cook ribs in five minutes flat.

He shook his head. "Where is the fun in that?"

I could see why he'd think so, but others might not. "Maybe there's a mother of five out there just trying to get it done. Cooking the ribs in five minutes flat could really help her."

Max nodded slowly. "Sure. I can see how that would help. Only I bet that tastes like hell, and they're zapping all the nutrition right out of it."

He ran his finger up my arm once, then again. And then

68

again. I loved the feeling. He didn't seem to be doing it consciously. His eyes and attention were glued to the screen. I leaned my head on his shoulder, and he leaned the side of his on top of mine. It was intimate in a way that I didn't think sex would have been.

Maybe tonight wasn't a total wash for me getting over things.

Do people ever really get over things?

There I was with my thoughts again.

"Why don't you sleep well? Or much?" I watched his fingers move on my arm instead of the television. It was somewhat hypnotizing. I really shouldn't have asked the question because he was going to ask me why too, and I didn't really want to tell him.

He sighed. "Combat has that effect on people sometimes. It's better than it used to be. The years pass, and with lots of help, I am better at managing it. I still don't sleep a lot, but that's okay. I function well enough. I seem to be healthy. I exercise. Things could be worse. I'm lying in my bed with a beautiful insomniac right now."

My cheeks immediately heated up, and since we'd positioned ourselves the way we were, I couldn't look up and see if he were laughing at me. "Are you making fun of me?"

"Not in the slightest."

He thought I was beautiful. It wasn't that I hadn't heard the words before. I had, and over the years, I'd come to actually hate it. Was it because I was considered so physically attractive that I'd been left open to just be...? Nope, I wasn't going there. I'd Scarlett O'Hara syndrome it—I'd think about it tomorrow. One of my nannies loved that movie.

Max saying I was beautiful felt different. It actually moved through me like it was something I should want. It was flattering. Yet, I still gave my answer the way I always did. "My mother was spectacularly pretty. She passed off a little bit to us, but you know what they say?"

He was quiet, but when he answered, it was with amusement in his voice. "No, Hope. What do they say?"

"Beauty and folly are old companions." I said the line and was comfortable with the idea that the conversation would move past my looks. No one really knew exactly what to say when flattered, right?

"And she quotes Benjamin Franklin."

Well, that is unusual. I shifted my head, separating us, and we both looked at each other instead of leaning on each other. "You know who said that."

"I do. I went to school." He winked at me. "And I'm not a guy who reads fiction. I like to read biographies and autobiographies. Anything about history." He took a strand of my hair in his hand. "Is that your way of telling me that you don't like to be complimented about how you look?"

I sighed. "I don't really know what to do with it. I get all this attention for how I look, but when I stare at myself, what I see is that parts of me look like my mom, parts of me resemble my siblings. My brown eyes are all my father. And…" I sighed. "I'm afraid, if this is all I am, then soon I will be nothing at all."

He furrowed his brow as I spoke and then eventually nodded. "Maybe it's what first strikes people about you, but it isn't what I think of when I think about you anymore. I mean, sure, I do think about what you look like. I'm crazy attracted to you, sometimes despite myself. But I keep thinking of how you managed to clear all that fruit from customs." He grinned at me. "It was insanity."

"So what you're saying is it starts with the pretty, but people stick around for the way I am absolutely out of my mind?"

70

He touched the end of my nose. "Totally that."

Somehow, what he said seemed about right. We ended up lying back down, but this time, I pressed up to his chest. His heartbeat was steady and strong against my ear.

Time passed slowly, as it always did at night. Max tangled his hand up in my hair, rubbing the back of my scalp gently. "Why don't you sleep?"

There was the question. He hadn't been put off, just delayed. Or maybe he'd been giving me time to think about it, knowing the query would be coming. I didn't know him well enough to have that answer.

"Would it be okay if I didn't say? There are lots of answers, and all of them are...distasteful."

He nodded. "We're all entitled to our secrets. It's one of the few things that belong just to us. Yes, you don't have to tell me." He kissed my forehead. "Friends respect each other's boundaries. Or at least we do *sometimes*. I don't always, but I will this time."

The thing about talking when I should have been sleeping was at some point, my mind wanted to shut off, even if it couldn't. I could get weird, rambling, and not even know what I was saying half the time. Like I was asleep and talking...but not, because I was actually awake.

I'd learned over the years to just shut down when that happened, so I didn't say things I would later regret. I snuggled down against him, and he shut off the light, leaving the room dark except for the flashing of the television. He changed the channel twice, finally landing on a black and white movie that featured a man on a horse. I didn't know what it was and I supposed I could ask, but my brain didn't want to work anymore.

If I were this shut down, why couldn't I sleep? It was so...frustrating. His breathing evened out, and I looked over to see he'd shut his eyes. That was good. I was glad that Max could actually get some sleep. I stared at the screen some more, trying and failing to make sense of the movie. Finally, I picked up his remote and turned it off. He didn't budge, which was good because sometimes, the sudden onset of silence registered as loud and disturbing to me.

I stared into the darkness. It was nice not to be alone. His breathing was even, not disturbing, and he didn't move around or jar me in any way. I'd never shared a bed like this. The hours passed, slowly. Some nights were fast, but this wasn't one of them.

Eventually, I lulled into being able to sleep, sort of. It was a funny kind of a thing on nights like this. I could sleep, but I was conscious of doing it, so it didn't make me feel particularly rested. I drifted on a boat, but it was like I'd put myself there. I could stop at any time. It wasn't fun, and I almost wished I hadn't done it at all. But the not dream continued, so I hoped it would transfer into actual sleep.

His alarm went off, interrupting my pseudo sleeping, and I lifted my head as he rolled over to turn it off. "Sorry." He sort of grunted as he spoke. "I should have told you. I always get up early."

I rubbed my eyes, trying to smile. Not sleeping was hard but it wasn't his fault, and I needed to not act like a psycho grump woman he'd rather not see again. I liked being friends with him, even if it didn't end in the sex I'd wanted. If anything, he was really upstanding to not push it when I was clearly not ready. "That's okay. I have things to do."

He tugged on the end of my hair until I looked at him. "You okay? Did I keep you up? I didn't mean to fall asleep without you. Guess you are warm and soothing, Hope."

I shook my head, trying to stifle a yawn. "No one has ever

72

called me that. Just give me one second to pull myself together, and I'll get out of your hair."

He sat up, pulling me against him. "Are you under the impression that I'm kicking you out? Eat breakfast with me and come to the gym. We can say goodbye later."

Now he had my full attention. Well, the best I could give it before I'd caffeinated through this haze of a morning that I could already tell was going to be one of those days. "I don't have anything to wear to workout. I'm going to exit this apartment in the dress I wore here. It is a great dress, but not conducive to the gym."

He laughed as he got out of bed. For all that he didn't sleep very much, he woke up in a much better mood than me. That could be an aggravating quality, and maybe the first thing about Max that I wasn't sure I could get behind. *Of course, it might also be because my middle name might as well be grumpy this morning. Hope Grumpy Radford.*

"Okay. We'll go back to your place, grab you some clothes, then go to the gym. All of that, though, after we eat." He was already halfway out of the room when he said the last bit.

"You're big on this gym thing, aren't you?"

"Oh," he called back to me. "You must go to the gym, Hope."

I managed to pull myself out of the bed and put on my dress, which looked a lot less pretty this morning. I did go to the gym. I hated every second, but I did it. I couldn't love food as much as I did, wear the clothes I needed to be seen in, and not do some kind of exercise, but I hated it. Despised the gym like I was being forced to participate in torture every week.

Layla loved to run, and as much as I couldn't get over all the hugely positive changes that happened to her since she got together with Zeke, running was not one I could understand.

The smell of coffee wafted into the room, and it made me move a little bit faster. I didn't know that I was up for a whole big meal, and I really wasn't sure on the gym thing. I might just tell him a resounding *no*. But I'd take the coffee. I'd never say no to that.

He stood at the stove, and as I entered the room, a second smell overtook the coffee. He was making eggs. I loved eggs. My stomach rumbled. Maybe I'd have to reconsider the not eating bit. Max stepped away from the pan, giving me a view of his backside.

There was no doubt he was a beautiful man, probably at least in part because he hated the gym less than me, since it was part of his morning routine.

"Cream?" he asked over his shoulder. "Milk? Sugar? Sweet and low?"

I'd spent the night in his bed, but neither of us knew even the most basic things about each other, not even the way we took our coffees. For some people, that might be normal, but for me it just felt…weird.

"Just cream." I didn't like the way sugar tasted in my coffee. If there was the smallest amount of bitterness, I actually preferred it.

He nodded, taking a container out of the fridge before he poured some in a cup he then passed to me. Max's every movement seemed fraught with purpose. He didn't squirm, didn't seem to make a move unless he had to, almost like he was a dancer on a stage instead of a man in the kitchen.

I shook my head. He was only making coffee. My mind on no sleep was not a pretty place to exist. I sipped the coffee. "Thanks."

"You're welcome." He lifted his gaze. "I'm making eggs I

think you'll like. If you don't, I can make them a different way the next time we eat breakfast together."

I took a seat at the counter across from where he was cooking. "Are we going to do this again?"

He smirked as he stared down at the eggs, touching them for one second with his spatula. "I think we both know that we're going to be doing this again. Last night wasn't the end of something, it was the beginning."

Max turned off the eggs and poured something on them before he put the fire back on. It was a white substance. "What's that?"

He lifted his eyebrows but didn't look up at me, instead stirring the eggs with his spatula. "A sauce I've perfected over the years."

"What's in it?"

He smirked. It was adorable. How did men do that? If I smirked, they'd call me bitchy. Well, I knew how they did it, but I was too tired to deal with all those reasons at the moment. I needed more sleep to smash the patriarchy.

He said, "I'll never reveal my secrets."

"When did you make sauce? You've been out here for two minutes."

He turned his back to put the container back in the fridge. "I make a lot of stuff on Sundays. Some for the restaurant, some for my personal use. I store it in the fridge if I don't bring it in to work. It's my prep day. Helps me feel very... prepared. I always have my favorite sauce on hand."

"And you're not going to tell me what's in it?" My mouth already salivated.

He turned off the stove top and spooned the eggs onto two plates, passing me one before he got out a fork for both of us. "Try that. I'm going to make some toast too."

I took a bite and then closed my eyes. The moan that I

released wasn't purposeful, it just happened. "Wow, that is good."

When I opened my eyes, he grinned at me. "It never gets old. When people like what I cook? It never ceases to be the best part of any day."

"What did you put on these? Plus, they're so light and airy!"

As we spoke, he moved about the kitchen, taking bites of his own eggs, toasting the bread, and pouring more coffee. He never seemed to have to look at anything as he did it, as if he knew exactly where everything was without needing to check. The whole thing was impressive and ridiculously sexy. "Thank you on the eggs, and the sauce is my version of what they'd call a Greek bechamel."

I'd never heard of it. "How is yours different from a traditional Greek version?"

He leaned onto the counter, smirking at me. "That is my secret."

I sipped my coffee, suddenly feeling full and happy. Good food did that to me. There was a euphoria to eating like this. "Thank you for breakfast."

Max leaned farther toward me and stole a kiss. "You're welcome. Finish your coffee."

I took a long drink of it. I never left coffee unfinished.

We rode together to my apartment in my car. Max leaned back and stared at the front seat, where my security had shut themselves behind a barrier and couldn't hear us. Or so they said. Maybe I read too many spy novels. I doubted everything these days.

"So they just follow you around and drive you where you want to go?" He pointed at the front seat. "These two?"

I yawned. "Mostly them, but obviously no one can be with me all of the time. They trade out with two other people,

76

but I know them the best. They are my most constant guards."

"What does having that kind of security cost, just out of curiosity? I know someone who does this for a living. He works for a security firm. We served together. I know he's earning a fortune doing it, and honestly, it's perfect for his personality. Good fit for him as a job."

I shook my head. "That's a good question. My brother-in-law pays for security for all of us. My sister Bridget, his wife, Layla, and myself. He would cover Justin too, but he's in Russia with my father." Thinking of him made me check my phone. Nothing from Justin. Why had he reached out if he didn't want to start a dialogue? Why send me that one thing and nothing else? "Zeke is very generous with us. I'm not sure..." Well, truthfully, he was someone else I didn't know how to pay back. These sorts of problems were adding up in my life.

Max shifted in his seat. "What kind of danger does he think you're in? Like you could get stolen off the street or gunned down in the car? Or they just want to drive you crazy until your father does whatever it is he has to do?"

"They pulled my sister off the street and kept her for several days until Michael Li, who runs our security, got her back. I guess they feel the same could happen to me." I rubbed my face. I hated talking about all of it. "They're working on putting a stop to this and then the security can stop. I'm grateful for the help."

"Ah, yes. I'm sure you are." He shook his head. "But your tone tells me that you have multiple feelings about it."

I startled, turning to look at him. "Am I that easy to read?"

"Little bit." He took my hand. "But enough about your guards. They hate me. The looks they shoot me? I get what they see. You're young, gorgeous. They think I'm some lecherous bastard bothering you."

I laughed, which surprised me. "Because you're ancient?"

"Right. Well, next to you I am, Hope. I'm going to be forty on my next birthday."

That was kind of what I'd thought when I'd tried to guess in my head. "Which is when? How many months are you from this date that will make you, in your mind, geriatric?"

His grin was worth the joke. "Ten months."

"Well, there you go. I don't think that's why they don't like you. They were there when you threw me out of the restaurant."

He tilted his head. "Well, that'll do it."

"Hey, maybe it makes sense to go to my gym. We're on my side of town now. Come with me to mine. It's closer."

"Sure." He nodded to the building as we pulled up. "This your place?"

"It is."

When he moved to open the door, I stopped him. "No, they have to open it."

He shook his head fast. "Not for me. They can stand in front of you and let you out, but I'm not going to sit here while they rush around opening doors for me. I'll never be able to show my face at home again. Besides, nothing is going to happen to you when I'm around. I'm not without my own skills, I assure you of that."

I opened and closed my mouth. What was I supposed to say to that? Max jumped out, but Theo helped me the way he usually did, and I met up with Max on the sidewalk. "Wouldn't want to undermine your male ego."

He laughed, throwing his head back. "Fair enough, Hope. Call me on my bullshit, but it's mine and I'll own it."

"Come on." I walked inside, nodding to the doorman. I

had a list of people who were allowed up—my security team and my sisters. I'd added Zeke. Not that he'd ever been to my apartment, nor did I expect him to come. Layla wouldn't either, most likely. They were going to stay in their vineyard and raise their family. I was sure Noah wouldn't be their last baby.

We took the elevator to my apartment, and I let us in. I'd no sooner closed the door than the need hit me. I hadn't thought about it, but bringing him into my apartment meant that I was going to have to deal with my need to lock my own door over and over again in front of him.

"Wow. That's a view." He walked to my window, and I tried to breathe. It wasn't going to work, but I tried.

When I had to lock and lock again and again, it was as though my brain simply couldn't move on until I did. I rushed to the lock. I had to. I just had to. I clicked the lock. Again. And then again. Four times. And then I swung around. He'd turned to look at me, but he didn't say anything.

I'll just pretend nothing happened. "Give me two seconds to change."

Max nodded. "Sure."

By the time I'd gotten to my closet, I had to wipe at my tears. *This is over now.* I never showed anyone my need to lock. I'd thought about showing Layla, even invited her to stay with me so that we could be open about it, but she had gone to Washington instead. I got it. Layla had more than earned her life.

But the first person to see it was Max, who would probably not be out there when I got back from changing. I threw my clothes on and put on my happy face. I was good at this—cry, then fake that I hadn't. I'd been doing it my whole life. I splashed water on my face, threw on my yoga pants, and my tank top that made a witty remark about day drinking, and headed back out.

Max stood staring at *September*. "I can't decide if I should be sad or not looking at this painting."

He'd read it correctly, and he was still there, which said something. "I'm sure she meant it to be.

"You know the painter?"

"It was my mother's. She's dead."

I had to unlock the door I'd just exposed myself locking. *This is a terrible idea.*

CHAPTER 7

My gym was always a who's who of the Upper East Side. I couldn't speak for the other neighborhoods of town, but I knew there was one just like it on the Upper West that did nearly the same things. I supposed I should know the names of all the gyms. Maybe I could drum up more people to invite to my gatherings. I had to think like this all the time.

I ran as hard as I could on the treadmill, which wasn't a particularly impressive feat. I wasn't an athlete. Since college, it seemed like everyone I knew had become a runner, including my sister. But the more I tried, the more I hated it. I wasn't going to be running 5ks, let alone marathons. I was not an athlete, and this wasn't pretty.

In the meantime, I ignored the fact that I was there with Max. He ran on the treadmill next to me, ear buds in his ears, and he didn't even seem out of breath, despite the fact that he ran twice as fast as me. It was pathetic really how bad at this I was.

I had another minute in me, and then I was going to have to call it a day. The lack of sleep wasn't helping either. I had too much to do to be so exhausted. I might break a rule and take a pill to put away the not sleeping problem for one night. I didn't like how I felt afterward, though. Being so deeply asleep, I was out of control worried me too. Of course, that was ridiculous. I lived in a building with a doorman and had the added benefit of security, who sat outside the building the whole time. No one was getting in my apartment. I could take a pill and be fine.

But my anxiety wasn't reasonable and never had been.

I could never bring myself to do it.

Of course, none of that had anything to do with the fact that my mother took too many pills and never woke up again. *Nothing the fuck to do with my fears at all.*

I stopped the treadmill. Another problem with running—I thought about too many things when I did run. I grabbed a towel and wiped my face before I headed to the mats where I'd do my sit ups, stretches, and lift some weights. Then I'd be done. I wasn't going to join a class or breathe through some yoga. I had this much in me and no more.

That was when I spotted her. My heart clenched, and I almost fled for the locker room, except that would be a lot worse than just hoping she didn't spot me.

Amanda Hill, gossip vlogger extraordinaire. She plagued my family. Luckily, she cared a lot less about me than she did about Layla. The woman had searched for Layla for the past year. My sister's location wasn't secret, but there was no way for her to catch her on video at their vineyard in Washington. For the moment, anyway, she and my nephew were hidden from the world, just like Layla wanted it. Amanda didn't even know that Noah existed, and I intended to make sure she didn't find out.

If Amanda didn't find me as interesting as Layla, she hated Bridget. I didn't know why, but I didn't plan to ask.

I didn't want to talk to Amanda Hill at all.

Max sat down next to me, stretching out his hands over his head. He winked at me, seemingly totally unaware the movement revealed the bottom half of his abs or that they were drool worthy, even in a room filled with people who could claim that title for themselves.

"This place is a lot fancier than mine. I feel like everyone is staring at each other."

I nodded and gave a little wave to an heiress who walked past. "They are, and it can be very helpful to me."

"Must be exhausting, yet you can't sleep."

That was the last thing I wanted to talk about. A thought dawned on me, and I almost didn't say it, but he had the right to know. "That woman over there with the long brown hair and the gray eyes? Pretty face. She's talking with her hands right now to the tall guy with the red shirt, do you see her?"

He blinked and then looked over at Amanda. "What about her?"

"She's a gossip vlogger."

Max shook his head. "And she just gets to…walk around here, into a room full of all the people she might want to talk about, and everyone acts like it's just fine?"

I smiled at him. "Sure. We all make nice. Thing is, if you wanted to pay me back—if you wanted to do to me what I did to you—then you could tell her something about me right now. You could ruin me if you want to. She is the one with the video who showed it to everyone. It's her most watched stream to date. She could do it again, this time on your behalf."

He dropped his arms from the stretch. "So you live in a world where you work out with people who talk badly about you publicly, and now someone you spent the night with might decide just hours later to destroy your life?"

I waited a second before I answered, because I had to

consider what to say. He seemed to have missed my point entirely. "I guess I do."

"That is really fucked up." He shook his head. "Somehow also not surprising, but you aren't like that, so why do you do this? I'd also like to know why you said it in the first place, but I know you're not going to answer me. You'll evade it. That's fine. I just wonder, that's all." He pointed at me. "Your eyes are brighter right now. I think you're feeling endorphins."

Was I? I didn't know, but I certainly did feel awake. That was nice for a change. "Are you? Feeling the good vibrations from exercise?"

He shook his head. "Takes a lot more exercise to bring on an endorphin rush for me. This wasn't my normal routine. This was more like…a jaunt at the gym."

I snorted and then covered my face with my hand like I could muffle the sound. "Did you just say a jaunt at the gym?"

"I did." His smile was huge as I dropped my hand. "Hope…"

"Oh my god, it's you!"

We'd been spotted. Amanda stood staring down at us like we were peasants at her feet—not the ideal way to be found by the gossip vlogger. Then again, I was the least interesting person in the gym at the moment, so I hadn't really expected her to focus on me.

I smiled because that was what I always did. What every good little socialite did. And that was how I made my living. "Amanda! Hello there. It's been a while since I saw you."

Her smile was cold, calculating. Mean. *If she didn't have legs, she'd slither on the ground like a snake. All she needed was a forked tongue and…*

"I've been looking for you. Coming at various times to try

to find you. I guessed you hadn't been working out." She looked me up and down. "I think I was right. Look at you, winded like you climbed Everest." She had an affectation where she put on a lisp. It was always present during her videos, but not so much when normally speaking. Why did she do that? Sometimes I couldn't figure people out.

I waved my hand. "I didn't see you on the treadmill. You're not sweating at all. Just getting started or are you some marvel that never sweats? It's supposed to be a good detoxing system."

Max rubbed my back, a light stroke. I didn't know his intent, but the effect was to remind me I should watch my tone.

She laughed. "Just getting started, but I run every day. I sweat. I love it." She lifted an eyebrow. "I have to admit I've been very concerned about Layla. She and I are such good friends." Oh boy, were they *not* friends. She knew it. I knew it. Anyone who watched her vlog knew it. "Where is she?"

Layla wasn't hiding from anyone. Not really. Her husband owned a vineyard, and the family lived on the property. They were eventually going to start selling wine. A real journalist could find her in under two minutes. Bill of sale. Companies registered legally—because Zeke was big on doing things by the book—in the United States. They'd get an address. If they could get past her security, they'd be able to ring her fucking doorbell and see Layla face-to-face.

Someday, they might even open a tasting room. Layla and I discussed decorating space for tastings together the last time I visited her.

The piece of shit in front of me made me madder than she usually did—probably because I was so tired—because she couldn't be bothered to do that kind of work. No, all she could do was take photos and videos or buy them while she picked apart Layla's life and said terrible things. She didn't know Layla married Zeke, so it might be a while before she figured out she had a new last name. And thank the universe, she didn't know about Noah.

I got to my feet, and Max rose next to me. "Layla is happy and well."

"I'd love to say hello."

I was done. If I'd had anything in my hands, I might have thrown it at her. Maybe it was a good thing the gym made us lock up our stuff in lockers when we came in. "If Layla wanted you to find her, she'd let you. Otherwise, I suggest you get some kind of life that doesn't involve destroying others and leave my sister the fuck alone."

The gym had gone completely silent. Yes, I'd just told off a woman who formed public opinion. She was a tastemaker, an influencer on Instagram. Like me, she was the kind of person who could squash me like a bug, if she wanted. Despite all that, she knew my sister didn't want her to find her, yet had the audacity to ask me anyway. We owed her nothing.

"Here's some advice, move on from Layla. She's off limits to you. Find something new to talk about. Surely you must have enough brain cells to find someone easier to chase."

Her smirk told me all I needed to know. I'd walked right into that one. *Damnit*. I knew better. What was the matter with me?

Tears threatened, but I held them back. Nope. It wasn't time for the great Hope freak-out. Not yet.

"Where is she?"

I pointed at her. "Off your radar."

Next to me, Max shifted his weight. *Oh no.* He was going to say something. I couldn't let him do that. I'd ruined his life once before, and I wouldn't do it again. I swung around to stare at him. "And you. It's bad enough that you threw me out of the best restaurant in town." Amanda would already know that. "You have to yell at me here?"

I threw him a look over my shoulder and hustled to the locker room. Hopefully, she'd think he wasn't involved with me and not take him down because he had the bad luck to be seated next to me on a mat at the gym. I pressed my back against the wall and tried to breathe for a second before I put on my clothes. I was sweaty and a mess. Although I needed a shower, I wanted out of this gym.

I needed to get home and start thinking about the rest of my day. I had an event that night. What was I doing? I had no business spending all this time with this man, anyway. I couldn't even have sex. What kind of total idiot couldn't do that? I grabbed my bag and hustled myself outside, where I immediately collided into Max.

He grabbed me. "Whoa, there. Don't hurt yourself. What was that? Are you okay?"

I wiped at my face. I was still managing not to cry. That was a small miracle. "I didn't want Amanda to come after you."

"I got that. She flirted with me for half a second and moved on. She tells me she's eaten there. But she moved on after she got what she wanted from you. Wow. She really pushed your buttons. Are you okay?"

I nodded. "I'm fine. I just need to go."

"Okay, let's go. Come on." He took my hand. "And I'm proud of how you stood up for your sister."

I shook my head. "It's the least I could do. I left her in Paris once with no money and entirely on her own."

"Why?" He waved to Theo, who was maneuvering

through traffic to bring us the car. "That doesn't sound like you."

"When I make mistakes, I make big ones. I wish I could say it was just every once in a while. I think I have a tendency to do it at least three times a week."

Max scrunched up his face. "Don't round up. Maybe it's more like two point five times?"

I laughed. Nothing should have been funny, but there it was. He'd just made me laugh when things were really, really not funny. "Maybe it's more like two point five."

"Come on. You've had enough today. That is for sure. I'll take you home, then I'll jump on a subway and go home. Don't let that small-minded person bother you. She's…sad."

Easy for him to say. His life didn't depend on people like her. "I have an event tonight, so I should get going."

He nodded. "Next time, we'll go to my gym. The only person you'll see there is a man named Joey who might talk your ear off about his grandson."

That sounded like a plan. I also liked the *next time* in that sentence, even if I knew it was pretty much impossible.

LATER THAT DAY, having showered and eaten cereal dry because I was out of milk, I tried to do my work for that evening. Everything was mostly done. We were raising money for children with cancer. It was a worthy cause, and I was glad to help the elderly socialite do it. She'd been nice enough, but when I talked to her, it felt like I might be looking at my own future and I didn't love the preview.

Sure, she was rich. She had a big apartment in the city with views of Central Park. Pretty furniture. Nice clothes. Four ex-husbands that made her roll her eyes when she talked about them. But no family around. No one to really talk to. People had moved on, and while maybe she was happy with her own constant company, I wasn't sure that I could be.

She'd never indicated to me that she wasn't happy.

I just wasn't sure I could be her and not be miserable all the time. What did that mean? I wasn't sure. Maybe I could find one husband that I could love for always, like Layla and Zeke. Maybe Bridget and I could share an apartment?

How is the dating life going? I sent the text to Bridget as I thought of her. I had suggested that she start looking for Australian surfers. She'd told me there weren't that many of them hanging around in Hong Kong on the trading floors.

Bridget didn't reach out much anymore. Was that because of me? Did my family just not want me around?

Was I making a nuisance of myself?

And how was it that Max's sweat smelled so good? We'd sat together in the car, and it was like I couldn't get the scent out of my head. I sighed. He had probably experienced the opposite with me. I had been pretty rank by the time I got home. I shook my head. *Time to concentrate.*

I needed to do my makeup and get on with this.

Was just going to text you. Bridget answered me. *Fuck that woman.*

I stared at the response. That didn't make a lot of sense, considering what I had asked her. What woman?

I'm going to fly back to New York and kick her so hard, her head spins.

I stared at the text. Well, that was violent, which was not like Bridget at all. *Whose butt are you going to kick?* I texted.

There was a long pause before she answered me. *Amanda Hill.*

Fuck. What had Amanda done? I'd just encountered her that morning in the gym, so I figured I'd get twenty-four hours before she posted about me. Hell, between then and now, some heiress could have fallen over drunk, kicked over a tray, and landed funny on the street. That would have taken her attention off me faster than anything else.

What had she done?

Ignore it if you haven't seen it.

I set down the phone and walked over to my computer, ignoring what was probably good advice from my sister. According to my father, who I was surprised could remember it, our birth order was Bridget, then me, and then Layla. She'd sometimes acted like my big sister, having breathed the air of the green Earth thirty seconds before I did.

But I needed to know what Amanda had done before I faced the event that evening. My reputation literally dictated my job. I'd yelled at her, and that was stupid. How big a hole had I dug with my fury?

Amanda looked at the camera. She wore gray, which looked good with her blonde hair and gray eyes. The woman always knew how to dress herself. Truth was I knew almost nothing about her. I'd never learned her background. I didn't know if Amanda was even her real name. Did she pay all her bills from advertising from her social media accounts, or did she have some other source of income that I knew nothing about?

"Well, what a morning I had." She smiled at the camera. "I know that I promised you that today we would talk about who wore what and who shouldn't have worn what they did at the gala two nights ago. I mean…it shouldn't be so hard to track down designers, but I digress."

I rolled my eyes. It wouldn't be hard if she knew the right people. There was some happiness to be found in the fact that I could have gotten to those designers immediately.

Not that it mattered.

"This morning, I was at the gym where I had the unfortunate luck to run into Hope Radford. That's right—my second favorite Redhead was at the gym." She smiled, and there was pure joy in it. "Layla, if you are seeing this, you are still my favorite, darling. New York isn't the same without you here, Redhead."

I rolled my eyes. Layla would never see this. She was deep in baby happiness and being loved by the man of her dreams. If the knowledge of my sister's happiness caused me the smallest amount of jealousy, then I was just going to add it to the growing list of all the things I didn't like about myself.

"So, anyway, I saw Hope. Can I just say thank god she was at the gym? She looks like hell. I mean…if I didn't know she was Layla's sister, I wouldn't believe it. Not. Pretty. Right. Now." She shook her head. "I know. I know. You're going to leave me comments telling me that I shouldn't say things like that about our fellow females. Girl Power. But seriously, yes, she looked like hell. She was there arguing with Max Broadley. Maybe it's a good thing he kicked her out of his restaurant? It would be wise if she stayed away from such fatty foods for a while."

I gasped and turned off the computer. Had she just called me fat and ugly? My ears rang. My phone buzzed and I was sure it was Bridget, but I ignored her because I had to think. I rushed to the mirror and stared at myself. I didn't look much different than I usually did. Granted, I had been at the gym, but I'd worn cute workout clothes.

Did I look like hell?

Fuck. I had to get out of this headspace. Maybe there would be a time when it wouldn't matter. When women could be raised to not care what people said about them physically. Maybe women would stop saying such things. Maybe men would. Maybe there were people out there who didn't care. I wasn't one of them.

It was pathetic and I'd add it to the ever growing list of my worst traits, but I *did* care. I had to care. Being pretty was part of my public persona.

Amanda was mean, petty. She meant to hurt me because I'd yelled at her. Well, she'd done it. I was this shallow. She'd called me ugly on a vlog that was picking up thousands of watches by the minute.

And it mattered.

I had to get dressed. If I'd known this was going to happen today, I'd have made a hair appointment and used a professional makeup artist. I knew how to put myself together, and I was going to be stuck with the job I could do on an evening when everyone would be looking.

I didn't read Bridget's text. I just sent her one back. *It's fine*.

Only it wasn't.

I sank to the ground. I could be proud of myself for all the times I'd managed not to cry over the last twenty-four hours, but I wasn't winning that war at the moment. *Hope cries—* that was what the nannies used to tell my father.

How were the kids? he'd ask, not really caring.

They're fine, mostly. I'd heard a rendition of this over and over during my growing up years. *Layla is flunking school. Bridget is too quiet. Justin is sneaking out at night. Hope cries*.

Yes, I did. I'd always been a marshmallow. I'd always been unable to be one of those tough, strong women that I saw in memes. *May we know them, may we raise them*. Well, I wasn't that. I could survive terrible things. I proved it, but I hadn't stood up, back straight, and marched on. No, I was a mess, and it was never going to be any other way.

I wasn't strong.

I put my head down on my knees and just sobbed. My shoulders shook, and my body vibrated. With my ears ringing, I was unable to even breathe, let alone think. I pounded on the floor with my fists. This was mean girl, high school shit, and it was never going to stop for me. I would always be at the mercy of what others thought of me.

And it turned out, I was lacking in a million ways. Inside and out.

CHAPTER 8

EVENTUALLY, I STOPPED CRYING. I WASHED MY FACE AND applied enough makeup that no one would guess I'd been crying. I put on the outfit I'd picked out and checked it five times to make sure that while it was attractive on me, no one would think I looked like a stuffed sausage. Yep, I'd let Amanda that far into my head. It wasn't pretty in my mind at that moment.

But my black dress was fashionable, my hair was pulled back, and I had diamonds that I almost never wore in my ears to make me feel like I was wearing *fuck you* jewelry. We were raising money for cancer, and I was ready to throw a hell of a party.

Or so I thought.

It turned out that being called fat and ugly publicly by Amanda Hill meant that people weren't going to show up for my party that evening. It was sad, really. I did my usual head count again and again, sure that the numbers had to be wrong. There should've been twice as many people there as there were.

And I was hardly the only one who noticed.

My client was pretty pissed. I walked to the corner to ignore her heated looks. I was sure I'd be taking abuse for this later. It wasn't that she wouldn't raise money for her cause. She would. It was embarrassing for her. Hell, it was the same for me.

I looked down at my phone

You know that you're gorgeous, right? Bridget's last text made me smile.

Well, I may need to sell my body to make a living, so I hope so.

That bad? Her texts were fast.

Apparently being fat and ugly means I'm suddenly on a list for people not coming to my parties.

You know you're better than your job, Bridget answered me.

I stared at her answer. Unreasonable rage rushed through me, and even as that happened, I knew that nothing Bridget texted deserved my anger. I took three deep breaths before I texted back, but still, when I did, I knew I was going to make her upset. Right then, I didn't care. *I could really do without the holier than thou right now. Not all of us can be investment bankers.*

My temper had risen. Between the crying and the anger, I was really worked up for me. Most of the time, I tried to just maintain. This was a lot of emotions for me to have all at once.

I didn't mean that. I'm sorry. I can see how you read it that way. I just mean you're amazing. You shouldn't be doing something that requires you to stay on the good side of such small, miserable people. I love you. You're amazing, Hope. The only one who doesn't know that is you.

I put away my phone. I wanted to cry again. Instead, I went to my client—the woman I was afraid that I might be some day. I tried to smile, but before I could say a word, she shook her head. "Well, don't feel too bad, dear. You're just done. It happens. Find a husband before you're not pretty anymore."

Yes, tonight sucked.

MY PHONE DINGED JUST as I poured whisky into a glass. I put on a black and white movie and sat down on my couch. I'd locked my door four times. No one was there to see me, so I could be happy about the four. I was holding steady at four. That was something I'd hold on to. I wiped my face. The tears were coming and going now. It was like, since I'd opened the faucet, they just felt free to stream down my face anytime they wanted.

This was glass two, and already, I was ridiculous. I'd stop at three because I'd be outright drunk at that time. Probably dance naked in my apartment. Take a bath where I'd send my sisters texts about ducks or other random things. Eventually, I'd fall asleep until two in the morning, when I'd wake up with a headache.

Tomorrow, I would regret drinking.

Now? I was fully invested.

I only drank alone or with my sisters. It was the only safe way to make sure I could feel like this and have nothing bad happen to me.

My phone rang. Someone was actually calling me? I looked down as Max's number popped up. "Hello?"

"Hey." He had the sexiest, richest voice. I could really listen to it all day. "What are you doing?"

"Drinking," I answered honestly. "What are you doing?" I looked at my clock. "Aren't you working?"

There was a bang in the background that sounded like someone had dropped something. "Watch it, Pete. I don't want to be buying another box of those. Yes, I'm working. I just wanted to check on you. Anna said that you had a bad day because of that vlog. I wanted to see if you were okay."

I sighed. "Great. It's so awesome hearing that the guy you almost slept with last night has heard how you are fat and ugly. Yes, I'm great. My party sucked. I'm apparently done, so now I'm drinking whisky. Straight up. So I'm going to go."

"Hold on." His tone lowered. "You know that's a bunch of bullshit. You're the prettiest woman in any room you walk into. Hands down. Where are you drinking? I'll meet you there in two hours."

I shook my head, but then it occurred to me that he couldn't see that. I smiled at the thought. "I only drink alone. Or with my sisters. But they don't live here anymore. In Manhattan. They never lived here."

He was quiet for a long second. "You only drink if you drink alone?"

"That's right." I put my legs up on the coffee table and sighed. "So I'm going to get back to it."

"Did you sleep today?"

"Nope." I looked out my window. The red lights of the city were always so inviting from this height. Like it was fake outside, not real.

But of course it was.

"And now you're drinking alone." He sighed. "Drinking alone is a very bad idea."

I groaned. "Okay, I'm going to go. Thanks for the lecture."

"That wasn't a lecture. I promise you that. That was an eye roll at best. Call down to your doorman and your security.

Tell them I'm going to be there in the morning and to let me up. We're having breakfast. Do it now."

Was he really ordering me around? I squirmed on the couch. What did it mean that I sort of liked it? "Okay."

"And go to bed."

"I'm not done."

"You are." He sighed. "You're more than done with today. Go to bed. Put me on the list, then sleep."

I yawned. Maybe he was right.

BY THE TIME he pounded on my door the next morning, I'd been up for six hours. Like I'd guessed would happen, I'd been tossing and turning since two in the morning. My head wasn't pounding as badly as it had been then. It was probably a good idea that I'd listened and cut it off after two drinks. Not drinking very often or regularly really lowered my tolerance.

I swung open the door, glad I'd showered and put on some makeup.

"You're okay." He let out a breath. "I spent the whole night wondering if you had drunk yourself to death because of some lowlife talking nonsense about you on a vlog."

I waved my hand. "It would take more than that to bring me down. What did you bring me to eat?"

He shook his head and strode inside. "Drinking alone is absolutely the worst way to do it. Who would know if you got in trouble?"

"I don't do that much of it. Are you avoiding the food issue?" He wasn't carrying any bags. Had he lied about the breakfast promise?

He extended his hand. "Put on your shoes. We're going

out to eat. Much as I love your red painted toes, I think you might tear up your feet if you went walking around like that. Plus, there is the whole no shoes no service issues."

I grinned at him. Truth was I'd been in a pretty bad mood rather consistently since the gym. But he was funny, even if he wasn't trying to be.

I wiggled my toes. "You like my toes?"

Max rolled his eyes. "Put on some shoes."

It was like I could get a compliment once from him and not again. Guess I wouldn't be digging for them because he only dished them out on his own terms. That was okay. He was there. None of my so-called friends had gotten in contact. My phone dinged. It was Layla texting me. I didn't have to look to know she'd found out about Amanda Hill. Unlike my caring for an infant sister, my friends had seen the post for sure and hadn't shown up at my party.

With friends like these, the question was, did I really need enemies? I focused on Max. "Okay, I'll get my sneakers."

I wore jeans and a T-shirt. I didn't really see the point of getting dressed up. People who were done rarely had to make any kind of effort on themselves. But I had put on makeup because I guessed I was just that level of pathetic.

With my shoes on, I locked up my apartment—only once in that direction, since my issues seemed to come with locking up when I was staying in—and followed him out. My guards were both leaning on the car, but he waved his hand.

"We're walking. It's three blocks."

Theo and Luke stared at each other. I'd been banned from doing too much walking. Max squeezed my hand. "You'll be fine. It's good for the soul to be able to walk on occasion. It'll take them twice as long to get you there, because they'll have to go up Park, turn around, and come back the other way. We'll be seated and eating by then. They can follow in the car. Text them the address when we get there, and they can wait outside in case anyone wants to Tony Soprano you inside the diner."

I laughed despite myself. He really did say the funniest things. "I don't think they've ever confirmed he's dead."

"Oh come on. He's dead." Max grinned at me. "He was obviously dead."

"We don't really know what happened. It could be any number of things." One thing about insomnia was that I watched a ton of television. Old. New. Interesting. Dull. I watched all of it. Cooking shows in particular. We crossed the street, heading for the diner where he must have meant for us to eat. I'd never been inside, although I'd always meant to give it a try. "How come you aren't on television? I'm shocked you haven't been on one of those cooking shows."

"They ask all the time, but I'm not the right personality for it. I really don't want to talk to the camera and say pithy things. I've had the same people working for me for years, and they can barely stand me in the kitchen. I don't want a camera crew."

I guessed he didn't need the publicity. His restaurant was kicking ass, and if some crazy socialite didn't screw it up for him, he was bound to continue to be successful. "Listen, about last night? Thanks for reaching out. I don't want to talk about it if that is possible. I have a therapist. At least I used to have one. I suppose I could call her, make an appointment to talk about being called mean words by a mean person and how it screwed up my precarious career. If it's all the same, talking to you about it seems somehow wrong."

He shook his head. "I don't want to talk about that woman. She bought film of you puking all those years ago. I mean...fuck. Who makes their living doing that? At least you're doing something helpful with your fame. She's a waste of space as far as I'm concerned."

I sighed as the waitress sat us. "She gives people what they want. To talk. To know. To judge. To keep their eyes on people who are famous. I could see it, if I'd done something to earn the attention, but my mother was a famous artist. She married my father. Had four redheaded children. Three of us were triplets. That caused some stir. Then she...died." Sometimes I could say 'killed herself,' and sometimes I absolutely could not say it. "We were left mostly alone. We moved around a lot because it turns out Dad is a crook. Once, we snuck out to a party when we were sixteen. Our brother helped us. We walked in—four redheads, all of us rich, with a dead mother. The whispers started. We were...newsworthy for living, somehow. Layla took the most heat. She was the prettiest, and that was our greatest value right off the bat."

He lifted an eyebrow as he picked up the menu. "She's not prettier than you. Ever eaten here?"

I shook my head. "No, but I'm craving pancakes, so I'm going to order some. Just carb it up every day."

Max groaned. "Yes, you'll do that until you feel terrible for having done that too much, and then you'll hate yourself for the overindulgence, having given that Amanda woman more power than she already has. Eat the pancakes. I'm sure they're fantastic. But don't eat them because she's making you feel small."

The waitress poured coffee, and I took a long sip. "I'm done with letting her in my head. Sort of. I've been up since two in the morning. She's had enough time today to bounce around in my subconscious."

"Great." He sipped his own coffee. "So the party went badly. I'm sorry about that."

I sighed. "I guess after your party—or Muffy's at your

restaurant—I'll find something else to do. I'm going to make sure yours is outstanding. One way or another, I'll work it out."

From about three to four in the morning, I'd strategized a plan. People owed me favors. They were going to show up at that party, or they'd live to regret it. Yep, that was how I was living now.

I was tired of talking about myself. I had plenty of me all the time. "So you were in the army, then you got out and went to culinary school?"

He cleared his throat. "There was a year in between where I did some other stuff. Worked for some people doing jobs no one wants to talk about in countries we shouldn't have been in. I can't tell you where or what, but after one year, I gave it all up. By then, Eric had gotten engaged to Anna. Then it seemed actually possible to be respectable, to do something worthwhile with myself. So I served, did some other things…"

Clearly, talking about it made him uncomfortable, because he abruptly became very preoccupied with getting the right amount of sugar into his coffee.

He continued. "And then culinary school. Once I graduated, I worked for some chefs until I bought my own place. And well, you know my story from there."

We placed our orders. I got the pancakes.

I took a deep breath. Much of the stress from earlier was gone. It was just nice to sit there. "But you started out in Maine with a big family."

"A really big one that is ever growing. I have so many nieces and nephews, I can't keep track. I'm kidding. I sort of can. I mean, if I'm in the room with them, I can tell who is who. I know their names, but trying to remember who is pregnant when? It gets confusing."

That was interesting. "I only have one nephew, and he is the best child that was ever born. He's beautiful. Perfect. There has never been a more beautiful baby ever."

He smiled slowly, stroking one broad fingertip across the rim of his cup thoughtfully before he said, "That is quite a proclamation. I'd bet you're going to change your mind when you have your own kids. You'll still love that boy, but nothing will ever compare to your baby."

I laughed. "Not having kids. God help any child I could conceive. They'll be so fucked up. From day one, they'd have a mother half out of her mind."

"Are you under the impression that only people who have their shit together have kids? Because I have news for you— most people are totally screwed up. If it were a requirement to be totally fine all the time, no one would have kids. You're the kind to have them. I can tell."

I leaned forward. "What about me tells you that?"

"I just know." He winked at me. "Consider me a soothsayer."

"Ooh, wow, I'm with a person who can see the future. We should hire you out to the police. Or put you on television. *The Predictive Chef.* You can chop onions and tell people what's going to happen in their lives at the same time."

He pointed at me. "Hope, you are so much more fun than I thought you would be. Don't drink alone, okay? I sat up last night thinking you'd passed out drunk in your bedroom and we'd find you dead this morning."

I shook my head. "I almost never drink. And I don't overdo when I do indulge."

"Well, the point remains. It's dangerous. I've seen too much shit." He shook his head. "So why do you choose not to drink with others?"

I swallowed. Anxiety surged through me. "I know that it's

totally shitty that I'm going to say this, but I'd really like… I'd like to not talk about it in detail. I get that we're sharing and I love it, but can I just say that I don't like to be out of control?"

"I can get that too." He took my hand across the table. "I can't understand why I tell you things."

"Well." I smiled. "We're friends who thought about having sex. It's probably not odd that you tell me things. Besides, I'm a good listener, and I keep a secret like I'm a vault."

He leaned forward. "I'm pretty good at keeping things private as well. Are you an alcoholic?"

That was certainly a leap. "What makes you think that?"

"I don't know. I've never seen you drink, and now you confess you have this strange thing about only drinking alone. I'm trying to make sense of it. Secret drinking? I wondered. Or maybe you're supposed to not be drinking and you only do it when you're by yourself so no one knows, but we have this strange relationship so you told me anyway."

I shook my head. "I don't think I'm an alcoholic. I almost never drink. Also, I very rarely think about it when I'm not drinking."

He sighed. "So not that, then."

"Not that." Maybe I *could* tell him. We had this odd relationship. He'd be the first person I spoke to about my problems who wasn't a therapist, but maybe it was time to…

His phone rang, and he let go of my hand to pick it up and then quickly put it on his ear. "Anna?"

The waiter set down our breakfast, and I took a big bite of my pancakes. They were good. I didn't give a shit why I was eating them. Food didn't have to be psychoanalyzed. I was happy to do that for the rest of my life, but not right then.

I loved these pancakes.

"I'll be right there."

I turned my attention to Max. "What's wrong?"

"Eric had a bad seizure. He's at Brooklyn Veteran's Hospital. He's asking for me. I've got to go." He looked around. "Where is the waitress? Do you mind paying? I'll get you back."

I shook my head. "I don't mind paying." In fact, I pulled cash out of my wallet and set it down on the table. Much more than this could possibly be. "And we'll take my car. I'll drop you there. It'll be the fastest way to get you there."

I'd always been good in a crisis that wasn't my own. "Come on," I urged him.

He nodded. "Thanks, Hope."

"It's nothing." I texted Theo to make sure he was outside, which he was. I would've been shocked if he weren't. They might have let me walk to the diner, but there was no way I was walking home since they'd found me. They took their jobs very seriously, and I couldn't pretend to be surprised about it. One of their own had been nearly killed taking care of Layla.

We got in the car fast. "You didn't eat anything. Let me go back in and get yours to go."

"Not hungry." He looked out the window as we pulled into traffic. "Amazing how quickly that can happen."

I actually understood him perfectly. "Eric was with you when he was injured, right? The injury that did this to him."

"He was. I was his XO. Sorry, that's an executive officer. I was building quite the career for myself, actually. I was good at it, and so was he. Although he was also a lieutenant, he was under me that day. I had seniority. Anyway, yes, he got hurt. On me."

"On you?" I hadn't been there, but I recognized guilt when I saw it. "You got him injured?"

"No, but I didn't protect him. It should have been me, not him. I can't give you details. Most of it is classified."

I nodded. That meant it was one of those secrets he wouldn't be sharing. We had that kind of relationship, both of us keeping our truths to ourselves. Maybe it didn't matter. Maybe all that counted was what came next. I had to find redemption, and perhaps he thought he had to as well.

"What do you think he is going to want to say to you?"

He closed his eyes for a long moment. "Every time he almost dies, he asks to see me and he tells me that it wasn't my fault."

"Then he must not think it is."

Max's eyes were dark, fathomless. I wasn't sure what he was going to say until he spoke. "It doesn't matter what he thinks. I know the truth."

"You employ Anna. We're going to raise money for him." So help me, we were. I'd figure out how to make Muffy's party a raging success. "I think you're a good friend to him. How many times has he almost died?"

Max rubbed his eyes. "Too many."

I went silent. Sometimes we needed silence. I sat back in the seat and watched him quietly as he looked out the window. Everything about him screamed *leave me alone*. To do anything else might get my head bit off. But then again, perhaps he was actually really needy in that moment and even he didn't know it.

I touched the strong muscles of his back, running my fingers up and down. He needed me right then, whether he knew it or not. I would be there for him, because sometimes you just needed someone to be.

His body tensed before he nodded and then smiled at me. There was no joy in the act but thanks just the same.

"Really can never make you out, Hope."

"I can't make you out either, Max. I guess we're both impossibly hard books to read."

His smile broadened. "I don't know. You seem to have me down pat." He took my hand and brought it to his mouth. "Come in with me."

"If that's what you want."

Right then, I'd give Max anything he wanted in the world. That should scare me, but it didn't. And I wasn't going to ask why, I was just going to roll around in it for a while.

CHAPTER 9

Unless I was going to visit a new baby—something I
had only done when Layla had Noah—I hated going to the
hospital. But that was okay. This wasn't about me. Max had
asked me to come, I'd said I would, and so I wouldn't make
this about me by acting like I didn't want to be there.

The good news was, by the time we arrived, Eric wasn't
in the ICU anymore. He'd stabilized and they'd put him on a
regular floor. That seemed awful fast to me, but when I asked
if that was normal, Max just sort of grunted, mumbled about
healthcare and them knowing there was nothing they could do
for him short of the surgery he needed, and not said another
word. I'd kept quiet after that.

Eric's room was quiet and sad. There weren't flowers
anywhere, and someone had pulled the shades closed so that
it was particularly dark, save for a small lamp illuminating
things and the light emanating from the constantly beeping
monitors. No one could possibly be expected to get any sleep
with the machines making so much noise.

He turned his head when we entered. The man must be
very sick, but he didn't look worn down. No, he was a big,

strong man with dark hair, dark eyes, and olive skin. Anna stood next to his bed, offering me a small smile when I gave her one.

"Hey, there." Max's voice was somehow even lower. "I heard you were doing this again, looking for all this attention, throwing yourself around."

Eric's face lit up at Max's clear joke just as the man I'd arrived with sat down on the side of Eric's bed. "Was hoping you'd show up. What was going on? Too busy to come see me?"

Max groaned. "Got here just as fast as I could, brother."

Eric nodded. "Likely story. Look, I know I've said this before, but it bears repeating. This is not your fault."

Max visibly paled, his jaw hardening, and yet neither Eric nor Anna seemed to have noticed it in the few seconds it took for Max to pull it together. "I'd do anything to be in that bed instead of you."

"It was my fault."

I stepped forward. "Hi, sorry. I wanted to introduce myself. I'm Hope Radford."

Eric's eyes widened, and he grinned at me. The conversation about blame stopped, at least temporarily, which had been my intention.

"You're Hope Radford—the woman who ruined this guy's life, but who Anna tells me he can't stay away from."

I sighed dramatically, even as the words sort of burned. I deserved it, but whatever. "Well, I guess it's a fly to the flame kind of thing. He knows it's bad for him, but he can't stay away. Like…like I'm carbohydrates."

Max closed his eyes and shook his head. "Not funny."

Anna crossed over to me and elbowed me gently in the side. "Carbs are fine in moderation."

"I'm in a room with two chefs. I should have gone for

some angle that wasn't about food." I crossed my arms over my chest in mock distress. "But now, how about that? Has anyone fed you, and if they haven't, can we get you something that isn't hospital related?"

He scrunched up his face. "I have no appetite. Sorry. And three chefs—before I was constantly in this condition, I was his first sous chef."

"The best one Max ever had," Anna agreed fast. "And he hasn't wanted to eat for a week or two. Things may be progressing." She made eye contact with Max before she smiled at Eric again. "He just doesn't like my cooking. Never did."

"You and Max with your fancy shit. I'd rather have a little pasta, a hamburger, and a beer any day of the week. That was the stuff we used to make at Hayley's to go with the fancy stuff."

They continued to joke back and forth. I watched sort of in awe of the whole thing. I didn't have friends to joke with like this. My friends only talked about people or clothes. Or vacations they were bored on. Lately, it seemed my sisters and I were just miserable all the time. Or that had been the case before Layla got happy. Bridget was checked out. Maybe it was just me who was miserable?

We were in the hospital, and they were making jokes. *Talk about making the best of a terrible situation.*

Anna looked at me. "They're always like this. It's kind of awesome. He does better with Eric in these situations than I do."

I took her hand. "I'm sure that's not true."

"I think sometimes loving someone is knowing when they don't need you, but when they need someone else. Like when Eric needs Max."

I swallowed. "I've never been in love."

"Max can't take his eyes off you. You've totally preoccupied him. Please be the version of the person I think you are and not the one that Max thought you were all these years."

I ran a hand through my hair. "I don't know who I am exactly. I never have. But I will raise money for Muffy and get your husband that surgery he needs, I promise you that. Whatever else I am or am not, I will do that. I promise. I keep the ones I make. Always."

She nodded. "Thank you, Hope."

WE STAYED ANOTHER HOUR, and I remained mostly quiet, watching. Max had wanted me there, but I didn't have much to say, which was really okay. I was comfortable, considering the circumstances. We were in the hospital, but it felt like we were just visiting with really nice people.

Until Eric had a seizure.

I'd seen someone have one once before. On a subway late at night. Then, I was pretty sure drugs had caused the seizure. This was different. One second, he was fine, the next, his eyes rolled to the back of his head and he just seized. I covered my mouth to keep quiet and stayed out of the way while the doctors and nurses tried to help him.

What was surprising was that it was so quiet in the room. All of us, everyone helping. It was practically silent.

Then it was over. The seizure stopped, his vitals eventually returned to normal, and we left him to sleep. Anna looked like she'd aged ten years in the past ten minutes. How did she leave him at all without being utterly terrified all of the time?

I almost asked, but as we left the hospital, I didn't think it was the time. We'd just had a lot of reality, so maybe we didn't have to pick apart the absolute smallest details of their lives right then.

We got in my car without speaking a word when Max sat forward. "Can you close the barrier so they can't see and hear us?"

I nodded and hit the button shutting Luke and Theo away from me. "What's going on?"

Max kissed me. I didn't expect it, and although my first response was shock, I quickly melted into it like it was the best moment of my life. It might actually have been. I smiled against his mouth, and he pulled off his seatbelt before unbuckling mine.

"We're going to live dangerously."

We were? My heart rate kicked up, but I wasn't afraid. I was…excited. He pulled me onto his lap and the car slowed down. I looked out the window. Traffic. So maybe we weren't going to live quite so dangerously. I faced him. We were so close, it was like we were breathing the same air.

Acting on instinct, since I had less than no experience, I ground against him. He moaned and closed his eyes. When he finally opened them, his gaze was heated and all-consuming. "I can see your nipples through your shirt. They're fucking hard."

I looked down. Yep, he was right. My cheeks must be turning red. There was no way I wasn't blushing right then. "Guess there's no hiding that."

"Nope." He pulled me by the back of the neck until our lips touched again. He kissed and kissed me. I let him lead, happy to just be in this moment. It was possible to get lost in him. I loved it.

He placed a hand under my shirt, touching my nipples through my bra. My hips were outright grinding into him now. He cupped my breast under my bra, and I pushed my chest into him.

I reached down, feeling the bulge in his jeans. He raised an eyebrow. "Want to go for another kind of ride in this car?"

That was so cheesy, and I kind of loved it. We were being so bad. I didn't know that I'd ever been not seat belted in a car before, let alone something like this, but I felt alive and powerful. I wasn't going to question it.

"Yes. I do. Right now." Before I could overthink it. I grabbed at his jeans, and he let me. He widened his eyes and grinned at me in that sexy, smoldering Max kind of a way, but he didn't suggest I was going too fast or note that I may have become frantic.

I wanted this. Wanted him. If it were going to happen right in the car, in traffic, so be it. I wasn't going to say no. The bulge in his pants seemed like it was growing, and as that was just what I wanted, I must've been doing something right.

"Next time we do this, we'll have lots of room. But if you'd ride me right now, honey, you'd make this miserable fucking day so much better. I don't expect it. We're in a car. People are driving us. There are folks walking on the street, and I mean—"

I kissed him to shut him up. Right then, I didn't want to be Hopeless Hope. No, I was going to be the woman who knew what she was doing. "Do you have a condom?"

"Coolest woman ever." He kissed my neck. "Seriously."

I hoped I was. But he was incredibly beautiful, and he wanted me. He kept proving that over and over. This was the second time, and he'd come to make sure I was okay this morning. For some reason, Max gave a shit when he should've been the last person in the world to feel that way.

Not to mention I was entitled to enjoy myself.

"Do you have a condom?" He still hadn't answered.

That would be a dealbreaker. I was sure he had one in his apartment, but we were in the car. This might be different.

"Yes." His low laugh moved through me. "Embarrassed to say I've been carrying one in my wallet since I was fourteen. Not the same one, mind you. I just make sure I always have one."

He squirmed a little and pulled his wallet out of his back pocket. After he pulled the condom out, he discarded the wallet onto the seat. I frowned. That was going to get lost. I grabbed it and shoved it back in his pocket.

"Thanks." He kissed me again. "For thinking of that."

"I'm a little strange." I shrugged.

"The best of us are." He slipped his hand down my pants, finding my pussy like he was an expert. Probably because he was. I smiled at the thought. Whatever happened before, right in this second, he was mine. I'd take these kinds of moments in my life.

It was almost unbelievable this was happening to me.

We managed to squeeze ourselves around—despite the closeness of the roof to my head, the door to our side, and the knowledge the tinted windows wouldn't hide us if someone got close enough to the car—to strip from the waist down. He tore the condom wrapper open with his teeth and then stopped to look at me.

"I should be romancing you more than this."

I shook my head and said the words that floated through my head. "No, don't."

I kissed him, hard, before he could argue with me. I didn't want him to change his mind. Max doing this once was one thing, twice might send me over some edge. He'd initiated this, and damnit, he wasn't taking it back.

I got up higher on my knees, positioning them on both

sides of him. He pulled back his head to look at me, the slightest frown between his eyebrows, but he didn't say anything, so I took that as him getting on board. He handed me the condom. "Going to need you to put this on me in this position."

Swallowing, I nodded. "Okay."

I wouldn't tell him I'd never done it before. I'd just wing it. Really, how hard could it be? Well, it turned out in a car that was jerking around and in our awkward position, it was actually pretty difficult. Still, I managed to not say a word to indicate I was having trouble not losing the condom or breaking it as I rolled it onto his rather large cock.

Was it going to fit inside of me?

"Are you wet, baby?" He pressed his finger inside of me, and I gasped. His smile told me that hadn't been the wrong thing to do. "You are. And...make those noises when I'm inside of you. I'm begging you."

I kissed him because I didn't know exactly what to say. *Noises. Yep.* I hadn't thought about that. What if I made some he didn't like? *Fuck.* I didn't worry about these things years ago, but then again, I hadn't known just how screwed up I was going to get.

With his condom where it needed to be, I got up on my knees. It seemed like it would be perfectly obvious what I should do, but I wasn't exactly sure at that moment. "Help me?"

Maybe he'd think it was the car that was the problem? He nodded, which made me hope that he did. It took some squirming, and I couldn't believe that any of that was actually very sexy-looking, but then I felt him. A second before he jerked his hips and pushed himself inside of me, he was just suddenly there. There was this moment right before we were joined when I realized we were about to be that I caught my breath and thanked the universe I got to have this moment.

And then he was inside of me. It was a strange feeling. It didn't hurt. I caught my breath and tried to appreciate the novelty of it as my body adjusted to the uniqueness. In books and movies, women just adjusted, they orgasmed. One two three done. It was remarkable. I wasn't at all certain what to do, and I didn't think I was going to just come because he was inside of me, although it felt good in a way I hadn't expected it to.

We were joined. Body to body. I liked that element of it.

"Fuck." He cursed in my ear. "You are so tight, beautiful. Hope, I'm dying for you."

That was a good thing, and I liked how he said it. My cheeks heated up. Before I could think of something to say, he grabbed on to my hips and moved me. I might have been on top, but he led our bodies, and thank goodness he did.

Oh yes, I liked that. Each stroke of our bodies against each other made this better and better. I let my head lean back and closed my eyes. I could feel the buildup happening inside of me. Tears came to my eyes, but I pulled them back. I didn't need to cry just because I could feel the pleasure. It was such a strange dichotomy of emotions. The fact that I could was enough to drive it away.

He picked up the pace of our thrusts, and I bit down on my lip to stop from crying out. Max bit my neck lightly, and I gasped. Yes, I liked that.

"Another time, and you're going to give me all your noises. As loud as you want to be." His voice sounded huskier, and it moved through me like he'd stroked me in the midst of all of this.

Truth was I had no idea what to say. Apparently, sex talk didn't come naturally to me, so I was just going to keep quiet and try to be present in this moment. I had this beautiful man having sex with me in the back of a car as we moved through —or sometimes didn't move through—traffic. It was a strange, bizarre moment, and although he'd likely never know it, a perfect one for me.

"Look at me."

I did as he said because how could I not? We held our gazes together, and as much as I couldn't read his thoughts, I was glad he didn't know mine.

"Fuck. I want to make you come." He kissed my mouth, my chin, everywhere he could reach as our bodies jerked together and sweat broke out on me. He slipped his finger against me, which meant with every movement we made, it rubbed against his thumb. But he'd found my clit. I often tried to pleasure myself that way, but I usually ended up feeling hollow. This was so much better. The pressure was just right.

"That's it," he whispered in my ear. "Come for me. You know you want to, and I want you to. Now. Come for me, Hope."

I gasped, my body contracting. I didn't know that I needed that much pressure, but it was good. The sudden assault on my senses drove the tears from my eyes that I'd held off, and I came on a gasp that accompanied a sob. He drove into me, hard, before he came.

We held each other through the shakes as I forced myself to stop crying. A million thoughts traveled through my mind. I'd make an excuse if he asked. Sure, I always cried during sex. It was just what I did.

But as he drew me to him, kissing my face, where the tears had streamed and where my lips were swollen, he didn't ask. For long moments, we stayed just like that—kissing and not otherwise speaking about what we'd just shared.

Eventually, it seemed like I was going to have to do something. The car had sped up, and we were going to cross a bridge. At fast speeds, this seemed less…okay. I pulled off him, and he winced but winked at me. We straightened and got dressed. I tried not to stare at him. What was I supposed to do in this moment? What would a worldly, sexually-fulfilled person do at this time?

He tugged me to him. I didn't know what he'd done with the condom, but he was dressed again, as was I.

"You okay?" He kissed me again. "Next time, it won't be so fast. I'm just…worked up, and you are so fucking hot."

My cheeks heated up. "Thanks." I swallowed. Nothing he said indicated he had any clue how completely inexperienced I was with doing this consensually. That was good. I couldn't explain in that moment why it was so important, but it was. I'd hash it out in therapy at some future date when I convinced myself to talk about things again.

He ran his finger down the slope of my nose. "You okay?"

I nodded. "Sure. How are you?"

Max slumped down in his seat. "Much better now."

I leaned my head against his shoulder. What had just happened was significant for me. It was the first time I'd had sex since…well, *since*. And I didn't want to tell him. I got to keep my secrets the same way he guarded his own.

"What are you cooking tonight?" It seemed a safe topic. "Something delicious?"

He laughed, throwing his head back. "It's all delicious when I make it."

I groaned. "Sorry, of course. Could you be more specific? What *exactly* are you cooking tonight?"

He brought my hand to his lips and kissed my knuckles.

"The special tonight is going to be salmon. Do you like salmon?"

"I love salmon."

He leaned his head down on mine. "Thank you for coming with me today, Hope, and for being there for me when I needed you. I...I don't usually ask for sex in the back of a car."

I laughed. "Oh no? It's all the rage on the Upper East Side."

Max groaned, and I smiled. We stayed quiet for the rest of the drive.

Luke dropped Max at his home and then quickly cut uptown to bring me to mine. I didn't say a word to either of my guards. If they knew what happened, they made no mention of it, and I managed to get upstairs to my apartment before I sank to the ground.

That happened. It had actually happened. I let out a breath. I'd never thought I'd be able to handle it. Sure, it wasn't the stuff of fiction. I wasn't suddenly fixed because I'd had sex with Max, but it did matter. I hadn't gotten scared, hadn't freaked out. I'd spent a little too much time lost in my own head, but I'd enjoyed myself, even had an orgasm.

I let out a breath I'd held.

I wanted to tell someone, but not even my sisters would have understood the importance of the moment, since I guarded my truth so tightly.

Shaking my head, I rose and headed for the bathroom, stopping only to stare at *September*, the painting that I'd moved mountains to acquire. It really was so sad, and even though most of the time I could feel its truth in my soul, at that moment, it was an absolute opposite to my current mood.

"I'm sorry you were sad, Mom." I touched the side of the frame, avoiding the painting itself. "I am a lot too. But we're

119

not the same, because I'm not going to let us be." I stepped away from the creation that filled in for my dead mother. Was I talking to her or to myself? Did it matter? "Why did you pick Dad, anyway? He's really not a good man."

I walked into the bathroom and turned on the shower. I'd just had sex. That was so…not me. I smiled as the water sprayed over me. I was going to spend the day getting people to show up to Max's restaurant.

If this was the last charity I raised money for, then I was going out with a bang.

And then I'd…

Well, I had no idea what I'd do, but I'd figure it out.

For once, I was feeling pretty great about things.

My phone dinged. Justin had sent a text. *I think Dad would let you die if it would make them happy.*

I stared at the words like I couldn't believe they existed. I set down my phone, my good mood fleeing. I was wet, standing in the shower, and staring at what amounted to what? Was it a death threat? Was it a warning? Was it a deranged ranting from my drug-addled brother? I pounded on the wall, the vehemence of how I punched it shocking me, even as I did it.

When I could get my hands to stop shaking enough to manage the act, I took a screenshot of the message Justin sent and sent it to Michael. Maybe Zeke didn't have to know, so Layla didn't have to know. I leaned against the side of my shower. The water hit me but no longer felt so wonderful or soothing.

CHAPTER 10

I LEANED AGAINST THE CAR AND WATCHED AS PEOPLE entered the party. Silently, I made note of who attended. The turnout was good, and I swallowed some of my anxiety away as I saw it. They'd go in, eat—or pretend to—mingle, check each other out, write checks, and leave. That was okay. That was all I needed them to do.

I'd threatened, cajoled, flirted, and practically begged to get some of them there. I'd called in favors, but so help me, I would have gone and dragged people out of their apartments if I'd had to. This would be my last party. I knew that. I'd done what I could, but I was old news now.

Funny...I didn't feel any different.

My phone dinged, and I looked down at it. *Where are you?* It was Max. *Shouldn't you be here?*

We'd had some back and forth over text for the last day, mostly about *Star Trek*. It was fun to talk to him about it. And not being in the room together meant we didn't have to address the elephant in it with us—the sex in the back of the car.

Well, I tried to come in, but your maître d' is under strict directions to not let me enter. So I'm outside in the car watching to see who arrives.

What? His response came fast. *Fuck. I'm sorry. Old rule. I'm correcting it.*

The door to the side opened, and Max poked his head out. Lightning flashed in the sky. It wasn't raining yet, but it felt like it was about to start. That feeling in my bones said that rain was coming. If I'd doubted the sensation, the lightning confirmed it. That was okay. It would keep people inside, writing checks and eating.

"Hope." Max looked up. "Come in before you get wet."

I strode toward him, looking over my shoulder at my guards. More and more lately, I wanted them to stay in the car. I guessed technically they shouldn't do that, but they'd let me have privacy at the hospital, and it looked like they'd do the same today. Maybe they got it. There was being careful and then there was choking to death from too much attention. Maybe choking was wrong. Maybe it would be more accurate to think about being smothered.

By the time I got inside, the first drops had started to hit the pavement. "Just made it."

His smile was huge as he stared at me. "Why didn't you call or text that you couldn't get in?"

The sound of the crowd laughing in the back reached my ears. That was a good sign. This was the afternoon, and they were drinking like it was dinner. *Phew.* Things were working out. "Oh, I don't know. I've been thrown out of here once before. Maybe your dislike for Spock warred so intensely with my love of him that you've banned me again."

His grin grew. "You're fantastic, smart, and beautiful. And also wrong. It's Kirk's show."

I rolled my eyes. "Think of it as a buddy drama."

Max took my hand, and I inhaled all of the deliciousness

wafting through the air while we walked to the center of the kitchen. Anna looked up from where she seared something and nodded to me. "Hope."

Dano smiled at me. "Hope."

Max pointed at him. "Aha. I knew it was you. I knew it."

I shook my head. "I have no idea what you're talking about and neither does he."

Max narrowed his gaze. "I *will* find out, I promise you that."

"No, you won't," Anna called out to him. "And I like the stuff she gets us, so don't fuck this up. Also, she's nicer than you are. I'm changing allegiances."

Just then, the door to the kitchen opened and the staff of about ten turned to regard the people who entered. It was my client, Muffy, and her son, Tim, who really had no business being here. Where was his nanny? He was dressed like he attended the opera, in a little suit with a bowtie. His expression seemed very serious for a child.

Muffy paid no attention to him at all. "Oh, Hope dear, here you are. This is wonderful. And the chef! I'm hearing from that Amanda Hill that you two are a thing. I'll forgive you for not telling me because this event is such a hit."

She squealed on the last word. Yes, Amanda was there. I'd almost barred her from coming, but her presence drew attention to the event and some guests called to ask if they could come because Amanda would be there. The celebrity gossip blogger had become a celebrity herself, which I imagined was sort of the point. She made money the more people wanted to watch her.

I could certainly understand trying to use notoriety to one's advantage. The difference being that I hadn't asked for mine, I'd just capitalized on it. She'd actively sought notoriety by saying mean things all of the time.

I smiled at Muffy. This would be the end of our relationship. Funny how sometimes you knew when it meant goodbye. Sometimes there was sadness. This was not one of those times.

Max visibly tensed next to me. It dawned on me, maybe too slowly, that chefs really didn't like people in their kitchens uninvited.

"Muffy, have you met Max?"

As they made their introductions and he managed to stay polite, I bent over to talk to Tim. He looked lost, standing there with all the tall adults running around the kitchen. "You doing okay?"

He shook his head. "Hungry."

Well, that broke my heart in two. "There is so much food out there. You don't want any of it? Where is your nanny?"

Muffy groaned. "She quit. Ran off with one of the doormen in the building. I'm having a hard time replacing her."

I took that in but stayed on topic. "You don't want any of the food that Max cooked? He's really good at it."

He silently shook his head, looking at me with wounded eyes. What did he think was going to happen to him if he told me he didn't want to eat?

"Timothy," Muffy said through clenched teeth. "We spoke about this."

Oh, I knew that look well. My father used to throw it at us. That was the *you are embarrassing me* look. I shuddered to remember being on the opposite end of that look.

Max knelt next to me. "How about some pasta?"

Tim's eyes lit up. "Really?"

He nodded. "For sure. Really. Yes, easy to do. Come with me, my man."

Muffy blinked fast. "Oh you don't have to—"

He interrupted her. "Easiest thing in the world. I don't blame him. I didn't want to eat fancy food when I was his age. Little pasta. Little red sauce. Easy as pie. Come on."

Although the noises in the kitchen—the banging and clanging—continued, I couldn't help but notice the conversation had ceased. Max's entire staff watched their exchange. He picked up Timothy as though that were the most natural thing to do and carried him over to an area of the kitchen not being used. Setting him down on the counter, he started to grab pots and pans, filled them with water, and began making pasta, as promised, despite the party happening in the next room.

"Well, if you've got him." Muffy waved her hand and exited the room, leaving her son in the care of two childless people she barely knew.

Max shook his head but said nothing, instead turning to Tim. "I have several nephews your age."

"Do they live close by?" Tim's eyes lit up as he asked the question.

"No, they're in Maine, unfortunately."

I walked over to them. "Have you been to Maine, Tim?" I pulled out my phone. Was it appropriate to let him play one of the games I had on there? Like the matching game that I couldn't put down when I played it and really needed to get off my phone... "Do you like Candy Games?"

He full-on grinned. "You're so nice, Hope."

"You are too." I patted his head. I loved kids, but I had next to no experience with them and really no idea what to do when I was around them. That was okay. I would spoil Noah, and that might be the extent of children I ever really knew. Ignoring the pain the thought brought me, I focused on Tim instead. "Did you do anything fun for summer this year?"

Max set some carrots down in front of Tim, who started

immediately munching on them. When had Max pulled out the carrots? It was funny, if I didn't watch Max intently in this kitchen, I missed things. He cooked the pasta, but his eyes never really stopped monitoring the kitchen. Waiters came in and out to collect food and drop off trays, and staff passed plates around to each other to serve and cook things. Max reminded me of a conductor with an orchestra.

"I went to my grandmother's. She lives at the beach."

Max side-eyed him, placing a piece of buttered toast on the plate that was now vacant of carrots. "I grew up on the beach."

"Actually on the beach?" I hadn't known that. Quaint town in Maine that turned into an artist's retreat was all I knew about his hometown.

"Rocky and good for fishing but there… It counted." He winked at Tim and turned off the heat on the pasta, spooning it out of the pot, while Anna came over and poured some red sauce on it. How had they communicated for her to know he wanted her to do that? Maybe it just came from working with someone for so long that you eventually knew what they wanted you to do without having to be asked to do it? "What was your grandmother's beach like, Tim?"

He stared at the pasta, his eyes widening with each inhale he took. "White."

"White. That sounds pretty. We're going to let this cool for a second. This is a carb heavy meal, but you are young and growing. Plus, you'll never believe it, but what Anna put in the sauce is good for you. It just looks red, so you like it. My mother's trick."

He really was good with children. In fact, as I watched the back and forth through Tim's whole meal, of which he ate all of it, it was very obvious that Max just knew how to talk to him. Still, when the food was done, Tim jumped at me, wrapping his arms around my neck and holding on.

I wasn't exactly sure what to do in that second or why Tim had grabbed me. As it was, the door opened and Muffy entered. Tim's body stiffened, and I set him down. Poor guy. He was definitely tense around his mother.

"Time to go." Muffy smiled at me and took Tim's hand. "Keep the escrow money until we get back."

I nodded. That was fine. The money was in an account and not going anywhere. All in all, Muffy's event had been cheap, not that I would tell her that. "Are you taking a trip?"

"Oh yes, of course. We're going to Slomestikan to give out the food with the charity workers. Didn't I tell you?" She leaned forward. "It's going to be so exciting."

No, she had absolutely not told me that she intended to visit a country that the State Department suggested we avoid visiting. "Um…you are going yourself?"

"Yes, of course. This is *my* charity donation. I want to be there to see the gratitude."

With that, she took Tim and walked back into the dining room. My body was cold, and I rubbed my arms to warm myself up.

"You're not wrong." Max placed a hand on my arm. "That's a really stupid thing to do. I've been there. She has no business going. Honestly, I'm not sure who the organization is that she hired at all, but I hope they know what they're doing."

He'd been there? "When you were in the army?"

"Afterward, actually." He touched the side of my face. "Not going to talk about it, but yeah. So I wish Muffy well, but boy…that's a dumb move. Kid was cute."

He was. I sighed. "I suppose I should go make an appearance at the party."

Max shrugged. "You could and I suppose you should, but you could also go sit at that little table in the corner and let me feed you."

He wanted to feed me? I stared at the door where the last party I'd be throwing like this was happening. And then I turned around and sat down at the table. Max wanted to feed me, and I was going to let him. With a smirk that shouldn't be as cute as it was, he headed to a different stovetop and started to cook.

After a moment, he looked up. "Ben, get Hope a seltzer. Oh and, Hope, you want a meal made entirely of pesto sauce right? Everything coated in pesto?"

"Ha, ha." I rolled my eyes at him. "I see the plan. Lure me here with promises of food and make me choke down pesto."

The seltzer was set down in front of me, and I took a sip, loving the bubbles. Max had seen me order this when we'd gone out. It was sweet he remembered it was usually my choice. Or at least as usual as he could know anything about me up until that point.

Soon, the food started rolling out. I should probably tell him not to do this. Surely they had to prep for dinner after finishing a catered lunch that they didn't usually serve. But I wasn't going to say anything. Max wanted to feed me, and I wanted to let him.

I let myself look around. The standards of cleanliness were clearly high. The kitchen, even with all the food passing and dishes being moved around, practically sparkled. Max would look up about every forty-five seconds from what he was doing. His staff moved fast. If they placed something in a storage box on the left side of the room, they wrote their initials next to it. Also, every box was labeled directly in the center of the box. That had to be purposeful.

I'd no sooner thought it than the first dish was set in front of me by Max himself. He leaned over the other side of the table and watched me look down at the dish, which was a little bit strange. I'd never had a chef present at the table in a restaurant to watch me eat before. It was somehow different at home.

"That's gazpacho with Maine lobster. A little melon to go with it. If I'd had more time, I would have added some other fish too, so I'm sorry. It's not everything I would have done."

He was sorry? It was gorgeous. Like a piece of artwork on the plate. "Did you just do all of this right this very second?"

"No." He shook his head. "I knew you were coming. I prepped." His smile was slow. "Take a bite."

I couldn't have refused him anything in that second. I took a bite. The flavors together exploded in my mouth. Lobster could be too chewy. This wasn't. The melon, a flavor I wouldn't have paired with shellfish, worked to make everything sweet at the same time. I closed my eyes. "That is really, really good."

He didn't answer me, so I lifted my lids. Finally, he spoke. "I know. Enjoy. Be right back with the next bit."

There was more? I really would have been happy to have just eaten this. All of the hype for his cooking was obviously well deserved. What would have happened to him if I hadn't fucked with his life? I tried not to let that thought sour my tastebuds as I finished eating the melon. Eating alone wasn't ideal. Also, I couldn't have said why, but I might have sworn that all eyes in the kitchen were on me at one time or another.

They all seemed to be busy and not paying attention to me, except they totally were. Layla could always tell when she was being stared at, and she said it felt like pinpricks on her skin. I didn't have her ability, but I did feel like there were perpetual eyes on me and I couldn't have said why.

I'd no sooner finished than a man I hadn't met delivered a salad in front of me. He spoke with an accent and a kind smile. "Kale salad. For you."

With a nod, he left it there in front of me. I didn't adore kale most of the time. It was fine, but it was like walking on the treadmill in terms of food. Not my favorite thing, yet I'd do it because it was good for me. In fact, given the fact that I was recently called fat by a gossip blogger, perhaps I *should* be eating more kale. It didn't matter. Right then, I ate like I hadn't a care in the world.

There was melon on the kale salad. That was new for me too. Melon wasn't something I usually put on salads. Clearly, it was something that Max was doing tonight. I took a bite and knew immediately I hadn't given kale a fair shake before. There were also small chips that were great because they added a crunch. I hadn't known I needed that crunch, but oh, I loved it.

"How's the melon?" Max asked as he swung back over.

As I was chewing, I shot him a thumbs-up gesture. Once I swallowed, I spoke. "The best kale I've ever eaten."

Max leaned over and kissed my cheek. "Glad you like it, beautiful."

With that, he rushed back to the station where he'd been working. Anne lifted her head, and this time, made direct eye contact with me before she lifted her eyebrows slowly. I swallowed some of my kale. I wasn't sure exactly what she was saying to me, but her nonverbal gesture seemed serious. Okay. I sort of got it. She didn't want me to fuck with him. I wasn't. I had no idea where things were headed with Max and me, but right then, I was totally serious in how head over heels I was falling for him.

Yep, that was a cliché, and that was okay. Sometimes the cheesy love sayings worked because they just did.

Oh no. I'd thought the L word. We had sex once, and he cooked for me. I wasn't in l... No, I wasn't even going to think it. *Nope. Nope. Nope.*

Then he set the duck down in front of me. I swallowed. This had to be one of my most favorite things. Had I told him that? No, I didn't think I had. Leave it to Max to just so happen to be cooking duck. I smiled up at him.

"I love duck."

He nodded. "Of course you do. You have excellent taste."

This still had the melon. That must have been the theme for the night. "Do you always do this? Same ingredient in all the dishes?"

"No." He eyed the duck. I hadn't tried it. This was a thing, clearly. Max wanted to watch me take a bite like he had with the kale and the lobster. This time, I took the bite but kept my eyes on his when I did. The room might as well have emptied out. It was like we were alone in it. I tasted plums and something else... Was that fennel in there too? Of course, also butter. "I just did that for you. The melon in everything."

I swallowed my food. "You're amazing. This is...really, really exceptional."

I didn't remember eating the rest of that duck. As good as it was, all I could see was Max as he stood in front of me. Time passed, the duck got eaten, and I was full in a happy, *I ate the best food in the world* kind of a way. But there was Max—tall, strong, talented, and totally focused on me.

I hadn't understood the seduction of his cooking, the power in the artistry.

I loved it.

WHEN I FINISHED, he leaned over again and kissed me on the lips. "Do you have somewhere you have to be right now?"

I didn't. "No."

"Okay then, after I give you this very good cake I didn't make, could you come back here, say at midnight, and let me take you out? I know it's very late, but that's how late I'll be working tonight."

My heart rate kicked up. "I think I can do that, Max. I don't see why I can't."

"Have one of your guards walk you to the door. I don't want you wandering around alone late like that. Walk you *to the door*. Okay?"

I nodded. Maybe I should scoff? Before the bodyguards, I'd been perfectly fine in Manhattan all by myself. Still, it was nice that he cared, and there were worse things than someone who cared if you might get hurt.

"I'll do that."

He cupped the side of my face. "Seriously, the cake is really, really good."

I laughed. I was sure it was. Even if he hadn't made it, I'd learned in these minutes watching him cook and actually eating his food that there was no way that Max would ever serve anything that wasn't exceptional. Still, I was sure when I thought back to these moments, it wouldn't actually be the food that I would remember. It would be this incredible eye contact with Max, the way he looked at me, the way he was affectionate in front of his work colleagues, the way... Well, all of it.

We'd had sex in a car, yet somehow, this seemed more intimate.

"What are we going to do so late at night?" I smirked at him. "Or maybe I know the answer already."

He laughed, a low sound. "Yes, before we got to bed, we could do that. But, no, I'm taking you out. You have your

New York, and I have mine. I think you might prefer my version of it. I'm getting you that cake now."

My phone dinged, and I looked down to see my cousin from the State Department had texted me. *You haven't needed any food lately.*

I smiled. No, it seemed like Max might have everything he needed. Maybe I could soon be one of those things.

CHAPTER 11

I SUPPOSED I COULD HAVE STAYED IN THE SAME CLOTHES I'D worn to the event, but if Max intended to take me out, I actually needed to dress down a bit. He wasn't going to be taking me anywhere where I needed to be so formal. I ended up putting on a pair of dark jeans with a black tank top. It might have been a little bit too chilly for it, but I'd been cold for fashion before. I didn't want to have to carry a jacket or a sweater around. Years of leaving my things all over the place and having to go back for the things I'd forgotten wherever I'd set them down had taught me it was better to just not bring the thing at all.

Rubbing my arms as I walked with my bodyguard to the side door of Hyperion made me wonder if I should have just brought the sweater. *Too late to change my mind now.*

I lifted my hand to knock when the door swung open. It was five minutes after midnight, and although the streets were somewhat more subdued, no one would call them empty.

"Hey." Max smiled at me. "I saw you pull up." He offered his hand. "You're five minutes late."

134

Oh, so he was that kind of punctual? That was an interesting fact to store away in the box labeled 'Max' in my mind. "There was traffic."

He winked at me before looking at my bodyguard. "You're new."

"They rotate at night sometimes. Can't expect the same two people to follow me around all day. This is Trey. Trey, Max."

With a slight tug, I found myself in the restaurant. "I've got her now. We'll be leaving soon. Nothing will happen to her while she's with me."

Trey, who was usually quiet in the way that told me he absolutely did not want to chat, nodded at Max. "I'll follow along from a distance you won't see. We don't take our eyes off her unless she's inside and secured."

Max nodded back, like he appreciated the answer, then turned back to me when my bodyguard left. "Aren't you going to be cold? It's a little bit chilly out there."

I shrugged. "I'll be fine."

"I've got something here you can wear." He left me to walk around the kitchen, staring in the sink. It was weird, after so much activity earlier, to see it so eerily quiet. But Max checked out every square inch of his kitchen before turning toward his office. I'd never been in there, but when he came back out seconds later, he wore a coat and handed me a dark black jacket. I wasn't small, but it was huge on me since Max was significantly bigger. "You benefit from the fact that I left this one here a year ago by accident."

I grinned at him. "A year ago, and you didn't bring it home?"

"I kept meaning to. I guess it's good, since you didn't properly dress tonight." He took my hand. "We're going to walk ten blocks. Will the bodyguards freak out?"

I really didn't think so. "This crew is less attached to me. They trade in and out from Michael's overall employees. They're not permanently assigned to me. Not that they don't take it seriously, but…"

He nodded, like he understood what I hadn't said. "The other two are getting paternal. I can see it with them. That's actually a good thing. Better they care than not."

Max locked up the place and then took my hand in his. It was nice to be in his jacket, almost like he had his arms around me in a hug. I rolled my eyes internally. Yep, I'd done the thing where I'd over-attached. This was not a man who did relationships, I didn't think. Truthfully, we didn't know each other all that well yet. Maybe we were on course to become friends.

Who slept together.

We walked quietly, but it wasn't awkward. Eventually, we arrived at what had to be the destination. I hadn't even thought to ask him where we were headed. What did that even mean? It was a jazz club, and we entered through the basement. The smell of smoke outside wafted around us while Max tried to pay the cover charge for us to enter. He must come there a lot, because the bouncer refused his money and just let us inside instead. They shook hands like old friends, and I'd been right to think that I was walking into his world tonight.

I'd never been to a place like this. It just wasn't something that I did with my friends. Maybe, for all of our money, we were pretty uncultured. That was an interesting thought. I'd dwell on it later. I was going to have a lot of time to do that since, as of now, I had no jobs lined up, and I was probably, for all intents and purposes, done with my job. Out of work.

It was always going to be temporary, which didn't mean it didn't burn a little bit in my gut.

We sat toward the back of the room. "Normally, I prefer being closer, but I want to be able to whisper in your ear without bothering anybody. Are you hungry?"

I was absolutely not. "Honestly, I'm still full from that decadent luncheon. I don't think I could eat anymore."

He waved his hand at the passing waiter. It looked like the musicians were between sets, and they must want to distribute all the food and drink then.

"Max," the man who wore his bow tie askew greeted my date. I smiled at the thought. *My date*. Yep, that was what this was. "What can I get you two tonight? Great timing. Joe is playing. He's killing it."

Greeting him as warmly, Max looked over at me before he answered. "I'm going to have a whisky. Neat. You know which one I want, if he has it. Bring me some peanuts or something to munch on. The lady will let you know what she wants."

I swallowed. This was exactly the kind of place where I wished I didn't freeze at the idea of drinking alcohol. It would probably be fun to have one, but I wasn't there yet. I might never be, and I had to be okay with that. I was here. That was really something. This place—I hadn't even looked at the name because I'd been so consumed with Max—was outside of my comfort zone. I was sort of proud I'd made it through the door.

"Do you have a ginger ale? If not, I can—"

"On it," he said, cutting me off, then hurried back to the bar.

"So you're still full? Really?"

I placed my hand over my stomach. "Yes, very. It was so delicious."

"I didn't ask you if you liked jazz."

No, he hadn't, and it didn't bother me at all. I loved it. Looking around, I couldn't say that I'd ever been to a place where so many different types of people all gathered at the same time. All ages, all kinds of outfits. Everyone stared at the stage with expressions that said they enjoyed the sounds. One woman with long gray hair, that fell past her waist, drummed along with her fingertips, while her companion, a much younger man with burgundy hair, tapped his leg. The music started softly and then got louder.

I turned my attention to the stage, watching the piano player intently. I might never choose to listen to jazz when I was alone, but I was perfectly happy to let it move around me, suck me in, and take all of my attention.

If I closed my eyes, I might be able to make out one instrument from another, but I didn't want that. No, I preferred to take it all in at once. It was loud and it almost shut off my brain, so I couldn't do anything but be present in the moment and exist through it. I bit down on my lip. My thoughts were downright crazy. I was listening to music, not having a transcendental moment that would alter the shape of time.

Still, I drifted through it, loving the power of the sounds and the people to change my mood entirely. Who knew? All this time, I should have been going to jazz clubs. Why wasn't this a thing in my life? Why had I spent so much time worrying about things when I looked in the mirror? So what if I wasn't Layla? Layla wasn't Bridget, and Bridget wasn't me. We were sisters, but just because we'd shared space in a uterus didn't mean we had to spend the rest of our lives worried about how we compared to the others. And…

Max squeezed my leg. His gaze focused on the stage. To me, he seemed almost casual, like he wasn't thinking a million miles a minute because the sheer magnitude of the sound had cleared up the background noise of his own head. *And there I go again.*

He leaned slightly toward me, tugging gently on the edge of my hair. I turned to look at him as he leaned over to whisper to me. "Do you like this? Or hate it? I should have asked. We can leave."

I shook my head. "I like it."

Even if it was doing something to me. Perhaps whatever that turned out to be was something that had to be done.

THE NIGHT WAS much quieter when we left. Well, maybe it was. Perhaps I had just lost some of my hearing, although I doubted that. Max raised his hand to call over my car. "Come home with me?"

I leaned against his arm. "That wasn't already implied?"

His smile was huge. "Hope, I'm going to confess, I can't always read you. Like, in there, I wasn't sure if you were liking it or not."

"I did. I actually found it a fully unique experience."

He laughed as the car pulled up next to us. "See? I have no idea what that means."

"That's a good thing, Max. I wouldn't ever want to be boring."

His smile stayed right where it was. "That's a good thing. I don't think you could ever be boring."

He had no idea. If he spent any time in my head, he might understand how completely screwed up my thoughts were.

Unlike the last time when we were in the car together, we didn't get naked on the drive to his place. So far, I'd resisted thinking about what we shared in this same car, like I'd already put it into a box labeled *did that really happen?* somewhere inside my brain.

But sitting next to him on the same seat made me fully cognizant of it. How he smelled—like sandalwood soap and something else that was just clean and purely Max—the way he moved, the way that he tilted his neck like he wanted to look at something closer. I'd seen him do that in the kitchen. When he really examined something, he had a particular way of moving his head.

I could easily become fascinated with him.

Oh hell, I probably already was.

We arrived at his apartment, and I followed him inside. Like last time, it was almost like walking into another world when I entered his place. He threw his coat on a chair, and I gently placed the one he'd loaned me over it. I'd been wrapped in his scent all night.

"Do you want—"

I didn't let him offer me something to drink or anything else. Instead, I practically threw myself into his arms. I'd had a taste in the car, and I wanted more. Also, it was better I not give my stupid anxiety too much time to rev up. Just because I'd had sex once and enjoyed it didn't mean I couldn't fall into a hole where I couldn't again.

I wanted him.

He must have felt the same way because he picked me up against him and pushed me against the wall. I smiled against his lips. His kiss felt powerful, consuming, and spoke of ownership. My body buzzed with excitement. Turned out I really, really liked this.

He pulled back to look at me. "Guess you're not thirsty?"

I shook my head and kissed him again. His smile told me he liked it as he carried me toward his bedroom. I met him, lips to lips. This time, I led and he followed. His body hardened against me.

But then the dynamic changed. I couldn't have said when it changed, but suddenly, he led the dance of our bodies. His tongue pushed between my lips, and I let him, melting into the power that was Max's strong body. Right then, I might have sworn that there was nothing in the world that could get to me, not so long as I had Max's arms around me and the soft mattress beneath my back.

He rubbed a finger over the outside of my shirt. My hard nipple increased in pain, and although I'd never have believed it, I loved the sensation. I arched my back to lift my breast closer to his hand. Max obliged me by squeezing the nipple that begged for his attention. Then he pulled my shirt over my head.

"I want a good look at them. I've already been dreaming about them."

My cheeks heated at what he said, even if it was cheesy. Maybe I was a person who needed a good dose of cheese in my life. I kissed his chin. "Better take my bra off then."

Max scrunched up his face. "Is it one of those front clips?"

It actually was. "Can I take from your expression that you don't like them?" I did him the favor of detaching the clip so that he didn't have to. I pulled my bra off and set it aside. The whole time, his eyes were on my breasts, watching them like he'd never seen a pair before.

I smirked at him, because how could I not? "Do they hold up to your expectations?"

"Hope, they are perfection." He bent over to suck my nipple into his mouth, and I moaned. Oh, this was going to be too much. I didn't imagine sex should be a rush, but I wanted more of this until we reached the end. Was that terrible?

Wasn't I supposed to crave foreplay? I didn't guess it mattered right then.

I reached between us. I was dressed from the waist down, and he was still fully clothed. With a tug, I indicated I wanted his shirt off.

He complied, and I ran my hands over his strong chest.

Max raised a dark eyebrow. "I know, I'm covered in scars. It's not pretty."

I didn't notice till he mentioned it. "We all have our scars. Max. Not one of us is perfect."

Some of us just hide our scars on the inside.

I kissed him to stop thinking and ran my hands over his warm skin, loving it when his muscles jumped underneath my touch. I did that to him. There was power in the knowledge and in being the kind of person who could make Max need. I didn't usually roll around in such a heady sensation, but I loved it and decided to let myself enjoy the moment while it lasted.

I kissed his chin, and he did the same to me, which made me giggle. He grinned. It was nice not to be so serious. I had to find a way to keep this lighter in my head before I started equating sex with Max with some kind of life-altering, universe shattering occurrence. I had to stay in the here and now, and that was a beautiful place to be.

I squirmed beneath him and pulled my pants off in an awkward way. He didn't seem to notice as he laid kisses all over my face.

But then he did that sexy thing again where he lifted one eyebrow while he looked at me. "In a hurry?"

"Aren't you?"

He shook his head, and a piece of his hair slowly fell over his eyes. "No. I want to savor every minute, but thanks for helping me get to where I wanted to be."

What did he mean by that if he wasn't also in a hurry to reach completion? Maybe my confusion showed on my face because he winked at me. "If your previous lovers aren't doing this with you, Hope, then they've been letting you down."

I still didn't understand until he pulled my panties down with his teeth. I sucked in a breath. Okay, now I fully grasped the situation. Really? He wanted to do *that*? My friends always complained that their boyfriends didn't go down on them, yet Max wanted to do it unprompted?

"You don't have to do this, if you don't want to."

The act seemed more intimate than our time in the car, or even of us being joined inside me. His mouth on my pussy would be a whole different thing altogether, and I didn't have time to consider really how I...

"There's no *have to* with me, beautiful. I tend to do just what I want, unless you don't want me to, which is a whole different situation."

I swallowed. I kind of *did* want to know what it would feel like. Nodding, slowly, I hoped my game face was in place. *Wow.* I was really fucked up when it came to this stuff. Max furrowed his brow for a second.

"If you don't like it, tell me to stop. You're not going to hurt my feelings." He held my gaze. "I can't explain how much I get off on knowing I'm making you wet for me. It works for me. Always has. And I think that it'll be even hotter with you."

His mouth was on me then. I thought I wouldn't like it, that I'd tell him to stop, but I did like it. I gasped, my hips rising, but his hand came down on me to hold me still. He licked me and then sucked. Oh yes, I liked the sucking. I liked that a *lot*. I closed my eyes. There was nowhere to go, nowhere to escape from this kind of pleasure. I couldn't turn it off. I grabbed on to the black sheets of his bed, like they could center me in the world, but quickly found I couldn't really hold on to them.

Pent up energy building inside me suddenly ached for release. The tension built, but it wasn't slow or gentle. I exploded around his tongue like a bomb. Unable to think, unable to even comprehend the fact that it was happening, I learned all at once that pleasure sometimes came with pain. Yet I loved it, craved that discomfort as much as the pleasure he gave me at the same time. I didn't know if I could have explained it, if pressed.

I hoped I never had to.

Max lifted his head to regard me. "I love how fast you come for me. It's such a gift."

I stroked my hand along his face, running my fingers through his hair. "Maybe you're just gifted?"

"And good for my ego too."

I leaned up on my elbows. "Come over here, and I'll return the favor."

He shook his head. "I'd love that…another time. Right now, I want to be inside you, if that's okay. You run this show, so to speak."

I swallowed. "I don't have all that much experience giving blow jobs." I wondered if everyone else out there practically choked on the words when they said it and hoped that I'd managed to fake being casual about it relatively well. I supposed I should tell him I had no experience. *None.* But that would undo the constant pretending I was doing, which now bordered on lying. Still, I wasn't going to deal with any of that at the moment.

He shook his head. "Not tonight, and I'm not worried about your inexperience. I have to tell you the truth—there is no such thing as a bad blow job, end of story. But it makes me beg the question, why are you with an old guy like me? Never mind. Don't answer. I like you with me in this here and now."

I liked it too, so I kissed him before he yanked off the rest of his clothing. I'd seen his cock in the car, but I was getting a better look at it. It was long, thick, veined, and I was glad we'd done this once before so I didn't have to wonder if it was going to fit. I still momentarily jarred at the thought. *How funny.* I was predictable in my anxiety, if nothing else.

I reached out to touch him, cupping the top of his cock with my hand. He closed his eyes. "The things that you do to me. I mean, fuck." He pushed my hand away and climbed on top of my body. "I can't get over how you want me."

Why wouldn't I? Had he looked in the mirror lately? Had he spent time talking to himself? Didn't he understand his complete, overall appeal? Maybe one of Max's most endearing qualities was that he really didn't have the slightest idea how fucking sexy he was. Maybe he didn't care? Either way, in a world of shallow, I loved his deep depths.

I wanted him inside of me.

I lifted an eyebrow. "Condom?"

He reached over me and opened his drawer, pulling one out. "Like before, will you open it for me?"

His hands weren't shaking. I took it from him. "You look pretty steady and capable to me."

"Sure, but I like watching you do it. Like watching you roll it on me. I didn't get enough of a look in the car. Pretty please?"

I laughed, most of my nerves vanishing. He was funny, and if he found anything lacking in me, I certainly couldn't see it on his face. "Gladly."

"Oh and, Hope? You'll have plenty of time to practice giving head with me if you want it."

I sucked in my breath. "Are you volunteering to be my guinea pig? For me to practice on you?" I licked my lips, not sure what had come over me but going with it just the same. "What if I bite?"

"What if I like that?"

Now my hands shook. I tore open the condom package. "Do you?"

"Maybe I do if you're the one biting. I guess we're both going to find out."

He pushed open my knees until I was as totally open to him as I'd been when he'd put his mouth on me. I sucked in my breath. "Max?"

"You're ready for me, Hope. And I want to fuck you like you've never been fucked before."

CHAPTER 12

MAX PUSHED INSIDE OF ME, AND I GASPED AT THE SENSATION.
Had I ever been this full? Had I thought this before? I didn't
even know. All I knew was that his big, strong body was on
top of mine and his cock was inside of me. Neither of us had
moved since he'd pushed gently inside. We breathed hard,
staring at each other, our faces so close, we practically shared
air without actually kissing. Our breaths came in unison.
Maybe if I moved my hand to place it over his chest, I'd feel
that his heart and mine beat together in that moment.

Fuck, I was such a poet in my own head.

I kissed him all over his face, everywhere I could reach.
Out of curiosity, I put my hand over his heart to feel it beat.
Like my own, it raced, but whether or not we were somehow
synchronous, I had no idea. At this point, I just liked feeling
it. He took my hand in his, keeping himself above me with
one arm, and brought it to his mouth to kiss it before he let it
go. His warm lips were practically imprinted on my skin.

"You are so hot around me. I love being inside you, but
I've got to move, beautiful. I've just got to."

I nodded. "Move."

He jerked his head in the smallest of movements before he jerked his cock inside of me. Slowly, ever so much so, he pulled out and then slid back in. Over and over. Each movement a stroke over my clit in a way that seemed to build up pressure. I closed my eyes to feel each stroke. Max stopped moving, which caused me to open my lids.

"You okay?" I stroked my hand down the side of his face.

"I need your eyes on me."

That I could do. I stared at his dark depths. He really was beautiful. Like he'd seen what he wanted, he shifted his cock slightly, and his movements hit me in a whole new spot. I gasped. *Yes, right there*. I squeezed him tighter, drawing him further inside. I wanted more of that. *Right now*.

"Oh, think I found a spot for you." His voice was a caress in my ear. "You like that."

I more than liked it, but I didn't have the words to tell him how much. It was like I'd lost the ability to communicate. *Just think and feel. Just think and feel.* I'd never know exactly what came over me, but I leaned forward and bit on his shoulder.

He laughed, throwing his head back. "I like that. Anytime you want to bite me, bite me."

Good, because otherwise this could get awkward. I didn't know why I'd bit him, but I loved it. A lot.

He jerked once inside me, hard, and I came like I hadn't just exploded minutes earlier on his tongue. I needed him, and I hadn't realized how much. I dug my fingers into him and resisted the urge to bite him again. Once was fine, but twice was too much. Or at least I thought those might be the rules. It was more like starts and stops in between gasping for air, seeing stars, and exploding from the inside out. Max had done this to me. He was just…he was just…something.

His body shuddered a second before he came, my name

on his lips, his head dropping briefly to my shoulder. Max was beautiful all the time but especially in that moment. I watched him like I was an outsider to the moment, to my own body, as though I observed both of us from a distance. I wanted to remember the moment always. I wrapped my arms around him and held on while we both breathed so hard, we might as well have run a marathon.

He lifted his head to regard me. "Wow."

I smiled at him. "Sorry I marked you."

He rolled off me, touching the bite mark while he did. "I told you, I liked it. Bite me any time."

I put my arm over my eyes. "It was…spontaneous."

"Good." Max exited to the bathroom, and when he returned, he didn't have the condom on anymore. He held a wet towel, and my mind must have been moving slowly, because I barely realized it was for me before he gently wiped my thighs with it. "I like spontaneous Hope in bed. Actually, I like all of you in bed, every gorgeous inch of you."

I grinned at him when he took the washcloth to the bathroom. Max crawled back into bed moments later. While he scooted close to me, anxiety, my dear old friend, found its way back into the moment. *What am I supposed to do now?*

He yawned. "I wish I didn't have to get up so early." I looked at the clock. It read three in the morning. Wow. Yes, it was late. "But I have to go talk to the fishermen directly. I just haven't been happy with… You know what, never mind. I'm not going to think about that right before bed.

Was he asking me to leave? Yes, I was pretty sure he was. That was a classic line, wasn't it? The *I have to get up early, so you should be going* cliché. "I'll grab my stuff."

He touched my arm. "Hold on. Where are you going?"

I swallowed. "Home. You said you have to get up early."

Max shook his head fast. "Oh, no. I was thinking out

149

loud, not suggesting you should go. I didn't mean that. I was just talking. No, I say what I mean. If I wanted you to leave, I'd say it." He paused. "Unless you *want* to leave. That's entirely your right, and all that."

We'd spun full circle and fast. I bit down on my lip. "I'll stay, if that's okay."

It wasn't like I was likely to sleep in general, but I liked the idea of staying right where I was for the night. His bed was warm, and Max was practically a furnace of heat that seeped into my skin in the best possible way. He turned off the light. "Do you want the TV on?"

"No, I'm good. I probably won't sleep, but sometimes I just want the quiet." I paused. "You know what I mean?"

The darkness covered us like a blanket, and as Max tucked me in against him, I let it fold over me. "I do, actually."

I WOKE UP SLOWLY. My eyes were practically glued shut, and I moaned, not wanting to give up the nothingness of sleep and the comfort it brought. When sleep was hard, actually falling into dreams was like a privilege, like the gods of rest wrapped their arms around me and temporarily granted me manna from heaven. I rubbed my eyes open, then realized where I was.

Max's bed.

Last night rushed back as it dawned on me that I must have literally passed out on Max, because I had no memory of falling asleep. That kind of sleep was so rare for me that I almost couldn't remember the last time it happened. *Months maybe?* As for Max, he wasn't there, which wasn't surprising since the light streamed bright into the room and he'd said he had to be up early.

Fuck. I hadn't even heard him get up. I shook my head. Okay. He hadn't woken me. Or maybe he'd tried and I'd just been so out of it, he'd left me there. How embarrassing would that be?

I groaned and threw my head back against the pillows again. I didn't do anything normally, not even wake up in the morning. I rolled over, grabbing my phone off the side table. I had no memory of putting it there. If anything, it was in the pocket of my pants, which had been on the floor. Unless I started sleepwalking on top of everything else, Max must've picked it up, plugged it into his charger, and left it there.

That was really...nice of him. He did things like that. Just gentle touches of care, like giving me his coat because I was ridiculous about fashion and hadn't wanted to mess up my outfit. I rubbed my eyes again. How had I become this person, and was it too late to do something about it?

A message lit up, and I looked down at my phone. He'd texted me.

Hey, hope I didn't wake you leaving. Coffee on in the kitchen. Left you breakfast on a plate in the fridge. Warm it up. Three minutes in the microwave. Busy tonight?

I was absolutely not busy. My heart fluttered at all the things he'd done for me so that I could stay asleep. Had anyone ever done that for me? Ever? I didn't think so.

I swung my legs out of bed, and after I used the bathroom —and the toothbrush he'd laid out for me—I texted him back. *Thanks for all of this. Sorry, I think I must have just conked out. Not busy tonight.*

The three little dots that showed he was writing popped up before he answered a second later. *Love that you fell asleep. I did too. Everything I could do to not turn off my alarm and sleep with you all day. Can I see you since you're not busy?*

I grinned, happiness flooding through me and pushing out, for once, my constant anxiety. *Sure. Sounds good.*

It really did.

I TRIED to make a list of all the jobs I might be qualified for and then gave up. I went to the gym and managed to avoid seeing anyone there. Showered, dressed, and with nowhere to go, I stared at my mother's painting, wishing it could tell me all her secrets. Why had she loved my father? What mistakes had she made? Or maybe there were more important questions. Had she loved my father? Had she stopped? Did she ever? Why did she do what she did?

The painting told me nothing. It never did, but it did prompt me to pick up the phone and actually call Bridget. We texted all the time, but when was the last time I'd heard her voice? Had I at all since she moved away? Morning in New York meant nighttime for her. Hopefully, it meant she'd be home from working.

"Hello?" She sounded awake, and I briefly heard a TV in the background before she shut it off. I could communicate in both French and Spanish, but neither would help me if I decided to go visit my sister.

"Hi." It was good to hear her voice. "How are you?"

"Are we actually talking on the phone? Voice to voice? Have we traveled back in time?"

I sank down to the floor. There had been a time the three of us—Bridget, Layla, and me—had been so close, but lately, we lived three separate lives, connected only because we were totally screwed over by our father and needed constant bodyguards to keep the Russian mob from killing us.

I laughed. "Don't you want to hear from me?"

Wincing, I wished I hadn't asked. Bridget was insanely honest. What would I do if she said no? Hang up? Go cry in the corner? I couldn't call Layla. She was busy being a mother, happy being in love. She'd be there for me, but phoning to say basically nothing would waste time she could spend with her family. She was so nice, she'd never admit it, and instead stress herself out trying to be there for me.

Bridget—maybe not so much.

"I do, actually." She sighed. "I had the worst date tonight. The man was so...dumb...I'm not sure how he is standing upright on a daily basis."

A giggle I didn't expect moved through me. "Really? Why did you go out with him?"

"Because he's really hot in that way that makes him seem like he's badass. I have a problem with bad boys. I've had a crush on one my whole life, or it feels that way, and I keep looking for him in other men. Or at least that's what my last therapist said."

I hadn't even known she'd been in therapy. "I went to one too, for a while."

"Yeah...we're all fucked up. Thanks, Mom and Dad."

Oh, she had no idea. "I went out with a guy last night. He doesn't really date. But we had great sex."

It seemed foreign to speak those words. Had I really just said them? I bit down on my lip.

"Honestly, Hope, I wasn't sure you even had sex. I thought you might be saving yourself or something. It was great sex? When was the last time I had great sex? I don't even know if I've ever had great sex. Maybe I'm defunct. Why doesn't he date?"

I blinked, trying to catch up to her conversation. "Why did you think I was saving myself?"

"I've never seen anyone as disinterested in dating as you seemed to be. I was wrong. Answer the other part. Why doesn't he date?"

I didn't know really. I had a vague sense of why Max wasn't going to get serious, but that was about it. "He just doesn't. Has a lot going on. He's a chef."

"Ooh, so he can feed you too."

Yes, he was certainly doing that. "He's really, really talented."

"So what else are you up to? Planned any great parties?"

I sighed. Maybe this was why I'd called. Talking about Max was fine, but now that we were doing it, I wasn't really sure what to say. Maybe that was because I didn't know at all what was happening with him, which might turn out to be nothing at all. For me, it would always be special in the sense that being with him had broken through a wall I'd kept erected for years, but would it be more than that? Internally, I sighed. Probably not.

"I'm going to need a new line of work. I was declared fat and over, so it's a mess. I'll find something else."

She was quiet. "But you love it. The event planning. Where the money goes after. And let's face it, Hopey, you have always been the one of us to like the media attention. You like to be that person."

It was hard to explain that while that was true, it was also not at the same time. When I was younger, it had been difficult to understand that there was plurality to life. Things could be…and also not be at the same time.

"Yes, I used to love to be in the spotlight. It felt like some kind of validation of, what? I didn't know exactly. But it was clear to me I didn't have Layla's talent or your genius."

"Hope," Bridget said, trying to interrupt me, but I kept talking.

"So, being the one they followed made me feel great. Truth is, and we both know this, it's Layla they'd also have preferred to be trailing, because she's prettier than I am."

This time, she sighed loudly. "That isn't true. I'm not even sure how I'd judge which one of you would be so-called prettier. What does it matter? One person seems prettier to someone and then not to the other."

I supposed that was true in some la-la land, but frankly, the fact that Bridget said it was surprising. Bridget only dealt in hard truths. "If you cared about such things, they'd prefer you to me too."

"And so what if these so-called *they* did? I'm sure if we took a poll of every *they* in the world, then we would see that…"

My phone beeped with an incoming call—Muffy. I didn't hold back my groan. I'd called Bridget to get a healthy dose of the medicine only she could give to me. Instead, I had to take a call from my last client ever. What did she want? I had a bunch of her money in an account that I would return to her shortly. If she wanted it today, I'd make it happen.

"Bridget, I've got to go."

"Yep." Short and to the point, that was Bridget. "Just, real quick, you might not believe this, but there are men and women out there who wouldn't find any of the three of us attractive at all. Somehow, I think the three of us will survive."

She disconnected, which transferred me immediately to Muffy's call. "Hi, this is Hope."

A loud, inexplicable noise sounded in the background. "Oh, Hope, good. I'm just calling to say goodbye. We're off. All of us. Here, Tim, say goodbye to Hope."

Tim? I blinked. "You brought your son?"

"Well, of course. I want him to see Mommy and Daddy doing good things."

How exactly were they going to do that? Were they going to haul the food and supplies out of the airplane? Were they going to chuck it while they were airborne? I couldn't get over these people. "Please be careful."

"I'll have you throw a welcome back party when we return."

I cleared my throat, a headache forming between my eyes. "Aren't you only going to be gone a few days?"

She'd already hung up. I stared at the phone for a second before I threw it onto the bed. Muffy was one thing, but Bridget had made some good points without really making any. Why did I care so much what other people thought? What was it about me that craved so much outside approval? What did other people do to get to the point where they were good just because that's what they were?

Maybe I should read some self-help books.

The thought made me giggle until I was outright laughing. I doubted they would work for me, but it was funny to imagine myself sitting there reading them for some reason. I could get a cool pair of glasses and sit in coffee houses until I went broke from not working and how fucking expensive New York City was as a home.

I groaned. Even my fantasies collapsed into dark realities, but no more of that. I'd take a shower. Go to the gym. And I'd have great sex again tonight. I hoped. There was probably a pretty good chance of it. Max seemed to like to see me.

Hell, maybe I'd pretend I was more like Bridget and be done with him instead of him being done with me. I'd make things work until they didn't for me anymore and walk away with my sense of self still intact.

Maybe. Or maybe pigs would fly out of my ass. I laughed at my own joke again. Okay. I was funny, at least in my own mind.

~

THAT NIGHT, I dressed for the weather. I wore a jacket, and I was okay with the look. Max hadn't seemed to care one way or the other about what I wore. I arrived at his restaurant a little early. Just in time to see Anna talking to someone by the doorway while she smoked a cigarette. I so rarely saw anyone do that in NYC anymore. In Europe, yes. New York, no. I must have stared because she threw it on the ground.

"I know. It'll kill me." She stepped on the butt. "But tomorrow is the operation, and I'm stressed. I've reverted ten years because of the stress. That was when I quit—a decade ago."

I held up my hands. "Not judging. I swear."

"Yes, you are, but I forgive you. Come on. Chef will want me to bring you right in." She swung open the door. "Just finishing up the last customers. Oh, and you should tell me which one of us was texting you what we needed and how you got it for us."

I shrugged. "I'll never tell. I'm great at keeping secrets."

"You are. I can tell that about you. Did you grow up here? I never heard that."

She jumped around in topics. It was enough to make my head spin. "No, not until I was in high school. And then..."

My voice trailed off, caught by the scene in front of me. There, in the middle of his kitchen, mild mannered Max laid into one of his cooks in a loud, angry voice.

"You ruined it," he shouted, and the younger man's face fell.

"I'm sorry, Chef."

Anna pursed her lips. "Whoops," she practically whispered, and it was more like she was saying it to herself than intended for me to hear her.

Max picked up the plate and dumped it into the garbage. "We can't serve that. Remake it, and if you ever try to serve one of my customers something like that again, you're out of here. Got it?"

He stormed into his office, leaving a visibly pale cook behind, who took a second before he rushed back to his stovetop.

Anna looked over at me. "I'll take care of this. It's my job. Why don't you go see him? Just be careful not to poke the bear right at this second."

I had no idea how to avoid that. "Are you sure it wouldn't be better if I came back later?"

"Absolutely not. Please, go now." She practically shoved me forward. "He was in a great mood today. Lance must really have fucked up."

I wouldn't want to be Lance for anything in the world in that moment. Max hadn't cursed or seemed violent, but his anger seemed to seethe throughout the room. All of his staff stared at their own workstations like they were afraid to look away, lest something happen. I hurried forward, poking my head in. "Good time, or should I come back?"

Did I sound light and airy? I was going for light and airy. I'd forgotten Max was the same guy who had thrown me out of his restaurant. He seemed so constantly easygoing that I'd forgotten there was no way he did this job with a blasé easygoingness. No way. He'd built up, not one, but *two* highly rated eateries.

He pointed at the door. "Shut that, would you?"

I did as he asked, closing it behind me. "Rough day?"

"Only the last two minutes, and it's better now. It pisses me off because I gave him a chance because his father asked me to hire him. We served together a million years ago. It's his stepson. Doesn't matter. Point is, I did it. And if I hadn't gone out to look at what he was doing because Anna was on her break, he'd have served that mess to a customer."

I sat down in the chair across from him. "I don't know anything about managing people, but maybe he's not ready. Is there something else he could do for you?"

"He gets it done or he doesn't work here." He shook his head. "Still want to see me tonight, or did I just become a monster?"

I leaned forward. "Still want to see you. No monsters here."

He nodded, once. "Great, because it would really bum me out if you cancelled while you're looking so incredibly beautiful."

I looked down at myself. *Jeans. White blouse. Black jacket. Plain, black shoes.* There was something magical about the fact that he always seemed to think I looked beautiful, even when I'd done almost nothing at all.

"Thanks, Chef."

His smile was huge. "Sexy when you say it."

Truly magical.

CHAPTER 13

I HADN'T KNOWN I COULD LIKE HAVING SEX AGAINST A WALL or on the floor. Or...well, hell, anywhere. I liked having sex everywhere with Max. It might become an addiction, and I wasn't in the mood to stop it.

We lay staring up at the ceiling together in his bed. I breathed hard and so did he, but when he flipped onto his side to look at me, he seemed calm. "So...I have a problem."

I lifted an eyebrow. "No, you don't. You seem to just get better and better."

His smile was huge. "Good one. And thank you, but seriously—a problem. See, Anna is going to be very busy because of Eric. For *weeks*. She's on leave—paid, of course. Anyway, I have to fire Lance, and this woman I don't think you've met named Cassie. Anyway, point being, I have to fire them, and it's the worst time to be down employees, because without Anna, I'm going to be even busier."

I rolled toward him. "So what you're saying is you can't see me anymore."

I spoke the words and hoped the horror that speaking

them caused in me didn't show on my face. I was the queen at hiding emotions. Surely I could do it again.

He was ending things while I was in his bed.

"I don't want to not see you. I'm hoping I still can, but I'm going to be wrecked. I know how much I rely on Anna, but I'm really feeling the fact that she won't be there for an extended period of time acutely right now." He cleared his throat. "She's going to get her mom to come next week, and I hope that she can return to work then, but we really don't know how he's going to do, so we can't count on that just yet."

I nodded, rolling over to reach for my clothes. I would have my meltdown in the car. I could hold on for that long. Somehow, I'd make it that far.

"Hope?" He grabbed my arm. "Where are you going?"

I looked over my shoulder. I'd forgotten how chiseled his abs were and how beautiful his face looked when the shadows of his whiskers came in after a day of growth. "Home."

"Why?" He didn't let go of my arm.

Enough game playing. "Because you just made it clear you wanted me to leave."

He blinked. "I didn't say anything like that. How do you get me wanting you to go from what I just said?"

"I understand subtext most of the time. You're busy. You're moving on. And you really weren't subtle about wanting me to leave, so why act like you meant something else?"

Max let go of my arm and sighed loudly. "I don't play games, Hope. If I wanted you to leave, I'd say go. I'm being one hundred percent up-front with you. If you want to leave, that's fine, but don't go because you think I'm talking around a subject. I don't do that. Who has the time?"

Did I want to go? No, I didn't. But I wouldn't be made a fool of. I'd had enough of that in my life to last a lifetime. "So you aren't just trying to find a nice way to tell me to go and that you're done with whatever it is that we're doing?"

He shook his head slowly. "You'll be tired of this before I will."

I didn't find that possibility likely. I couldn't imagine ever not wanting to lie next to him in the dark. Just the thought of giving up what we'd shared scared the shit out of me. "Why is that?"

"Because I'm not a relationship guy, and you are absolutely a woman who will want one. Until you realize that, I'm going to be selfish and keep you...at least until you tell me to bug off."

He was so confusing. I wasn't sure I understood what any of that meant at all. "You not being a relationship man means what? You're doing this with multiple people at the same time as me?"

So far, we'd been really, really careful. But if he was dicking around with multiple women, I was going to carry a package of condoms on me so I was sure we were never accidentally without. Maybe he had a girl he slept with at lunch every day.

He shook his head. "I think trying to do this with anyone other than you might just kill me, beautiful. I'm old, remember?" He held up his hand. "That's a compliment by the way."

It was? I was going to have to digest that. "And that tells me nothing at all and doesn't answer my question."

"No, it didn't. Really, it means that we don't have future plans. By that, I don't mean we can't schedule dinner together. It's that we aren't going to be planning buying a house or raising kids. Trust me, I've seen that life. It's not for me. I'm too…fucked up for that. Hope, I might seem like I've got it together because I've learned to put on a good show, but I am not. Basically, we're friends. Who do this." He ran his thumb over my hand, and shivers moved through my body. He only had to gently touch me, and I was always ready to go. He leaned over to kiss where he'd just stroked my hand. "You're going to get tired of my bullshit eventually. Move on. That's okay. It'll be this strange moment in time for both of us. How we met. What happened between us. This interlude. We'll both remember it, and at some point, wonder how it took place at all."

He really had no idea. "Since we're friends…" I almost choked on the words, but he wasn't the only one who could fake being normal. Truly, Max had no idea how much we really had in common. "I want to be clear I'm not your booty call." I might be lying. I'd probably come running if he called. Or maybe not. "We can't go without speaking for weeks and then just have sex. I don't think I'm built like that."

As I spoke the words, I knew they were true. That was something. It was like I had to learn myself in these moments because I'd never had them before.

He nodded once. "Not a problem. I'll be too busy to get together for a bit, but I will make time to communicate. I don't expect you to fuck and go. That's not me, either. Oh and, Hope, when you meet someone else, just end it with me. I'll get it. I don't want to share, but I'm not ridiculous. Move on from me whenever that happens."

Max was being so reasonable about our connection, I wasn't sure if I wanted to kiss him or slap him. I'd do neither because they were both sort of nuts. Instead, I crawled into the bed next to him. It was enough for tonight. I might not sleep, but the danger with insomnia was not knowing that sometimes I was just plain too tired to continue on with conversations that were complicated and required finesse. I never wanted to regret saying something just because I was exhausted, although I suspected it happened more than I thought it did.

He shifted so I could snuggle up against him. I'd asked, and he'd answered my question. Now I had to figure out what to do with what he said.

Tomorrow.

I didn't expect to sleep, and this time, I was right.

I THUMBED through the mail on the desk in my office. *Junk. Magazine. Junk.* Almost no one used snail mail anymore for anything other than bills. I had one for my cell phone, but it was a double because they emailed me too. Plus, I had it on autopay. Maybe I should call and see if I could go paperless. Yep, I'd put that on the list of things to do. I had lots of time. I was unemployed. No one had called or emailed to ask me to book a party.

It was official. I was done.

I should probably get rid of the office. I had no reason to keep it anymore, and it was an expense I didn't need. I'd do that today. Call the agent in charge, and let her know I wouldn't be renewing at the end of the year.

My phone rang, and I grabbed it off the table where I'd set it down. I was doing a great job of not thinking about Max today. The number didn't ring a bell, but I answered it anyway. If I got one more party to plan, I could live in denial just a little bit longer. As long as they had a charity associated with it, I was good.

"Hi, this is Hope."

There was a pause before the person spoke. "Hope?" The woman's voice sounded strained. It cracked halfway through my name.

"Yes? I'm sorry, who is this?"

"Oh, yes. I never called you directly. Muffy always took care of it. This is Sara, Tim's nanny."

The woman who was always distracted at our lunches. One thing I would say for Muffy, she might have treated Tim like an accessory, but she brought him everywhere. Tons of kids in his position were just left home with the nanny. Then they got sent to the schools I'd attended. Being left home with the nanny had been my destiny. A ton of nannies, actually. We'd moved so much, we had a new one every year or two. Some of them were great, and some of them were... Well, better not to think about that.

"Hi, Sara. How are you?" I picked up a letter and discarded it into the trash. No, I didn't want to change my cell phone carrier. Should I be tearing or shredding these things? Could someone steal my identity based on that offer? Did Max like all kinds of whisky? Not that I should be spending money on things I didn't have to right then, but maybe he'd like a bottle of something? Things were going to be hard. How was the surgery going? And didn't this woman quit? Was she rehired?

"Not well." She sounded like she was crying, and my attention immediately shifted over to her. "You didn't hear?"

My body went cold. I didn't know what she was about to say, but her sobs didn't bode well. "Didn't hear what?"

"It's on the news."

I hadn't watched the news, nor had I turned on my computer. After getting a million and one notifications on my phone when Layla had been kidnapped, I'd turned off headline news notifications. "What happened?"

"They're dead. Muffy. Martin." Yes, that was her husband's name. I stuttered on the thought. That wasn't really very important at the moment, but it was all I could think about right then. *Muffy's husband's name is Martin. Was, anyway.* I could never remember his name, and so I just never thought about it. I was good at that.

But, oh no. They were dead.

"They're dead?" I sank to the floor, my knees suddenly not wanting to hold my weight anymore. How could they be dead? *I just saw them. Focus.* I had to get a hold of myself.

"They took Tim." The nanny sniffed.

My body went cold as I asked, "How did this happen? *What* happened?"

She sniffed. "Tim's okay. I think. He didn't die. The people who killed the others have them. There are pictures. They're online." *Fuck.* I really had to get back into things and start paying attention again. *How did I miss all of this?* "Muffy and Tim liked you so much. I wanted to make sure you had heard."

The nanny hung up the phone, and I shivered on the ground where I had sunk. Muffy was dead. Killed. And Tim was alone in that country, taken by men who would do who knew what with him. All of this was my fault. I'd raised money for her, but I hadn't questioned her about any of it. I never did. Rich people used me, they got publicity and big checks that they didn't need because they were already rich. Who knew if they actually used those checks to do what they said they were going to do with them? I never followed up at all.

Muffy booked herself an airplane to go on an adventure so she could be photographed doing good. She died. Her kid was taken. Maybe if I had asked…

Did Muffy even know where she had been flying?

I put my head between my knees.

My phone dinged. *Eric's surgery went great.*

I swallowed. Max had thought to text me.

I answered him with, *Such good news.*

I didn't text him about Muffy. He had enough on his plate, and he just got great news. I couldn't bring him down, not after he'd worried so much about the surgery. Besides, he hardly knew these people. I had to think. There had to be something I could do.

I texted my cousin. *I knew them.*

He'd know who I meant. He answered fast. *Yes. Such a tragedy.*

I stared at his words before I quickly typed back. *What are you going to do to get the kid back?* Surely they would. They were the State Department. They didn't just leave American citizens to rot in countries until they were killed. Wasn't rescuing them something they did?

Nothing. Would love to, but we are not in contact with them. No real central government to deal with, and any communication with them would elevate the warlord to levels that we are not prepared for at this time.

Would they feed him pasta? That was the stupidest thought ever. Of course they weren't going to feed him pasta, if they fed him at all. I rushed to the bathroom and puked. For ten straight minutes, I puked. Then, when I lifted my head, I grabbed my phone again.

If a private citizen with no business getting involved wanted to do something, what could that person do?

My phone rang, and I picked it up despite the unknown number. My cousin spoke without perfunctory greetings. "You're going to do it anyway, aren't you, whether I answer you or not."

He didn't phrase it as a question, which was good,

because it wasn't one. I might be nuts, but I did the right thing as much as I could. I wouldn't leave that little boy there. I even had Muffy's own money to get things done.

If there were a way that I could get Tim back, I would get him.

"Call Michael Li, that man Zeke has taking care of all of you. He isn't just a man paid to hire bodyguards. If anyone could get in and out of there with that kid, it is Michael Li and the people he's employed. If he doesn't help you, I'll give you other names."

My hands shook as I got off the phone. *This is insane.* I needed to call my therapist. I needed to breathe. I needed to be more like Layla and go for a run. I could shower. Call Bridget in Hong Kong. Have a drink.

I didn't do any of those things.

Instead, I called Michael Li.

"Hope?" He sounded like he was in the middle of something. There was a lot of noise in the background. "Are you okay?"

"No." I spoke low, hoping he could hear me. "I need your help. If you won't help me, I can find someone who will." I needed him to understand I was serious. "I've heard you're actually the person to get this done."

I didn't hear background noise anymore. "What the fuck is going on, kid?"

He probably never called Bridget 'kid.' I was pretty sure he was in love with her. I also thought she had all those feelings right back for him, even though she'd never admit it. Those two were not going to confess to each other how they felt. But Layla and me? Yeah…he called us 'kid.'

We weren't children anymore.

I told him what I needed.

As I STARED at the ten men in the living room, I quickly calculated money. Michael had told me what this was going to cost. *The men. The time. The guns. The plane.* I had it, thanks to Muffy. She hadn't known she was giving me the money to bring her child back from a life worse than death in a foreign country, but that was what she had done.

Because of her complete mismanagement of money.

I'd spoken to her mother and told her my plans. She agreed I should do as I planned with Muffy's money, even emailed me a signed and notarized document giving me permission to do so as Muffy's living relative and guardian of the child who was missing.

I hadn't thought about needing that, but she had.

Ten men. Michael looked different than I was used to seeing him. Only when he'd plotted to get Layla back had I seen him so completely focused. With him, he brought a medic, Mitch, and the snipers Jefferson and Clayton. His fighters had other roles, but that's how I thought of them. I couldn't quite remember their names yet.

It was Clayton who looked up from the plans and spoke. "This is a child. He'll be terrified. That adds an element to this I don't like."

"How do you imagine countering any possible problems that arise from his age? Intel tells us he's here." Michael pointed at the document in front of him. "We grab him, and we go."

"Ever grabbed a kid, boss?" Jefferson chewed gum thoughtfully. He blew a bubble, then sucked it back into his mouth before continuing. "Not so easy. They're small and squirmy."

Michael sighed. "Are you saying you want out?"

"No." Clayton sighed. "I want in, but I think we need to bring someone that the kid knows. Make a huge difference in possible outcomes, I think."

All the eyes in the room turned to me. Michael shook his head. "Absolutely not."

"If she were anyone else, would you say no?" Mitch questioned. "I know you've known them a long time, but she hired us. Maybe she wants to help? We can keep her safe. It'll make a big difference with the kid."

Michael had been born in Hong Kong, but he'd moved to the US when he was three. His father was American, and his mother had been a Chinese citizen until she'd become an American citizen some years ago. That was about all I knew of his background. Right then, he looked less like a serious security officer and more like an absolute warrior.

"You're right—I've known her since she was sixteen, and I won't put her life at risk."

I shook where I stood. God, I was such a coward, because I absolutely didn't want to go. Terrible, but it was true. I didn't want to go to that country and have what happened to Muffy happen to me. I wanted to pay these brave men to do it for me.

"Out of my way, Luke," Max said, storming into the room. He had a bag under his arm and a bottle of wine. He stopped short as he took in the room. His gaze found mine at last, holding me in its intensity. "What the fuck is going on?"

"L.T." Clayton jumped to his feet. "It's you. Look, Mitch, it's Max."

Max pulled his gaze from mine to the other two men, who were suddenly in front of him, embracing him tightly.

"Hope," Michael said, catching my attention. "Who the fuck is this?"

"He's my friend," I supplied. How else was I to explain my strange connection to Max?

Luke cleared his throat. "Sometimes they spend the night together, boss."

My cheeks heated up. That was really not anyone else's fucking business.

"I'm supposed to be told if those things develop."

I held up my hand. "He's my friend." I couldn't stress the point enough.

"We served together for a long time." Clayton seemed downright joyful. "The L.T. is good people. Tough. And we did that other shit together too, until he lost his taste for it. Some bigtime chef now."

"Hope?" Max ignored Mitch to speak just to me. "What the fuck is going on?"

I sighed, exhaustion hitting me like a ton of bricks. I needed a vacation. "Muffy and her husband were killed. Tim is a prisoner of some very bad people. I'm getting him back."

There, I explained it.

"What?" He set down what he was carrying and walked over to me. "When did this happen?"

"Yesterday." Every time I thought about it, I wanted to cry, which wasn't helpful. "I have some of her money and her mother's permission to get her grandson back. So I called Michael—he's in charge of my security, and I guess he's good at this kind of thing. He's arranged all of this, and we're going." I swallowed. "We're all going. They need me."

When Max spoke, it was through gritted teeth. "The fuck you are."

CHAPTER 14

"Excuse me?" He'd shouted at me, so I shouted right back.

When he spoke to me again, it was through gritted teeth. "You aren't going with them to Slomestikan. That is insanity. It's dangerous, and I forbid it."

My mouth fell open. "You *forbid* me? Who are you to forbid me to do anything?"

Clayton whistled through his teeth. "Damn."

"Maybe you two would like to talk in the hall?" Michael suggested. "And you are going to watch how you speak to her, got me?"

Max rounded on Michael. "Look, I don't know why you think you can talk to me like that. Maybe you're in love with her? I don't really give a shit. Right now, all I see is that you're the imbecile suggesting this civilian should go with you to a country the State Department doesn't even acknowledge exists."

I held up my hand. "In the hall. *Now.*"

Max followed me to the hallway outside my apartment. I

could hardly breathe from the anger surging through my veins. It was like my entire body was on fire, and not in the same way it was when I was in the bed with Max.

"You understand that, in order to get his dick in you, that man is suggesting you risk your life."

I pointed my finger right into his face. "First of all, he's not in love with me, and he doesn't want to stick his dick in me. I've known him since I was sixteen. Besides, if he's in love with anyone, it's my sister Bridget. He's helping me out. Plus, he saved Layla's life, so whatever macho thing is going in your head about Michael, you can let it go. Not to mention you have no right to come in here and order me around like some sort of caveman!"

He flared his nostrils. "It's insanity. Why do you care so much about this, anyway? This isn't your problem. Give the grandmother the money and let her hire her own mercenaries."

"She's a little old lady who can hardly speak today from grief. She isn't going to be hiring anyone to do anything, and Tim is there alone."

Max shook his head. "You know, I knew you had a self-destructive side that could make you do stupid things, but I didn't imagine you could be this...ridiculous."

My body went cold as the insult hit just where he intended it to—in my gut. "Remember, friend, when you told me that there would come a time that I wouldn't want to do this anymore? Yeah...this is that time. I'm done. Goodnight and goodbye, Max. I'll always regret ruining your life. If I can ever help you, please let me know, but this thing between us, yeah, it's over. Please send Anna and Eric my regards."

With my back somehow straight and my emotions hidden away until I could lose it later, I shut the door in his face.

The room of mercenaries—I'd not thought of that word myself until Max introduced it—stared at me as I entered.

"You okay, Hopey?" Michael spoke in a low voice. "Want me to go take care of him?"

Mitch shook his head. "I don't know which one of you I would pick in a fight. Max has been out of the game for a while, but he was lethal. So are you. It's fifty-fifty which one of you would win."

"No one is fighting," I informed the room. I was the boss in this, after all. Or something like that. Who knew what I was anymore? I sure as hell didn't know.

Michael rocked back on his feet. "You don't have to go."

"I think I do."

That must have been the right answer because Clayton and Mitch nodded like they agreed. It looked like I was going to Slomestikan to rescue a little boy that shouldn't have been there in the first place. These men were going to help me get him, and I'd bring him to his grandmother on her white sand beach.

Another mistake I could try to amend.

Somehow.

Excusing myself, I left the guys in my living room, my mother's painting staring down at them with the lights of the city behind them. Someone had opened my curtain.

We were leaving in the morning.

No time for heartbreak. No time to wonder if he'd lingered in the hall at all or just left. No time to remember that he thought I was self-destructive and ridiculous. Just the hours of the night ahead of me to not let myself feel pain.

～

HOW MICHAEL HAD GOTTEN SO much equipment so fast was beyond me, but the plane I boarded was state-of-the-art and huge. We were taking off from a small private airport in New Jersey. The guys had their gear stashed under their seats, and there was an entire wing of the plane that would be used as a makeshift airport if need be. The pilot's name was Buck, and I hadn't learned the co-pilot's name yet. It was going to be a fifteen-hour flight. I'd been on longer. It took over a day for me to get to Australia, and I'd been a bunch of times. Plus, I'd visited Bridget a lot. Still, long was long. I was glad to have my Kindle app.

Quickly, and before I could overthink it, I shot out a text to Bridget and Layla. *Love you.*

It was really all there was to say. I put my phone on airplane mode and resolved not to turn it back on Wi-Fi until after I had Tim. Then I'd message them again.

"I'm going to message your brother-in-law that this is happening about two seconds before we take off. Then I'm not going to look at that phone again until later." Michael sat down in his seat. "He's not going to be happy about this. He might fire me, but you were going to do this anyway, and I know these guys. I trust them." It looked like we'd had the same kind of thought.

I nodded. "I know I put your back against the wall."

"You Radfords know how to do that. It's in the blood." He smiled at me. "You'll be safe here. We won't let you off this plane until the fighting, if any, is over. Plus, it looks like you're going to have your own bodyguard."

What? That was news to me. "How does that work?"

"Well, here he is." A man climbed into the plane, and Clayton closed the door behind him, essentially sealing us inside.

I gasped and sat forward, my brain trying to deny what

my eyes could clearly see. *Max. He is here. On this plane. Heading for Slomestikan.* How was that possible?

He plopped down in the seat next to me, still not making eye contact with me or acknowledging my existence, and Michael exited his seat, leaving us as alone on this plane as it was possible for two people to be.

"What are you doing here?" I kept my voice low.

He lifted his eyebrows. "If you are doing this fucking stupid thing, then I am doing it with you to keep you safe."

Now which one of us is being ridiculous? "You can't do this."

"I can't?" He looked left and right. "Looks like I am."

That wasn't what I meant, and he knew that. "How can you leave the restaurant?"

"Anna has it." He stashed his bag under his seat and stretched out his legs. "Her mother is good with Eric, who is recovering well, and this is going to be fast. In and out. I'll be back in three days. I'm paying her really well to cover for me. When I explained to her that I was trying to keep you alive, she was all for it."

I put my head in my hands. "You didn't have to do this. I told you, we are done."

"Hope." He said my name, and then waited until I looked at him. Like a force connected us, I had no choice but to lift my gaze and meet his. "I want to apologize for what I said in the hall. It was completely uncalled for. I was mean, and I didn't mean it."

Well, what was I supposed to do with that? I swallowed. "I'm not self-destructive. Not at all, actually. Most of the time, I hide in my house. I am ridiculous, that is true. Like a walking caricature or someone to be mocked in literature. I get it. I might be ridiculous, but I try to do the right things.

The next right thing. Day by day. Maybe someday, someone will appreciate that about me."

He squeezed my hand. "You're not any of those things. I mean it. None. And I appreciate that you care about your fellow humans more than you'll ever know."

"Did you come here because you felt guilt about what you said?"

The plane took off fast, and I closed my eyes against the onslaught. Other people loved this moment, but it was my least favorite part of travel. The anxiety passed quickly, and I opened my eyes.

He waited to speak until I did. "I told you, I came here to keep you alive. You get the kid, and I'll make sure you're still intact when you do it."

Max closed his eyes like he was done with the conversation. In turn, I stared out the window. The coastline disappeared beneath us, and a hush fell over the guys. They were all going to sleep. I wondered if that was part of the training they'd all had from whatever they'd done before— sleep as much as they could, whenever they could, in preparation for whatever might come next.

It was too bad I was an insomniac. It still applied to planes.

Max, however, seemed perfectly content to sleep right then.

He was there, and as much as I was still sore from what he'd said, his apology helped. Plus, just his presence was an incredible gift. He cared about me enough to do this incredible thing for me. I couldn't remember the last time anyone else had been willing to go so far for me.

Maybe it was weird—our relationship that wasn't one, really. I didn't understand it myself, and right then, I didn't care if I ever did.

Sometime about halfway through the trip, while I was playing my fifteenth game of *BitLife*, Max opened his lids to regard me. "Sleep at all?" He kept his voice low, and I shook my head as an answer. He frowned. "I don't sleep much, but you take it to a new level. Was I snoring?"

I smiled at him. "Totally. So loud, the whole plane complained about it."

He scowled at me before he grinned. "Why didn't you tell me?"

"About the snoring? I thought it would be rude." I could play this game if he wanted.

He shook his head. "No, in all seriousness—about Muffy and Tim. Why didn't you tell me they died? I didn't see anything about it until afterward. I was swamped and busy, but we texted about things. Why didn't you tell me?"

I shifted in my seat. "Because you were so busy. Because Eric had surgery. Because I don't know where the line is with us, what I should and shouldn't share with you. You're my friend, not my boyfriend. You can't become my one and only person. You said it yourself—this will end. I can't rely on you." I looked down. "Even if you do amazing things like this."

He took my hand in his again. "Did you not tell me because you thought I might stop you? Or talk you out of this?"

"Maybe there was a part of me that thought about that, but I was doing this. I won't leave that child there."

He tugged on the end of my hair. "No, of course not. This is you, and for some reason, you feel entirely compelled to try to solve the world's problems. Why is that?"

"There has to be a reason, a purpose for things. I fuck up a lot. When I do, I have to make it better. I have to believe that I can, otherwise I get sucked down to bad places

178

thinking about how much worse the world is everywhere I go."

His face fell. "Hope…"

"All right, everybody, we're halfway there. Everybody up. Let's go over the plan one more time. Then we eat and get ready to hit the ground." Michael spoke to the group, essentially cutting off our conversation. It was a relief. I couldn't believe I had said that. What had I been thinking?

The hours passed, and the planning continued. Every detail was attended and then attended to again. I didn't know how things worked when they were actually enlisted, but they really were trying to not leave anything to chance. My cousin had been right—Michael had a lot of contacts, and he was even able to pinpoint the area where Tim was being held. There might be other children there too.

"They sell them, kill them, ransom them, or train them. Frankly, it depends on the kid." Michael rubbed his eyes. "And I thought I was done seeing this shit when I left. I thought I was just going to take care of a rich guy and his kids. Arrange for guards to go to parties. I had no idea I'd be right back in the thick of it with this and other things." He winked at me. "But her family keeps things interesting. Plus, my side jobs are always all over the place."

The truth was I knew very little of what Michael did for others. He ran a whole company, and not all of it had to do with us.

"You might not have to do this anymore." I finally spoke for the first time in hours. Sitting next to Max at a makeshift table that they'd pulled out to act as the center focus of things, I hadn't needed to say a word. My only job was to be available when they needed me to make myself known to Tim. Otherwise, my job was to stay in the plane.

With Max, just in case something happened. Although,

179

from the looks of their planned approach, I wasn't at all certain how it could get fucked up. They were going to grab Tim and go.

If they could take other children while they were there, they would, but Tim was the objective, and everyone understood in this fucked-up world that might have to be enough.

Michael nodded, a smirk coming to his usually stoic face. "Because Zeke might fire my ass. Yes, I know, but I'm still not going anywhere. This is my job, as far as I'm concerned. He said to watch you and keep you safe, so you didn't get taken. I'm doing just that. If he fires me for it, I'll still hang around a bit until you're all fine."

I lifted an eyebrow. "Until we're all fine or until Bridget is fine?"

He shook his head. "Until you're all fine, including Bridget." He pointed at me. "You were always the problem out of the group."

"Me?" Now *that* was shocking. His words made the group laugh. Even Max, who had been very quiet this whole time. I had no earthly idea what he was thinking, or if he was greatly regretting whatever impulse brought him to my side. "I was a very well-behaved teenager."

"You were until you were about nineteen. Then you… Well, a senator's son and random trips here, there, and everywhere before you started devoting yourself to making a living in a way that meant you could be out till two in the morning every night. Yes, you. Not until recently did Bridget… Well, never mind. We all know what happened with Layla." He patted my knee. "You, Hope, you were the toughest one to keep safe from moment one."

I cleared my throat. "She's having terrible dates, but

eventually, she's going to have a good one. Isn't there something you want to do about that?"

"She's got you, boss." Mitch grinned. "Isn't there something you want to do about that?"

"Bridget Radford is safe from me." He met my gaze. "That is just how these things go, unfortunately. Maybe in another world, one where I didn't end up on planes like this one? Eventually, she'll find her version of Zeke, and then I'll keep them both safe."

I rolled my eyes. "If that is some kind of pseudo Knights of the Round Table bullshit, I would try to find a different kind of chivalry. Bridget can handle whatever you dish out. She's tough. Maybe tougher than you, Li. Besides, you might remember how it worked out for Guinevere and Lancelot."

"Heads up," Buck called from up front, and everyone got moving. With nowhere particularly I needed to be, I got back in my seat and buckled in for landing. Max sat next to me and got in his harness.

"I'm amazed he lets you talk to him like that. Do you not realize he's intimidating? I mean…not to me, but I think most people would give him a wide berth."

I smiled. "Michael has been with me a lot of places I'd rather not be. Lately, it's Theo and Luke. But it used to be the three of us and Michael. Then he started just guarding our father. Dress fittings. The prom. College. I think it was right around then when he decided he liked Bridget. When she got really serious, he took note of her. Everyone knows how he feels…except Bridget. I think Michael is the only one who won't acknowledge it would be completely reciprocated if he'd get off his butt and do something."

He shook his head. "Not nice to drag a partner to dark places with you, emotionally. Sometimes it's better to just go through your life without inflicting your unhealed wounds on others."

"I agree, actually. I wouldn't want to drag anyone down to my level." I closed my eyes.

He touched my hand. "What darkness do you know? I mean other than the Russian problem, which hit Layla. What hurt you, Hope? And a senator's son?"

I sighed. "They are overrated. Trust me on that." Technically, we could trace the ruin of Max's life to that guy, but I wouldn't go there right now. "And I guess I don't have darkness. You know me, just a flippant, snarky, bratty girl with too much time on my hands."

Max groaned and nudged my foot with his own. "Knock it off."

I grinned at him. "I think we're landing."

We were. I stared out the window at the landscape below. Fifteen hours airborne, but it looked like we were really nowhere at all. The view consisted of bleak, desolate landscape with an occasional broken tree and burned-out building. Michael spoke into his phone, a SAT version I suspected wasn't quite legal, and said a lot of things I couldn't understand to the person on the other end.

Letters and codes.

"Roger that." He hung it up. "We may have a problem," he said to the group. "They moved. They're actually on the airfield. Not expecting us, but a different group is arriving to take some of the kids and move some drugs. They aren't going to be happy to see it's us and not them, although they might not realize why we're there, initially."

"How does he know?" I asked Max.

His jawline hardened. "Just be glad he does. Probably some sort of satellite surveillance. Maybe someone quietly whispering on the ground. I don't want to know. I used to be him. It's too much shit, and of course, this whole thing is fucked up. It's always fucked up."

Mitch yelled out from across the plane. "Bringing back memories, L.T.?"

Max rolled his eyes. "Fuck off, Mitchell." There wasn't any meanness in his tone. Mitchell sounded downright excited, and I wondered if there was some sort of drive for their kind of work. Adrenaline or something else that made it almost addictive—like people got really excited to jump out of planes or attempt Everest. The need for the rush of being a hero the same as any other drug that people did on the street, only their addiction made them a lot of money too.

Max grabbed his bag and pulled out his guns. Multiple versions. He strapped them to himself and then placed a helmet on my head. "Keep that on."

"Isn't this yours?"

"Right now, it's yours, Hope." He shook his head, like I'd annoyed him again.

It hadn't occurred to me that I might need to be armed, but as the wheels hit the ground, I really wished I had reconsidered the situation. Then I remembered Tim. He was out there, maybe on the runway. He knew his parents were dead, leaving him alone in the world with people who did not wish the best for him. Thinking of him—this little boy I barely knew but who needed me—steeled my resolve. He had no choice but to be brave, and certainly I could be brave for him until we were airborne again.

We weren't stopped long when Michael threw open the door and they were all out on the makeshift tarmac in the middle of nowhere. I glanced out the window and then ducked as Max pushed my head down.

"Do not give them a target."

None of this had been the plan. We were supposed to

land, then encounter the enemy group about twenty miles from the landing point, when the snipers would have the high ground. None of it should happen at the small airport in the middle of nowhere.

Gunfire rang out, and I jerked automatically. I wished it were the first time I'd ever heard it, but I had been there when they rescued Layla. From a distance, but I'd heard it then too. This was different. I'd been terrified then for Layla but not at risk myself. The ping of the bullets hitting the plane was not something I could have prepared myself for.

"Can they…can they break into the plane with their shots? Stop us from taking off?" When I looked out the window, I saw a gathering of men. More than I could count, all standing in a circle. They had us hugely outnumbered. It hadn't occurred to me that any of us were actually going to die. The stealthy nature of the original plan meant no real risk to my team.

But now? This was really, truly fucked.

Max was ducked down low with me, his very large gun swung over his shoulder. "I wouldn't worry about that. If they take us down, there won't be anyone left to take us off anyway." He squeezed my shoulder. "But I've worked with a lot of them, and the ones I haven't…well, they seem pretty qualified. My guess is this is going to go just fine."

He thought this was going to go *just fine*? "Max…"

"Not everyone out there knows how to fire a gun and end a life. They've thought about it, but they haven't done it. They're a lot of bullies, picking on small children and women. Everyone here knows how to shoot and move onward. That's what they're doing right now."

Something exploded, and I winced. "I'm sorry about this, Max. Really sorry you're here when you should be, I don't know, making a bouillabaisse."

He laughed, which surprised me. The situation really wasn't funny. "You know I used to think a lot about food in moments like this? What I'd like to be eating instead of what I was doing. Then I'd stop and concentrate, but it was almost a pregame ritual for me. What would you like to be eating right now, Hope?"

I gaped at him. "I might never eat again."

CHAPTER 15

"NOW THAT WOULD BE A SHAME. FOOD, YOU'VE TOLD ME, IS your favorite thing in life. You can't give up your favorite thing entirely. If you want to, say, cut one thing out of your diet because of this experience, that is fine. I'll agree to that and only that. What thing will you be permanently eliminating after today?"

He was trying to distract me, that much I understood. "Is this a technique you've used often? To distract someone from the gunfire and explosions happening outside?" I looked away from him. "Tim's okay, right?"

Max took my hand. "One thing. What will you give up to always honor how much this fucking sucks?"

Was he serious? "Ah...I guess shellfish."

"No," he mock gasped. "Not shellfish."

Something exploded again, and I winced. He placed a comforting hand on my shoulder. I managed to say, "Not shellfish?"

"No, I make great shellfish. Something else."

This was making my head hurt. "I guess I would get rid of beets."

He nodded. "I like beets, but I can see getting rid of them. Fine. You'll eliminate beets, and every time you see them on a menu and don't eat them, you'll remember this moment and the severity of it. You'll say to yourself, *I'm not doing that shit again*."

"You're insane."

He winked at me. "Little bit. That's why I left this behind. I think they're done."

Sure enough, it had gotten quiet outside. I tried to ignore the fact that I was actually shaking. My whole body vibrated like I was a machine that needed some oil. Hell, I was thinking nutty things too. Something pinged on Max's belt, and he looked down at it. "They need you, and Michael says it's safe to let you out."

It was? How had any of this happened? I hadn't watched any of it, but it seemed rather unlikely that everything could already be fine. Max walked out in front of me, and I stared past him at the scene. Not everyone was dead. In fact, a quick headcount told me all of our people were fine. Dead bodies lay scattered everywhere, but others were just on their knees, their hands behind their heads. Clayton and the others walked behind them, big guns drawn, ready to fire at any time. Clayton was the one who caught my attention because he was actually whistling.

As though nothing tremendous had happened at all.

My vibrating limbs cooperated, and I spotted Michael squatted down, talking to three children, but his hand sat on Tim's shoulder. The little boy lit up when he saw me, then he took off in my direction.

I'd always thought it a ridiculous expression, but my heart really did fill up with gratitude. He was right there, and he was fine. I opened my arms to greet his incoming hug when I saw what was about to happen. It was funny, almost like it was happening in slow motion. Mitch treated the wound on one of the enemies who had been shot, so he didn't see the guy next to him pulled his gun.

I saw it, but I was the only one. He wasn't pointing it at me or at Max. No, he intended to shoot down the beautiful child rushing toward me.

I've heard that people can do tremendous things under stress, that adrenaline could make us sometimes almost superhuman. I didn't know if that was what made my legs move, but I ran like someone's life depended on it. I managed to knock Tim to the ground just in time to hear the gunfire. Max called out my name, and it sounded like it was in slow motion too, as though we'd suddenly found ourselves on a movie set where someone had reduced the sound.

More gunfire, and a screaming child beneath me.

"Okay. Okay," I said to Tim. "I'm sorry. But I had to protect you. You're okay. You're okay."

"Hope." His little voice called out to me as Max rolled me off the child. His face was pale, his eyes huge. *Why does he look like that? What is wrong?*

Had Tim been hit? I stared over at the child we'd come all this way to save. He was covered in blood. No. It couldn't end like this. He couldn't be so tiny and shot.

"Tim, it's going to be okay. You'll be okay. We'll help you."

The little boy pointed at me. "You're bleeding."

Me? I looked down at my gut. Sure enough, I was bleeding. Right above my hip and on my arm. Two places. "How did that happen?"

It was like acknowledging the wounds made them hurt, made them real. They burned, and I cried out from the sheer agony of them. Max pushed me back, his hands coming down on my side above my hip, while Michael, who had seemingly appeared out of nowhere, did the same on my arm. Everyone talked at once.

Mitch asked them to move, so he could see, but Max screamed at him for losing control of his guys while at the same time telling me it was somehow all his fault. Michael said the same. Everyone competed to take responsibility for the fact that I was shot. The world tilted sideways, and despite my pain, I tried to smile at Tim while Max lifted me off the ground.

"It's going to be okay," I told him. "You're going home to your grandmother."

I wished I could have actually blacked out, but I'd never been a fainter. I tended to stay awake through ordeals. Apparently, Mitch poking at my bullet wounds as the airplane took off, leaving behind the disaster we'd left in our wake, was something I was going to have to handle fully conscious. I shook as he touched each one.

"Stay with me," Max instructed, his tone different than any I'd ever heard from him. He sounded absolutely in charge. It was different than the kitchen. I could see why people listened to him. He just acted like they should, and I wanted to do just what he said.

"I'm not going to faint." My voice shook, but I got the words out. Next to me, Mitch pulled out an IV bag.

"This will help. But, yes, stay awake as long as you can."

I stared at him. "You think staying conscious will become a struggle?"

"The pain meds will knock you out. That's okay. Both bullets went straight through. That is very, very good news, Hope. I am so sorry about this. Despite what Max said, it's my fault not his."

I laughed, which was strange considering that absolutely fucking nothing was funny. "This is my fault. But we got Tim. That was the point."

Michael paced back and forth. I wasn't sure where he went when he wasn't near us, but he kept coming and going.

My head felt woozy, like gravity wasn't right. "Am I going to die?" I had to ask. Not finding out wouldn't make it any less true.

"No," Max answered, and I rolled my eyes at him. He was the least likely person there to know. Still, I decided to believe him. Maybe the painkillers were hitting me fast.

Mitch touched my undamaged shoulder. "Rest. Lie back. Deep breaths. If you pass out, that's okay. When you wake up, we'll be in Germany."

Why were we going there? I almost asked, then I decided I didn't care. Germany was lovely this time of year. I'd actually lived there for a while.

Max was pretty much all I could see then, except for Michael when he would come into view before he disappeared again.

There were things he had to know if I was going to die. I'd thought to take them to death, but maybe it was better to just get it out. Let him understand how things had been, so that he understood I hadn't meant it, but why I had to make it better.

"Max." I lifted my hand, and he took it. "I want to tell you something."

He scooted a chair over to sit with me as the plane hit turbulence. I winced. That hurt, despite the fact that I wasn't particularly feeling anything much right then. "It's truth time, is it? That's the drugs, baby."

I didn't know what any of that meant. "Five years ago, I was dating Shawn Callihan Jr."

Max tilted his head. "Oh, that senator's son. Sure. I know the one. Big on family values." Yes, funny he was known for that, really, but I had no inclination to laugh. "He was my first boyfriend. I was nineteen. A virgin." I had been sort of proud of it, not because I placed any judgement on when women decided to have sex for the first time or not. My pride came from valuing myself in some way, from having agency about who would touch me and who wouldn't. "I guess I wasn't getting with the program fast enough."

His face fell. He'd already looked pale and hard, but somehow, he became more of both. "Hope," he said as he stroked my hair. "Fuck."

"Drugged me. I don't remember much except the sense of what was happening. The sense that he raped me. The sense that he let his friends touch and play with me in the back of a bar. When I came to, I pulled up my underpants and left."

Michael's face appeared then, angry, hard. Max pushed him back a bit. That was a strange interaction. What was happening?

"I...I just got on with things. Asked my cousin in the State Department for help. He wasn't interested in helping. Shawn's family is untouchable. He can, however, produce oranges and onions." I laughed at my own joke. "I was pregnant, but I wouldn't know that for weeks. That night outside your restaurant—"

He cut me off. "You don't have to do this."

"Let me finish. I don't even remember being there. The doctors used lots of big words about the total blankness that is that time for me. Just a total and complete blank. Pretty sure I was puking because of the baby. Losing the baby, almost bled to death—that is how I got some help. Then they sent me away. To a spa, they told everyone, even my sisters.

When I came back, I was expected to be fine again. So I've been pretending ever since."

Max breathed hard. In and out. I could hear each breath, as though they were audible, as though he struggled to breathe past the weight of my words. "I…"

Once again, I stopped him. Somewhere in the back of my mind, I knew the meds were working, that I might not get this out. I had to finish before I couldn't, before being in my right mind, whatever that meant, told me I had to keep this to myself. "But I can't remember what I did. Didn't know until I saw the video. Watched it over and over until I can recite every line. I can feel remorse, even though I can't remember any of it. I know that I did it. I ruined your life, and I have to try to fix it. Like I had to get Tim. I have to. The things I do, plowing through life, with no regard for the mess I leave everywhere? I can't allow it to continue. Someday, when I die alone in some Upper East Side apartment eaten by my cats, I have to know that things weren't worse in this world just because I lived in it."

He rose, bending even closer, his hand remaining in my hair. "Hope." He said my name and then paused like it was hard to get out the words. "I've seen many brave things in my life, most of which I can't speak about. Twice today, you have stolen my breath by the sheer force of your strength and courage. Saving this boy? Like this? People don't do this, sweetheart. They don't. They don't send fruit to a stranger because they have to make amends. You consistently take my breath away. There isn't anything else you have to do in this lifetime. You do not owe the world something for allowing you to exist in it. I think at this point, the world owes it to you."

That was so nice of him to say and the last thing I heard before the medicine swept me under to a dreamless sleep.

I woke up to the sound of beeping. That was what registered first. My eyelids were weighted down. It took energy I wasn't sure I had to wrench them open. I was hot, itchy. What was happening?

"I think she's waking up." Layla's voice. It was low, soothing. "Hopey? Can you hear me?"

I nodded, or tried to nod. Finally, I managed to look at my sister. She sat on the edge of a hospital bed. I was in the bed. It was like my brain thought in short sentences. One thought, then the next, nothing adding up together in a sequence that made any sense.

"There she is." This time it was Bridget. She wiped my hair off my forehead. "You scared us, sweetheart. Got an infection, and you've been battling it. Can you hear me now?"

My mouth was dry. "Give her this." *Max*. I couldn't see him, but he must have handed Layla the glass of water with the straw that was soon in my mouth.

I sipped. "Hot."

"Well, you're still running a little fever. A lot lower than yesterday. You'll be better soon." Layla kissed my cheek.

"Just sleep, Hope. No one needs anything from you." Max told me to, so I did just that.

The next time I roused, I felt better. Thirsty and achy, but not hot. I forced myself awake, which was less than stellar because I was covered in sweat, and that was gross.

Layla, who sat to my left, looked up first. Followed immediately by Bridget. Layla held Noah, who she quickly passed behind her to Zeke. Michael was to my right, behind Bridget, and he nodded to me. And Max, like a statue at the end of my bed, stared at me silently.

I cleared my throat. My shoulder throbbed. I could feel my hip area was sore, but fuck, my shoulder hurt. It had felt like my arm when I was shot, but now I could feel it in my shoulder.

"Have you ever felt like a zoo animal?"

Max grinned and then immediately stopped, shaking his head.

"You scared us." Layla smiled. "It's nice to see your eyes clear."

I lowered my eyes. "I'm sorry, guys. I didn't mean to."

"You aren't responsible for how anyone here feels about what happened to you. In no way are you responsible for their feelings. That belongs to them. The only thing you're responsible for right now is getting better." Max crossed his arms over his chest.

Everyone turned to stare at him and then looked back at me. It was Bridget who finally broke the silence that followed his statement. "Are you in pain? Let's call the doctor." She leaned over and pushed a button. There were dark circles under her eyes.

"Max's speech aside, I really don't like to worry people, and I am sorry that I got shot. That you're all here in... Are we in Germany?"

Zeke nodded. "Germany."

"Why was it Germany?" I couldn't remember if I knew that.

It was Michael who supplied the answer. "We contract with this private clinic to take care of us if things go askew on a mission. They're always at ready for us. Fully equipped, and it was closer than trying to get home."

Zeke bounced the baby, but he shot daggers at Michael. "She should never have been allowed to do this to begin with."

"We've talked about this." Michael didn't regard him, keeping his gaze either on Bridget's back or on me. "She's a grown woman. She was doing it with or without me. End of story. I chose with me."

Zeke pointed at him. "This very scenario is what I pay you to avoid. You are supposed to be keeping the family safe."

Bridget jumped to her feet. "In what world can anyone really keep anyone else safe? I mean, really? We make choices every day. If I fall down the fucking stairs, it's not Michael and his men's fault that it happened. Hope decided to do a dumb fucking thing because she's big hearted. Michael tried to help her not die. She's not dead. Looks like it succeeded."

"Hey." Max stepped forward. "You don't get to lay judgment on what she did or did not do as you sit on some throne of superiority. She wanted to save that child because she believed it to be her job when no one else in the universe was going to help him. It was brave. She's constantly brave. Maybe you don't know that because you ran away to Hong Kong to live your life where no one has to see or remark on what you do."

I held up my hand as Bridget's face fell. "Whoa. Everyone stop. Please."

The doctor chose that moment to enter. *Saved by the man in the white coat.* He spoke to me for a while and told me several times how lucky I had been. I was half convinced that what he really wanted to say to me was that I'd done a really stupid thing and most people would be dead if they'd done the same. Since I already knew this, I mostly nodded.

Michael's phone pinged, and he left the room to go deal with whatever it was. Zeke watched him go with no amount of overt hostility chasing him from the room. The doctor finished up, letting me know I would be there a week, possibly more, and that he'd see me later.

I rubbed at my face. "Zeke, you know that I insisted on this."

He stared at me. "I know. I'm not firing Michael, but I don't have to like it. Do you know what it would do to the people who love you if you got yourself killed?"

"Do you know what emotional manipulation looks and sounds like?" Max shot that question right to Zeke, who pointed at him.

"What the fuck are you even doing here?"

Layla touched her husband's arm. "Obviously, they care about each other."

"Care about each other so much that he just went along with this plan?"

Max shook his head. "It isn't my job to tell Hope what she can and can't do. She's a grown woman. I went along to help, and I am here because I want to be."

The two men might punch each other any second. I tried to sit up more, and that was when I really felt my hip pain. Yes, this really, really fucking sucked.

Michael stormed back in. "We have another problem."

Zeke tugged his son tighter against him. "What now?"

Michael held up his phone. A video played, and it took me half a second to realize it was Tim's grandmother.

"She saved my grandson." Her smile was huge. "The woman's name is Hope Radford, and I own her everything. A real hero."

That was sweet but not the reason I'd done it. Why was this a problem? Max gripped the end of the bed, and Zeke cursed and then kissed his son's head.

"I think I'm missing something," I told the room, not caring who explained it to me.

Layla nodded. "Me too. Is there some issue with the State Department?"

"I suppose that could be." Max shook his head. "But I don't think that's the current problem, right, Michael?"

Michael sank into a chair. "Putting your name out there like that. It seems to have stirred up the Russians. They had really put you on a backburner, but now your name is all over the dark web. Plans are being made. It's a flood of Hope everywhere. This is bad. We're going to have to lock you away even further. Probably take you out of here early and then lock you up in a place where you can be hidden."

Max rubbed his eyes. "She needs physical therapy. You heard the doctor. They need to get range of motions back. She can't be locked up where that can't happen."

My brother-in-law handed Noah to Layla. "She can come to Washington. I'll move a physical therapist in to stay full time until the threat passes, and she can work with her on site."

"Well, this is a fine mess." Bridget patted my knee. "And Hope is here. She can participate in this conversation."

I could, but actually, a headache had formed right behind my eyes. I closed them for a second. "How long do you think I'll have to be locked away?"

My business was over. That was for sure. By the time I got back, I'd be so much a nothing, no one would hire me ever again. I sighed and forced myself to watch as my life was battered back and forth.

"Or she can come home with me," Max supplied. "My sister is a PT. She works with vets and all kinds of injured people. Won an award last year. She can help Hope, and she'll be nice and out of sight."

Michael shook his head. "Nowhere in New York is she out of sight."

"Not in New York. In Maine. My hometown. No one will see her there. Not for months and months. And if you're any good at your job, you'll have handled this by then, right?"

A muscle ticked in Michael's jaw. "You cannot believe the layers of complicated this mess has been. Their father and brother are in on this. Yes, I would like to be done with this too."

Bridget winced. I was pretty sure I was the only one to notice. Some other time, I was going to have to force her to tell me things about her and Michael. We were so good at leaving each other alone when we didn't want to talk that too many things went askew.

That was another thing that occurred to me. I'd told Max my secret. I swallowed. I'd broken the dam on that plane, and I was pretty sure that Michael knew everything now too. Probably the whole plane heard me, for that matter.

"Max." I interrupted the discussion. "You can't take me to Maine. You have to work. The restaurant. In fact, you should be there now."

"Leave that to me to worry about. That isn't for you to concern yourself with." He shook his head. "There is nothing here you have to fix."

Michael stared at Max. "Clayton said that you might have a contact that could make this go away. Something about a high member of the underground there owing you a favor."

Max Broadley. Chef extraordinaire. Former special forces. Underground operative? Who was this man I wasn't dating?

"I would if I could, but he vanished years ago. I'd gladly make this stop. But I don't know how I'd even find him."

"Guys." It was time for me to stop this endless talking. "I need to tell my sisters some things. And then, Max, can you come see me so we can talk about whether this is going to work. I'd love to come with you to Maine, although of course

I appreciate Zeke's offer and his constant willingness to help."

I just wasn't sure it could be. But before I could even consider it, I needed to tell the two people closest to me in the world what I'd never said.

CHAPTER 16

IT HAD BEEN EASIER TO TELL MAX. MAYBE IT HAD BEEN THE drugs on the airplane, or maybe he was just a person to whom I could more easily share secrets. In any case, Layla cried, Bridget kept grabbing my knee, and by the time I was done telling them what had happened with Shawn and me, I was a blubbering mess.

It wasn't a great time for me to feel that way. I needed to go back to sleep for an extended period of time and maybe an increase in my pain medicine.

"Why didn't you tell us?" Bridget finally spoke. "I'm not trying to make this about me, but all these years, you've hidden your pain from us. I...I wouldn't have said what I did to you about not putting out if I'd known. I would have been there for you. I wouldn't have run off to Hong Kong and left you alone."

I swallowed. "That's why. I didn't want to be treated like I wasn't able to take care of myself. Funny, right after the treatment was actually when I felt the top of my game. I was on like this rush of a high. I'd pulled it off. No one knew. Over time, it really hit me, and I had some help. But probably not enough help. And truth be known, I could really use some medication too. I lock my doors. Over and over and over."

Bridget grabbed my hand and squeezed it. "We love you. We would have been here for you. But we will be now. Do you want to live with me? Do you want me to move back to New York and live with you?"

Layla dabbed her eyes. "You asked me to come live with you, and I turned you down. I'm sorry. You needed me, and I didn't know."

I pulled myself into a sitting up position that was easier said than done. "My loves, we all have to live our own lives. It was my choice to be silent. Well, Dad encouraged it. But it's on me. I'm trying to do better, I'm trying to find some kind of...I don't know...redemption for things that I do."

"Like what? What terrible thing could you have done?" Bridget's voice rose. "You're terribly nice. Almost too nice."

"Well." I didn't really want to get into the whole story of Max right then. "Layla, I left you in France. Broke. Alone."

Bridget shook her head. "We both thought that A, it would be worse if we didn't leave with Dad, and B, that we could reason with him and make it better on the plane. We didn't know that our dingbat brother was going to do that to you, and the second you found out, Hope, you texted Zeke and sent him to her."

"And," Layla kissed my cheek, "it turned out to be the best thing to ever happen to me. On that note, you have to go home with Max. Don't get me wrong, I want you with me, but he is something. I think you need to spend more time with that man."

I closed my eyes. "It's complicated."

"Of course it is. Hope, look at me." Layla demanded so I did as she wanted. "There is good complicated and bad complicated. I think this is good complicated. I mean...he followed you across the world to a place we're not supposed to visit and has, for the last week, been there every waking moment for you. Good complicated."

That was probably true. But given the history between us, I wasn't sure if even good complicated wasn't just too complicated.

∼

"ARE YOU SURE ABOUT THIS?" I realized it was the fifth time I was asking him, but the plane was going to take off and if he really couldn't do this, I'd rather know it before we were in the air.

Max shot me a look. "I'm sure. I wouldn't offer if I couldn't do it."

I chewed on my lip. "But Hyperion?"

"Anna is doing a great job with it, and Eric feels so good, he keeps trying to leave the house. It will survive a few weeks without me. I'll even work on some new recipes while I'm there. It'll be productive. No one will get to you where we will be. If they somehow do find you, they won't get through me."

I stared at his hard profile as the airplane took off, and I tried to ignore how much I hated takeoffs. He winked at me. "You hate this part."

"That obvious?"

He yawned. "Yes, very. Come here. Put your head on my shoulder if it's comfortable. Close your eyes. Get some sleep."

I'd taken a pain pill not too long ago, which meant I was going to pass out any minute anyway. I stretched out my legs, but there was no good way for me to sit comfortably. I'd be glad to be unconscious soon.

I winced. "I don't think I can. It's awkward. I pretty much have to stay like this."

He nodded. "Been there, unfortunately."

That was right. One of the things I'd learned in the last days was that Max had been shot twice. Both times had been superficial because he was, his words, "a lucky bastard." But he knew how much healing sucked.

We were alone on the airplane set up by Zeke to bring us to Max's home in Maine. I wasn't sure where we were landing. It didn't really matter to my tired brain. Where, who cared? Just so long as we landed.

"Can I ask you something?" He pressed his nose into my hair.

"I think at this point, you've earned the right to ask me anything." Yep. My hip area had officially replaced my shoulder for the most painful injury.

He breathed out and then kissed my head before pulling back. "Was your first time in the back of that car?"

I blinked as it took me a second to realize what he was asking me. "Since the bar and the incident? Yes, it was."

He closed his eyes like they pained him. "Fuck."

I squeezed his knee. "Why is it upsetting you? That was great."

Max slowly lifted his lids. "Because if I had known, I would've never suggested the back of the car for your first time. I might have...I don't know...found a more appropriate place."

I tilted my head. "I didn't want you to know, and I wouldn't change a thing about the car. Please don't redo that in your mind so that you would. It would...I don't know... steal something from the moment."

He took my hand, bringing it to his mouth. "Fair enough. It was...really incredible."

I closed my eyes, the medicine sucking me under. When I woke up, it was hours later. The seat divider between Max and me was gone. I was stretched out on him like his lap was my pillow as the rest of my body lay straight across the seats. How and when had this happened?

His eyes were closed, one hand in my hair, one on my good shoulder. It really didn't matter. These drugs were going to get old quickly. Yes, I needed them to heal, but losing time was really pretty awful. I didn't just fall asleep, but I did things when I was asleep I wouldn't normally do. Sure, I was an insomniac, and it was great to be sleeping all the time. However, I would take being tired over the time gaps.

I had to pee. Hating to wake him, I really had no choice but to jostle him slightly when I got up because I was on his lap and he was touching me.

His eyes opened slowly. "You okay?"

"Got to pee." My voice was rough. I must have been sleeping for hours.

He nodded and placed a hand on my lower back, helping me to sit up a little bit easier. He unbuckled himself, which was when it occurred to me that I hadn't had mine on. That was pretty bad. What if we hit unexpected turbulence?

I forced my stiff, beaten up body to move and shuffled rather ungracefully to the bathroom, where we, of course, hit unexpected turbulence, which forced me to cling to the wall on my walk back. Max rose and came quickly over to me, grabbing my waist and helping me get back to our seats. He didn't even seem bothered by the shakes. Was he somehow so superhuman, he wasn't even bothered by the laws of gravity that took down every other being on the planet? I laughed at my own joke, and he shot me a look but didn't comment.

After he'd buckled us both in, he put his arm around me. "We'll be landing soon."

"In Maine?" I just wanted to confirm I hadn't been delirious through a change of plans that was now landing us someplace else.

He nodded. "In Portland. Then I'll drive us to my place. Your security will meet us there. They'll hang around the perimeter. And we'll wait for Michael to get this handled." A muscle ticked in Max's jaw. I wasn't sure why. "There is a doctor in Portland who understands the situation and will treat you with my sister, who is lined up on the other end ready to help with the PT. That is the plan." He side-eyed me. "Do you not remember it? Or are you just checking?"

"Just checking. I am...losing time."

Max winced. "Yeah, that sucks. We'll see what the doctor says in a few days about when we can cut back your pain pills. I hated them too."

"You and I are quite a pair. We'd both take pain and not sleeping over being out of control."

He nodded. "We are quite a pair."

And we were landing in Portland, so I could go into hiding for who knew how long. Truth was I was almost too drugged to really care, but even in my state, I knew I still would. This one was going to chafe.

I couldn't really remember landing, but then we were in the car. It was waiting for us on the tarmac—thank you, Zeke —and we'd driven off toward his hometown. I shivered until it heated up inside. In New York, it had started to get cold, but here it already really was. I was in long sleeves, but I wished I had a jacket.

In fact, I didn't have any clothes at all, just the sweatpants and shirt I was in. The clinic in Germany had given them to me.

"I don't have clothes or toiletries. Or really anything."

Max took my hand for a second before he put it back on

the steering wheel. "You do. My sisters and mom have dropped off some things for you. If you need more, we'll get other things. I think you'll be okay." He turned up the heat. "I won't let you be cold. My house is warm. I promise."

I rubbed my eyes. "I guess I never focused on the fact that you told me that you have a house in Maine. It just sits empty?"

"My brother James watches out for it for me. I bought it after Hayley's closed. Thought I might just go home and chop wood forever."

I groaned. "Max…"

"Not your fault. I chopped wood for a week and then I got busy plotting my return, but I bought the house anyway. I like having it in my hometown. It makes me feel like I can come back and not be a visitor even if, having spent a good six months really living there, I know I never want to live there full-time. Not ever." He winked at me. "So you see, it was a time of clarifying certainty for me."

I sighed. "If you say so."

"I do."

We drove in silence most of the rest of the way, and I dozed on and off. Eventually, the pain came back. I wrenched my eyes open to check the clock. Was this one of those moments when I was due for more meds, or was it one of those meds not strong enough to hold out over the time between doses? It was the first, and before I could even ask, Max opened the container and handed one to me. He pointed to an open water bottle sitting between us.

I shook my head. "You're amazing, you know that?"

"I remembered you needed meds. That's not amazing. And we're here." He pointed ahead. "Just down this road."

I rubbed at my eyes and forced myself to be present. I might not have called it a road. It looked more like a path.

206

Trees surrounded us, but eventually, we came up to a house lit from within.

"My brother got it ready for us." He shrugged. "He owes me like, a thousand favors."

We pulled into a garage that closed behind us, and I took a deep breath. "Thanks for doing this."

"Don't thank me again. I'm thanked. I never do anything I don't want to do, and seeing you through to the end of this mess is important to me. Come on. You're going to sleep with me." He got out of the car and flung open the door to the garage that led into the house. I followed him more slowly, taking in the surroundings as best I could, given the haze that was my brain.

It was a lovely wood cabin, or at least it looked like one from the outside. On the inside, I found a fully modern house with three bedrooms, two and a half bathrooms, and a working fireplace. That much I gleaned from what he told me as he chatted around opening and closing closets to make sure it was all as it was supposed to be.

What I saw was a warm, inviting room that had pictures of Max with other people all around it. Max bent down, still telling me about the house, and lit a fire in the fireplace easily. He barely even looked at the maneuver as he did it. Soon, a blaze lit up the comfortable room. He crossed to the fridge and opened it. One picture in particular caught my attention. It was on display above the fireplace. In it, Max posed with people who had to be his relatives. They had a look about them that said they were family—the long face, the cheekbones, the smiles. They all looked like a combo of their mom and dad. All eight kids. Two girls. Six boys.

I remembered he'd told me about his family once, but it felt like a million years ago.

"Remind me their names?" I held up the photo, so he'd know what I was asking.

He smirked. "My mother must have put that photo there. I didn't really decorate the place. She comes in here when I'm not in town and decorates it because, evidently, the fact that it's bare makes her uncomfortable. In any case, that photo? We are actually standing in age order with my parents on either side of us."

That much I had figured out—not the age order, but his parents on either side. "What are everyone's names?"

"My parents are Hayley and James, the same name as my oldest brother. But people call my father Jim, and my brother is James, which is what they called my grandfather—James." He winked at me and walked over with a glass of water in his hand, placing it in mine. "Did you follow that?"

I nodded. "Think so."

"Good. Then, in order, we have James. My older sister, Susan. Me." He grinned. "I was lucky number three. Two boys after me. David. Cameron. Then Trina. Vaughn. Jerome." He pointed at the glass. "Drink that. They're all married. They all have kids. We can go through all of them if you like."

I swallowed the drink. "No. Please not yet. At some point, if I'm going to meet them, then yes, but not yet. I'm not sure I'll remember them all."

"Yeah, we're going to get those pain meds decreased just as soon as it makes sense."

I put the picture back where his mother had placed it and sat on the couch. I didn't know what time it was, if I should have been hungry, sleeping, or running in a circle. I had no idea whatsoever what I should be doing. But the couch was comfortable, the fire inviting, and I thought maybe sitting in front of it was just what I should be doing right then.

He plopped down next to me and put his feet up on the coffee table between us and the fire. Since he'd done that, I did the same, although I'd never have presumed to do that if he hadn't.

"You will probably meet all of them. I'll hold them off as long as I can, at least until you're feeling more yourself. But there is no way that I'm going to be here with a woman and they aren't all going to want to see who that is with their own eyes. I don't bring people here, ever."

I sipped more of my water. "You'll just have to explain I'm your friend who occasionally screws up your life."

He laughed, a deep belly version of it, and I grinned. "Sure. I can promise you that Trina has already told them some things. She was living with me when Hayley's went under."

That's when it occurred to me what I should have realized moments ago—Hayley was his mother's name. The restaurant that had tanked had been named after his mother. I closed my eyes. This was going to be uncomfortable to say the least.

What did I owe his family for having caused him so much pain? It had probably affected all of them to see that happen, and the restaurant had been named after his mom, a gift for her in that way. Max would probably say nothing, but was that true?

"You're thinking deep thoughts. Are you plotting something that is going to put both of us on the back of a motorcycle heading up a ski mountain, or is it past even what I can imagine?"

I put my head on his shoulder. "Nothing of the kind."

"I'm not sure I believe you." He kissed my hand again. "Do let me know ahead of time."

I groaned. "I'm not up for anything like that."

"But you'd admit the possibility if you were."

I smiled. "Maybe."

∽

I MUST HAVE DOZED off because I woke up some time later. It was quiet in the room. We were both on the couch. My head was on his shoulder, and the fire crackled gently in the fireplace. It was warm, and I wasn't in much pain at that moment. Still, my neck was stiff from the angle I'd been sleeping.

Max made a noise, and it wasn't a happy one. His face was scrunched up like he was himself in pain, and he shook his head back and forth several times before he cried out again. I sat up, realization dawning on me. He was having a bad dream, and it was a doozy.

I put my hand on his shoulder. "Max."

He didn't open his eyes. If anything, he thrashed harder with his head. With no choice, I shook him gently but firmly. "Max. You're having a bad dream. Wake up." I kissed his cheek. "Come on, wake up."

With a startle, he jerked awake. He breathed heavily, like he'd been running, and then threw his arms around me, pulling me against him. I winced but didn't complain. It wasn't the best hold for me right then, but I wasn't going to complain when he needed me.

"Are you okay?" I whispered. It was hard to wake up suddenly, whether you needed to or not.

He nodded. "I'm okay. Bad dream. Thanks for waking me."

"Seemed like a bad one." I held on to him right back. "Want to talk about it?"

He shook his head. "No. Fuck no. I really don't. Couldn't if I wanted to. More of a memory than a dream. That year."

The one he'd never tell me about, the one probably responsible for why he called himself fucked up when he had it together better than anyone I knew.

"Okay."

He pulled back. "Sorry, wasn't thinking." Max let me go. "Just grabbed you like that. Not okay. It's late. I guess we both dozed off on the couch. Want anything? Hungry?"

I didn't. "No, I'm okay."

"Tomorrow, I'm going to feed you really well."

Honestly, I wasn't sure I was going to be able to eat. "Kind of borderline nauseated all the time."

"That's because you don't have food in your stomach. Tomorrow, we'll get you settled. You're going to need food if you're going to make it through cold weather in Maine."

I let him lead me toward his bedroom. "Am I going to be shoveling snow?"

"I wouldn't put it past my sister to eventually decide that was part of your treatment." He picked me up, and I yelped in surprise before I giggled. "So maybe hope really hard that it doesn't actually snow."

He was trying hard to be upbeat, but I could see the shadows in his gaze. Whatever he'd been dreaming had shaken him up.

"You sure you're okay?"

"I will be. It's been a while since that happened, but yeah, I'll be fine."

His bedroom was simple. A king sized bed. A bureau. Closed windows with drawn curtains. Max set me down on the bed. "I'm going to go deal with the fire downstairs."

I rolled, carefully, off where he'd put me and made my way into the bathroom. I needed a shower, and I'd been given instructions on how to do that. It was tricky. I couldn't let my wounds get wet, but I had to get clean, which meant sponge baths for the near future. I got busy getting the uncomfortable activity done and swore I would never take a bath for granted again. Every time I sank into the hot water, I'd feel grateful for the ability to do so.

When I was sure I was clean enough, I stuck my head in the shower to wash my hair and then wished I had waited until I could have had some help. Still, I got it done. I officially smelled better. Max hadn't lied—I had everything I needed. Even a bathrobe hung on the back of the door, ready for me. I wrapped myself up in it and went back into the room. Max lay face-down on the bed, his head turned away from me, his shoes kicked off. He'd gone back to bed. The thought made me smile. Like me, when I wasn't drugged, sleep was hard for him. It was nice to see him comfortable again.

As quietly as I could, I searched his drawers for my clothes. They were in the right part of the bureau, and I dressed myself as quietly as I could.

Finally done, it was a little bit like I'd just been to the gym. My whole body hurt. I climbed in next to Max. He lifted his head, his eyes opening. "You would have called out if you needed my help, right?"

"I would have."

He nodded. "Good."

We were warm, on the ground, and at least for now, no one was going to hurt us. That was enough.

CHAPTER 17

FOUR DAYS LATER, I COULDN'T REMEMBER WHY I HAD begged the doctor in Portland to cut back my pain meds. I ached all the time, and grouchy had become my middle name.

Max eyed me from the kitchen but didn't speak to me, which was probably smart, since I'd bitten his head off when he asked me if I wanted breakfast. Apparently, I didn't do pain well.

"Sorry," I called out to him, hoping he'd know what I was apologizing for, since I didn't have more in me right then.

"Yep," he answered fast. "My sister will be here soon to start PT. Are you sure I can't offer you some eggs?"

My stomach clenched at the thought. "Absolutely not."

The toast I had managed to keep down, despite how awful I felt, was all that I would be attempting any time soon.

He nodded. "She'll probably have my mother with her."

I darted to my feet, which was easier said than done. My shoulder was actually coming along a lot easier than the flesh wound over my hip. I'd never understand the why of it, and the doctor hadn't seemed to have a lot of answers about that either. I limped toward the bedroom and made quick work of putting on some makeup and fixing my hair. I could live with his sister thinking I'd never seen the inside of a salon. His mother? No, not so much.

Even though we were friends and not dating, so it shouldn't really matter. It just kind of did. Not to mention it really was starting to feel like we were just friends. He'd made absolutely no moves to act like he wanted sex since we'd arrived.

Of course, before yesterday, I'd been pretty out of it and apparently looking like the horror I'd seen in the mirror before I started applying makeup.

"Is it going to run down your face when you are doing your exercises?"

I jumped, not expecting to find Max in the doorway.

"I hope it's smudge proof." I hadn't bought the cosmetics myself. Someone else purchased the items, and I'd simply made do with what they'd provided. Truth was, they weren't really my colors, but beggars couldn't be choosers. I was lucky someone thought of cosmetics at all.

He came over and stood behind me so that I could see him in the mirror. "I don't think anyone would judge you for being not put together right now. You're gorgeous. So beautiful that you really don't need makeup."

I lifted an eyebrow. "Is that so?"

"You sound like you don't believe me." He leaned his cheek against mine. "I realize you have very little self-confidence, which continues to blow me away because there is so much that is out of this world amazing about you, Hope, but I would think you would at least know that."

He smelled fantastic, and for a second, I closed my eyes and breathed him in. "Sometimes you say the sweetest things." I opened my lids. "And sometimes you drive me crazy about eating eggs, I can't meet your mother looking like you dragged me out of a river."

Max swatted my rear end gently, and we grinned at each other. "They're really good eggs. You're going to hurt after this. PT fucking hurts."

That I already knew. But I couldn't help but let his words roll through me for a short second. Not long but enough to nearly bring me to my knees. I was going to hurt after this. Yes, he'd meant today and the workout. What if it had more meaning and he didn't even know it? I was going to hurt after this.

Somehow, I already knew that. When Max was done with me, I was going to hurt. A lot.

HIS MOTHER THREW her arms around me, and I stopped breathing. Hayley Broadley was a hugger. "I am so happy to meet you, Hope. I am so glad you came here to heal, and I am so happy that you brought my boy home."

"Ah…" I wasn't sure what to say. I'd never been embraced quite this way before, not instantly upon meeting me.

"Mother." Susan, Max's sister, sighed. "I'm sure that can't be comfortable, given her shoulder injury. Let her go."

Hayley jumped back, and Max put his arm around her. "It's okay, Mom. Go easy on the hugging with Hope. She isn't used to the Broadley brand of hugging strangers the first time we meet them."

His mother patted him on the arm. "That is how you make sure you've never met a stranger. You simply don't allow them to stay that way."

Susan rolled her eyes, but there was mirth in them. "You

should see how that goes when a stranger happens to wander into our little grocery store here in town. God forbid we don't know their whole life story by the time they leave, have their cell phone numbers, and a date to see them when next they're in town."

"I... That sounds sort of awesome, actually."

Max shook his head. "Don't encourage my mother, Hope."

He was not a hugger, per se, and he didn't make friends with everyone he knew. Maybe there was a time he'd been like that and he wasn't anymore. I didn't know, but it was another piece in the Max puzzle I'd have to try to piece together at some point.

"Come." Susan took my hand. "Let's get you sorted out. Maybe do some light stretches. It'll hurt, unfortunately, but it will give my mother a chance to give Max the Broadley inquisition about why it took his girlfriend getting shot for him to come home."

I caught my breath. "We're just friends."

"Uh-huh. Whatever." She rolled her eyes. "I was once friends with my husband too. Five children later, and he alternates between being my best friend and the bane of my existence."

Five? How did she balance kids and her work? I followed after her as quickly as I could, which was staggeringly slow, unfortunately.

Susan Broadley-Finache turned out to alternate between sweet friend and drill sergeant in a heartbeat of time. She had served, as all her brothers had, in the army and was a no-nonsense therapist who I was sure would get me back to full movement. I got the impression right away I wasn't to whine, but I was to tell her if I had true pain.

As everything hurt, it was hard to judge how much pain

required notification. Still, I figured I'd eventually work it out.

"So, you and my brother?" She didn't bring that up until we were headed back to the living room. "What do you see in that grump?"

I shook my head. "Max has been...amazing to me."

"Yes well, they do that when they are properly motivated, don't they?" She winked at me. "I don't know what I expected from you, Hope, but you are very different than whatever preconceptions I had. I followed you the last few years on social media. Well, I guess I sort of followed the Redheads in general. I got the impression you were incredibly shallow. Then you go and save a kid and get yourself shot up doing it. Somehow, you got tangled up with my brother. Although that last bit hasn't yet blown up on social media."

I didn't know what to say when people spoke to me so bluntly. I preferred it to a bunch of bullshit, yet there never seemed to be a good answer. "Maybe it's possible to be really shallow and still not want kids to die. And as for your brother, there is social media involving the two of us, which I am sure you know about."

She nodded. "I do. I appreciate you owning it like that instead of pretending you don't know what I'm talking about."

"Max knows I'd do anything to make it right."

Susan put her hand on my shoulder. "When I look at the video, I don't see you, not as I see you standing here now. I know it was years ago and people change, but I'm wondering...were you feeling okay? Obviously, you were puking. But other than that? Your eyes right now, in pain and worried about what I'm going to say next, it still doesn't look like you in that recording."

I swallowed. "I'm not really ready to share the answer to that with you."

She touched my arm. "Fair enough. I'm guessing you shared it with Max and that's why you're here. The way he looks at you? Whatever you've told him is clearly good enough for him, that makes you great in my book."

"Thanks." I nodded at her. "And I appreciate you doing this for me."

Susan smiled. "I know we're keeping your presence here secret, but it's a bit of a kick for me to know I worked with one of the Redheads."

"There's only one as far as I'm concerned." Max walked toward us from where he had clearly been listening to our conversation on the porch. "Just one." He held up a finger like he was going to illustrate that. "And the Broadleys are far too nosy for their own good. Hope doesn't owe anyone explanations for anything. Her life story isn't fodder for conversation on long winter nights."

Susan held up her hand. "You know I'm not going to be the worst of it."

His mother stepped outside, pulling her sweater around her. "Worst of what? Ooh, it is getting chilly out here. Get your girl inside, Max, before she catches a chill."

Was it cold? Since we'd started moving around, I hadn't noticed it. In fact, I should have paid more attention to a lot of things, like the fact that the leaves on the trees and the ground were stunning in color. Yellow. Red. Orange. I saw them change every year in Central Park, but it wasn't like this. They were everywhere, like we were intruders in the world of the leaves.

"Are you cold, Hope?" Max walked down toward us. "Or are you just falling in love with the colors right now?"

I pointed at him. "You only read me that well because you were out staring at them yourself."

He smirked. "I wasn't staring at the leaves."

"Sure you weren't." I patted his arm in a dramatic way, and he grinned.

"You two, you know you have to come to dinner Sunday." Hayley smiled at us. "Since you're here, you have to."

Max rocked back on his feet. "I don't know, Mom."

"It's my birthday." Hayley said in a sing-song voice. "When you're in town on your mother's birthday, you have to come to her house for dinner. That is one of those must do things."

He ran a hand through his hair, and I watched as a million different responses crossed his face, finally ending with him nodding and putting on a smile. "Sure, we'll be there, Mom. But I want it clear to everyone that they are to go easy on my friend here. The last thing she needs while she's healing is to be overwhelmed by the Broadleys."

"Oh." His mother came down the stairs toward us. "She is pretty tough. Made of strong material that doesn't fall apart. I think being overwhelmed by the Broadleys might be just what she needs."

I'D JUST GOTTEN out of the shower when the first scent of whatever delicious thing Max cooked wafted into the bathroom, taking my attention from the strawberry shampoo I'd used just minutes before. I ran a hand through my hair to comb it rather than going through the process of using a brush. I put on shorts and a T-shirt before I wrapped myself in a huge bathrobe. Probably Max's robe, based on the sheer size of the thing.

I watched his back quietly as he placed something that looked like russet potatoes in the oven. A bottle of truffle oil sat next to the sink, and without watching what he was doing at all, he put the oil away into another cabinet.

Max was almost never at his home in Maine. How did he still manage to cook in it so naturally? Did the man instinctively find his way around any kitchen? Or maybe it didn't matter where he put the oil, since it was his kitchen, so wherever he put it became where it belonged?

"Smells good."

He looked over his shoulder. "That is the barbecue sauce on the pork you're smelling. I made it on the stovetop. I haven't really started cooking anything else, except those potatoes."

A bottle of wine sat open on the counter, and he had a glass next to him, while next to the wine he'd poured a glass of seltzer over ice. I walked over and picked it up. It was cool on my tongue. "Thanks."

"You're welcome. It's nothing." He sipped his wine. "How are you feeling? How much pain are you in?"

I stretched my arms over my head. "I can do that, which is apparently a very good sign. And some of my other muscles are sore, but I'd say the areas where I'm shot don't hurt additionally."

He swung around and picked me up by my waist and set me on the counter. I grinned at him. "What are you doing?"

"I'm fucking hungry." His gaze held mine like I was captured in it.

"Then I guess it's a good thing you're making dinner." I smiled at him.

He shook his head. "Not for food."

Max bent over, pushing my legs apart gently. "Let me know if this causes you any pain."

Pain wasn't on my mind a second later when he kissed my thigh. I actually trembled. He laid a long, warm kiss on the other thigh before he took an audible deep breath. "Can never get enough of this. Missed this."

He pulled my shorts off, dropping them on the floor. I hadn't put on panties, preferring instead to sleep commando under the shorts. Now I was glad I hadn't put them on. This was a lot easier. I loved Max having access if this was what was on his mind.

Max kissed my clit, finding it with his mouth, and I sighed. *Yes.* This was just what I wanted. So much had happened since the last time he touched me like this. We'd been in New York, and I hadn't known yet what my decisions were going to do to my life. There were bullets and missing children. Air travel. Pain. But there was also this moment. Fuck. There was Max's clever tongue swirling around my clit like he knew just how I needed his touch.

This was life. This was pleasure. This existed too. It wasn't always hard. Sometimes it was downright incredible. I grabbed on to the back of Max's head and held him right there. It helped to hold on to him, otherwise I could get lost in the sensations. There was such a thing as too much pleasure for me.

He moaned, and I quit thinking. Max thrust his hips into the counter as he ate at me. He held on to my thighs, keeping me open to him, but dropped one of them right then just to cup himself on the outside of his pants. He groaned like it hurt him and put his hand back where it was.

"Stop." I spoke quickly, and he pulled back to look at me.

"What's the matter? Did I do something you don't like?" He panted.

I shook my head. "Together. Not just me. Both of us."

Max smiled at me. "You…you are always surprising me."

Max had me off the counter in seconds, and both of us were back on his couch.

He lay on top of me, pressing his finger inside of me, and I reached for his cock, which took a lot of maneuvering. It was hard to get his pants off, but I managed it. By the time I'd freed him of the clothing, we grinned at each other like stupid idiots.

It always seemed so romantic when people did this on television or in the movies. We were sort of goofy, and I loved it. I stroked him from his balls to his tip. He moaned. "You do things to me, Hope. I can't begin to explain to you what you..."

He kissed me rather than finishing the thought. I wanted to know what he wanted to say, but I wanted what his mouth was doing to me more. Kissing me all the way down my neck, stopping right at that point where my neck met my shoulder. I gripped him harder, closing my eyes to feel that moment.

Max kissed me there again. And again. Apparently, I had a spot, and he'd found it. I squirmed, and he sucked in a long breath. "I love when you make those noises."

I couldn't have stopped if I wanted to, not when he was making love to my body, pressing his fingers right where I needed them on my clit. Over and over again. "Such a good girl. I love how prettily you moan against me."

"Inside of me," I told him. "Please. Inside of me."

He shook his head. "Not until you come for me, Hope. You come for me, then I'll press inside of you and stretch out your pussy with my cock until you are screaming for it a second time."

I caught my breath. His words were hot, scalding hot, but it wasn't his words that threw me over the edge of pleasure. His fingers did their work too, but what really got me was how he looked at me. I'd never seen myself in someone else's gaze before, but right then, it felt as though he threw the warmest adoration at me that I'd ever experienced. I came, but it wasn't sudden or explosive, more like a release of everything inside of me that had been tied up with nowhere to go.

Maybe he understood I was having a moment because he kept his gaze affixed to mine, neither of us able to look away from one another. Max cupped my cheeks. "So fucking beautiful."

"You," was what I managed to say. It wasn't much, but I must have made myself clear because he nodded and reached over me to pull out his wallet from his pants where they'd been discarded. In two seconds, he'd gotten a condom out and then dropped his wallet again. I watched all of this like I was looking through a fog. Maybe haze was a better word. The haze of wanting to fuck Max. Right then. No more waiting.

He sheathed himself and then was on me like he rode the same edge of desperation drowning me. It didn't matter that I'd just come. It had been exactly what I needed, and yet I required more now. I had to feel him, experience the connection that only happened when Max was deep inside of me.

Wasting no time, he pushed inside of me. I cried out at the feeling, both from the fact that he'd met my craving and also because he was big, it had been a little while since we'd done this, and my muscles weren't ready for him yet.

Staring at each other, I panted like I was running a race, while he smoothed my hair off my face. "Just breathe with me, baby. I'm going to make you feel so good."

I loved when he used endearments like that in these moments. Like he wasn't guarding what he said, like he wasn't weighing if he should. It was Max just being Max. I breathed with him, and then he moved again. In and out of me, each thrust passing by the bundle of nerves that made me gasp, made me dig my fingers into his back so hard, I was sure I would leave a mark. I couldn't help it. Max took me like I belonged to him, and I only needed to hold on for the ride.

I wrapped my legs around him tighter, drawing him even deeper inside of me. His moans matched my own. We both practically shouted. I arched my back as pleasure drove me to the peak of what I could handle and grinned when I felt him finish.

Falling back down, my back hit the couch cushions, and I grinned some more. Actually, I couldn't stop grinning. He held himself off my body, finally kissing me all over my face. "I think I made you giddy."

"You did." I kissed his chin. "What did I make you?"

"I don't know that I have words for it." He kissed my nose, then groaned as he pulled himself out of me. Faster than I would have liked, Max got off the couch and went to deal with the condom. "Did I hurt you?" he called over his shoulder.

I shook my head. Not that he could see that, which meant I actually had to answer. "Right now, I'm feeling no pain."

"Good." This time he answered me from the kitchen. "That was fun, Hope."

It was. For me, it had been a lot more than fun, though. But I knew this trap, and I wasn't falling into it. Too many of my girlfriends felt ecstatically emotional after sex and ended up on their own that way because the guy had already moved on to what or whoever he was doing next. I didn't have the slightest intention of being one of those women.

I knew the score with Max. He wasn't in this for the long

term except as my friend. Eventually, we'd have to stop having sex, and the thought pushed my euphoria away. Wow. That had been fast. I got off the couch and dressed slowly. Max had left his clothes where they were on the floor, wearing pajama pants he must have grabbed from the bathroom instead.

They were the same brand but differently colored than the ones he'd had on this morning when he'd gotten out of bed before me. We'd been sleeping like two people who didn't know each other since we'd gotten here. Me on one side of the bed, him on the other, and never the two shall meet.

I sort of hated it. Did cuddling have to be off the table? Or maybe it was that I—thanks to the drugs—had been sleeping, and I had no idea if he had because I passed out every night and didn't wake up till morning. That would probably stop since I'd cut back the drugs. Maybe we'd go back to late night conversations and dozing together.

Pretending I hadn't needed more hugging after we'd just had sex, I slid onto the stool to watch him cook. He smiled at me. "This is something I've been working on for Hyperion, so be brutally honest when we eat, okay?"

"Sure." Of course, it was the only thing I was going to be brutally honest about since I had to lie, even to myself, about what was going on between us. Sure, I could be easygoing Hope who didn't get her heart involved.

But I had to ask, why did the guy who followed me into gunfire and brought me home to care for me have to be off limits? Why did it have to be no?

He said he was fucked up, but I saw no evidence of that. Not really. "How long have you been working on the recipe?"

I really was a coward sometimes.

CHAPTER 18

WE NEEDED TO GET HIS MOTHER A GIFT. IT WAS HER birthday. The thought occurred to me the day before we were supposed to have dinner at her home, where I would meet the rest of his very large family. Max had been twitchy all day, and when I reminded him about the need for the present, he immediately suggested we should go to Portland to buy it. This was going to be my third time in Portland, since I counted landing there in the plane as one. The doctor had been the second visit, and now we were shopping for his mom.

I'd never gone shopping for someone else's mother before. Moms had been a foreign concept to me growing up. Something other people had, sure, but I never did. I used to make Mother's Day cards in school, because we had to, and then throw them out. Teachers would say things that were meant to be helpful, like how I could make a card for a grandmother—we really didn't see them very much, either, and then they were both gone from this world—or that I should make a card for my mother in heaven. I'd burst into tears with that one—maybe I'd been in second grade?—and

Bridget had told off the teacher. Not all holidays were celebrated in all countries, but Mother's Day was one of those celebrated most places. I just never knew exactly what day I was going to have to face that pain.

So picking out a gift for Hayley Broadley was a novel experience, and Max wasn't helpful when it came to deciding what to get her. I got a lot of *I don't knows* when I asked specific questions, which eventually led me to buying her a soft, warm designer blanket that was tan in color and hopefully she wouldn't hate. She could put it into a trunk, if she hated it, and people always needed extra blankets. I was pretty sure they did, anyway.

The small store was happy to giftwrap the gift, so we left. I was bundled in what I was pretty sure was an old coat of Susan's, and it was sort of hard to believe that just a little over a week ago, I had been in Germany dealing with having been shot. I was still dealing with it, but it was a world of difference now.

His sister had been over every day to work with me a little bit, and I liked her more and more each visit.

Max remained incredibly quiet. "Something wrong?" I finally asked him.

"No, I love it here."

Well, I hadn't expected that answer. Not in the least. "Good to be back in Maine?"

"I meant Portland. I do love Portland. Always did. Used to think that this would be the perfect spot to open a restaurant." We headed toward the car. "Close enough to my family that I could visit, or they could come see me a lot, but not close enough that my mother is in and out of my house all the time."

So far, his mother had dropped over once a day. She was always bringing us stuff, like jam she'd found in the grocery store she thought he would like. She'd realized that I didn't have enough socks and brought some over. I'd kind of loved the attention, but I was probably desperate to be mothered, and she wasn't mine anyway. Who was I to say what too much of a good thing was for Max?

"Then why didn't you? Open here? Why choose New York City?"

He grinned. "Ego."

"What?" I didn't know how ego played into business management.

"I went from culinary school to working in kitchens in Manhattan. Feels a little bit like the center of the universe there, sometimes. And I wanted to make it there. Like the song or whatever. I wanted to be a hit there."

I squeezed his hand. "You did that. How is it going, by the way? Anna still okay?"

"Anna is loving life, and I'm pretty sure the staff prefers me being away too. Eric came back yesterday to work a little bit. He cooked for an hour and then went home. Huge moment."

So something I did had made a big difference. I'd helped to make that happen, in a small way. "That is incredible."

Do you need to go back? I almost asked him the question aloud, but then I didn't. He'd just tell me to worry about recovery. I didn't have to keep questioning him about things when I knew what his answer would be before he gave it, even if the answer was somewhat dissatisfying.

We headed back to his home together in the car, mostly talking about nothing important. It would have been a perfect moment, if I didn't have a million things to say to him that I just didn't feel like I could. A minefield of things remained unsaid, and if I swayed at all in the wrong direction, I might explode the ease we pretended to have with one another.

Well, an ease that included really hot sex that kept popping up here and there.

Like on the kitchen table that morning.

Or maybe it was just me pretending. Maybe Max really was content in our current setup. In this…pattern of whatever it was we were doing, because friends really didn't behave like this. Not really.

I was afraid I'd already plummeted into a problem because I was pretty sure I was in love with him. Pathetically in love with a man who said he wasn't interested in love. Was this a thing with my family? Layla had done the same thing, the only difference was Zeke already really loved Layla. He'd made a terrible mistake when he'd hurt her, but he'd fixed it, in a big way, and spent a lot of time proving his feelings to my sister. I just couldn't see Max doing that.

Zeke had been so used to feeling lonely, he'd thought he had to stay that way forever. Or at least that was how Layla described it. I wasn't sure why Max continued to give me so much attention if he didn't love me, but it was clear he wasn't lonely.

He had friends and family to fill his life anytime he wanted and the ability to scuttle off to be by himself, if he preferred solitude.

When we took another walk together to look at the leaves that afternoon, I let myself pretend for just a bit that we were happy and we could do this kind of thing together forever. Pretending was only going to make my heart hurt more later, yet I couldn't bring myself to break out of the bubble of illusions. Not yet.

Right then, I could breathe. I had no need to lock and unlock his doors over and over at night. It had never been a problem for me in other people's houses, only my own space, and that meant that I didn't really feel at home there yet.

When that changed, I'd have to acknowledge it was time for me to speak up.

I made deals like that with myself all the time.

How many times I locked the door was how I judged if I needed help or not.

How many times I cried...how many calories I ate...how many times I went to the gym. Did other people live like this, or was this just my own brand of cray-cray that I hid from the world?

It didn't really matter, because I fell asleep that night pressed against him as we watched a movie together. I might have stayed like that all night if he hadn't gotten hit with another nightmare.

He woke easily when I said his name. He jolted to awareness, then placed his head in his hands for a good thirty seconds before he would speak to me. Eventually, he did. "Thanks."

"Are you okay?" I sat up so that we'd be more face-to-face, and the blanket slipped down a little bit. I had to pull it back because it was cold in the room. In the week we'd been there, it was getting significantly colder in Maine.

He nodded. "Yep. The nightmares are back, and I really hoped they were gone. If it keeps up, I'll call the doctor and do something about them again. Sorry I keep waking you up."

I touched his arm. "Don't worry about me, I just want to make sure you're okay."

"Yep." He got out of bed. "Go back to sleep. I'm going to do some stuff for a while, and I might sleep in the guestroom if I sleep at all so I don't keep you up."

The idea filled me with coldness that had nothing to do with the room. "Don't do that. I mean, get up if you want to, but come back here. I'll sleep in the guest room before you will. This is your house."

He rubbed his eyes. "You sure? You need more rest than me. You're healing."

I was pretty sure I wasn't the only one healing, but his wounds were more internal at the moment. Not that I had any intention of saying that right then. "I'm sure."

"Okay." He walked from the room, his shirt off, like he didn't know the temperature had dropped ten degrees. Maybe he just didn't care.

Max never came back to bed.

His mother's party was everything I'd imagined it was going to be. We walked through the door, and everyone in the house seemed to yell *hello* all at once. I smiled, and Max didn't. In fact, he'd been tense all day.

I'd wondered if he was going to make an effort to be pleasant with his family, and the answer turned out to be sort of no. He was nice to his parents, but that was about it. His siblings got grunts as answers when they pulled him into hugs, but they pretended not to notice he was being rude. They did that for me too. Big hugs. Everyone in the whole house—and there were so many of them, I lost count—hugged me.

Except for his sister Trina. She barely said hello and then turned her back on me like I wasn't even there.

It hurt, since I'd decided to pretend for the afternoon that I belonged there, and then I remembered that she had been the one living with Max when it had all gone sour with Hayley's. Yep. I was never going to be her favorite person. Her husband, whose name I was pretty sure was Hal, was very friendly, and I liked her daughters, who were three and one.

In fact, I spent a lot of the time before dinner with a tiara on my head, playing with the children who had decided I was new, sparkly, and exactly who they should be spending all their time with. Their parents would come in and out, sit with us, and make small talk. Max looked the most like his brother David, but the whole family had a familial look that really worked for all of them.

Eventually, the kids ran off to play outside in the snow that had started coming down. A dusting, they were calling it. I didn't know what that meant to Mainers, as they called themselves. I followed noise toward the large living room.

But I stopped outside his father's office when I heard Max's voice.

"What is it that you want?" He sounded annoyed. I was glad he wasn't talking to me like that.

"I just don't know what you're trying to prove by bringing that bitch to our mother's house." I recognized Trina's voice, and I winced. *Ouch.*

Max sighed. "Don't talk about her like that. You don't know her."

"Oh, but I do know her. I was there, remember? I lived through all of it with you. She destroyed your life. Why are you bringing her here, Max?"

He didn't say anything for a long moment. "I appreciate that you were there for me when it all fell apart, but it's so much more complicated than you understand. She's my friend. That's all there is to it. You don't have to understand more than that."

I should really have walked away or announced I was there. I did neither thing. I just stood there like a high schooler eavesdropping on gossip that happened to be about me. I couldn't even blame Trina for how she felt. I had hurt him, and if someone did that to one of my sisters, I wouldn't want to have them in my house either.

Well…this was technically her parents' home, but same difference in the end.

"Does she know what she cost you? What it is still costing you? How you had to sign up with investors who are eating you alive? How you aren't even earning on your own fucking restaurant yet?"

This time he sounded tired. "Enough. Thank you for caring, but Hope knows what she needs to know. I don't want her to know I'm struggling. She'll try to fix it, and like I said, it's complicated. She has enough on her plate already."

I scurried away, my heart beating fast. He wasn't making money? *Damnit.* Why hadn't he told me? I shook my head. Well, I knew why. He didn't want me to know.

"Hope," his mother called to me when I wound up in the living room. "Come sit. I was just looking at old pictures. Look at this one of Max."

I wasn't sure I could smile and fake it right that second. I had to think about what Trina had said. I had to figure out what to do. Max was never going to be honest about his situation, but that didn't mean that I couldn't help. Of course, I'd promised him when we started sleeping together that it would stop.

Damnit.

"Here." Hayley patted the seat next to her and Cameron's wife—whose name I now couldn't remember—popped up to let me sit there.

There wasn't anything I could do if he didn't want me to. I had to…butt out.

With that thought, I forced myself to look at Hayley's family photos. Max had been a very cute kid. Big, bright eyes and happy smiles. He always seemed to be holding a fishing pole or lying in a hammock in these sets of photos.

Hayley pointed to one where he held a cat. "That was his third cat he brought home that summer."

I blinked. "What?"

"Oh, Max was always bringing home strays. Whatever animal he thought needed him, he took it home. Third cat. Five dogs. A rat. A chicken. Sometimes they were other people's pets and he just didn't know. It was cute."

"Ugh." Max walked into the room. "Are you seriously showing Hope family photos?"

I smiled. "That's okay. This is lovely. No one has photos of me from when I was young. I think there are maybe three photos from my whole childhood."

"Maybe that's why you love to be photographed so much now," Trina sort of sneered. "Trying to make up for the attention you didn't get?"

Their mother gasped, but I forced myself to smile. "Maybe. I know you teach drama, but maybe you should have majored in psychology. Seems like you might be on to something."

Everybody laughed, even though I hadn't really meant to be funny. Still, it was better because it set Hayley at ease. It was finally time for dinner. Amazingly enough, in a room of people being kind and nice, the only person I could focus on was the one who didn't like me. Like she took all the air from the room and only she remained in it.

Max bent over. "Sorry about that. Trina is snarky."

"No big deal." I was good at faking happy. I'd lost my appetite, but I'd fake eating too.

Maybe I wasn't cut out for being around big families.

THE SNOW GOT WORSE, and we all left quickly after dinner. Max drove through it like it was no problem, and we were back at his place before I knew it.

"My family is a lot." He told me after we'd settled inside. "You were great with them. Particularly when my father started grilling you at dinner about why you had never been out on a fishing boat. Handled that like a champ, although you should expect him to insist you go fishing with him this summer."

I doubted I would be there by then. Certainly, Max couldn't still be there. He had to get back to his restaurant. "Your family is amazing." I meant that. Completely. "And they adore you."

"Even in my bad moods. They're used to them, I'm afraid. Everyone knows I'm just a little fucked up." I stared out the window at the snow. Amazing how it felt like I was going up as I stared at it. I hadn't noticed the optical illusion since I was a kid. Then again, I hadn't really been focused on the snow. It was more like something that stopped me from doing whatever I needed to do and kept me stuck inside.

Max came up behind me. "Trina was intense tonight. She was there with me when—"

"I fucked things up," I said, interrupting him. "Yes, I remembered that, and if I hadn't, I would've figured it out fast. Don't worry about it. Not everyone has to like me." Even if I wished they did. Maybe she'd been right about my need for attention.

He put his arms around me. "You did well with it."

"I'm not sure if I should say thank you. I didn't know I was being judged."

Max laughed. "Fair enough."

"Why do you call yourself fucked up?" Maybe it was the snow making me brave enough to ask questions I should have kept to myself, but he said we were friends— currently my least favorite F word—and friends talked to each other.

He put his chin on my shoulder. "Lots of reasons. The nightmares. The bad moods. The fact that I absolutely hate the thought of the things that other people want."

Well, that last one was a new piece of information. "Like what?"

"Like I don't think I could get through a week if I had to do the marriage thing." He stepped back and went into the kitchen.

I took a beat before I asked the obvious. "The marriage thing?"

"The whole *what do you want for dinner tonight, honey? How would that even work?* I'm cooking for hundreds of people. Or the *where should we go on vacation?* thing. Or the *you're working too many hours* thing. Or the *you left the bathroom a mess* thing. Why does anyone want to go through their lives having to be accountable to someone else's needs and wants? Whatever it is that makes someone want to do that, I don't have it. Like us, for example. This is fine. It's been actually fun being together. But if you wanted to go, you could go. You don't have to check with me. I'm not in charge of you. If I took off tomorrow, there isn't anything you'd say about it."

Well…that wasn't true. If he left me in the woods without him, I'd have something to say about it. That wasn't, however, what I wanted to focus on right then. "Look I don't have a lot of experience myself. My parents were unhappy, and I was a baby and don't remember. Your parents seem happy. Your siblings seem like they're in love. My sister has never been better than she is right now."

"Right, I get it. That's why I'm saying I'm fucked up. I don't date or do relationships outside of friendship for this reason. There is something inherently missing inside of me. I don't want that...whatever it is that makes people get married."

I was pretty sure that Max was astute enough to know that the things he said hurt me, particularly because I wasn't putting on my best fake happy right then. But if he was going to pretend this was fine, then I would too.

"I think that people get married for lots of reasons. Sometimes they get married for the wrong reasons."

He poured himself a drink of whisky. "What are the right reasons?"

"I guess it would have to be that the very idea of living without that person day in and day out is so abhorrent that it creates such a void in your existence, you have to declare to the world that you are in it together forever. Because if you don't, you're not sure you can get through another day."

He held up his hands and actually grinned at me. "It's like you're speaking a foreign language."

His point was taken. Direct hit to my heart. We were friends. We were never going to be like his siblings and their significant others or his parents. Or Layla.

"I'm going to bed."

Max frowned. "Don't you want to watch a movie?"

"Not tonight. I have PT tomorrow. I need to be rested. That's what I'm here to do, after all. Physical therapy and hiding from the Russian mob."

Not to start daydreaming about things that were not going to be mine. At least not with Max. The second part of that thought was the one that hurt me because I didn't want to do any of those marriage things, as he'd put it, with anyone else. He'd woken me up inside. So what did it mean that he didn't want me that way?

Still, that night when he climbed into bed, as I pretended

to sleep in the way only insomniacs could, he tugged me against him, making me the small spoon in his embrace, I almost cried because it was so fucking unfair.

"Why do you feel like you have to fix everything?" he whispered in my ear, negating my belief that I'd fooled him. He smelled like whisky, cinnamon, and sandalwood. Somehow, it was a heady combination.

I opened my eyes. "I have to be worthy."

"Of what?" He snuggled closer.

"Of having lived. When I'm gone, I have to know that I did something worthy of having been here. If I've made a mess, I have to fix it myself. That's how I'm built."

He was quiet. "Of having lived? So that when you're dead, some faceless people can lay judgment on your life? Or is this a religious thing?"

I shook my head. "Not a religious thing. I don't know if there is or isn't an afterlife. I wasn't raised with any particular faith. I guess it's the nameless, faceless people. Sure. But maybe they won't be nameless or faceless. Maybe they'll be my family."

"Still worrying that you'll care what people think after you're dead?"

I pulled out of his embrace. "There is nothing wrong with wanting to do better. There is nothing wrong with wanting to be a better version of myself. Of saying sorry. Of making amends. Of wanting the people you leave behind to say, hey, she was here and thank goodness she was. I grew up with a ghost in my house. All my houses. She walked behind us all the time. Her red hair, gorgeous eyes, and talent cast a shadow over everything I did. People remembered her. They pay thousands of dollars still for her work. It mattered that she was here, even if her time was brief. I can't do what she did, I don't have an inch of talent, but there isn't anything wrong with wanting to do what I can while I'm here. Maybe someday, Tim will remember me. They're going to remember you, by the way. Your food. What you did. I'm sorry if it doesn't make sense to you, like the marriage thing doesn't, but it's just a truth to me. If you live with a constant ghost, you learn to believe that someday, you will be one too. Maybe because of it, you also want to have made a difference while you were here."

He rolled onto his back. "Just another thing I'm never going to understand."

CHAPTER 19

AFTER THE BIRTHDAY PARTY, HIS FAMILY STARTED COMING over every day. Different members visited at different times. I was always glad to see them because it was a distraction from the fact that Max and I weren't talking about what we'd discussed that night after the party. Susan declared me fit to stop PT by the end of that week, which was surprising for how fast it went, but I really was moving around better.

"Like this?" Max put a spoonful of something he was cooking in my mouth, and I ate it fast. This was typical with him. He liked my opinion on what he was making, even if he never wanted to discuss with me where we should go on vacation.

I did like it. "Delicious. Is that…soup?"

"It is. I think soups are really nice in the winter. I was thinking of adding two. That's a pumpkin soup."

"Outstanding."

He grinned. "Awesome."

When he smiled that way, I could forget all of the things that worried me about us going forward. This part of Max

was easy. I didn't know how I was going to do without this…
I was still here, and already, I could feel the anticipatory ache.

At what point did we put an end to what we were doing?
"Do you hear anything from Michael about the mob?"

"Nothing new." He walked back to the kitchen. "He's working on it."

"And you knew someone in that part of the world who could have at some point helped?" I suddenly remembered the conversation from the hospital.

Max turned off the oven and came around to me. "Hope, if there were anything I could do, I would do it. I hope you know that. The guy I knew, the one who owes me a lot at this point, has vanished. That's what guys like him do. They vanish. I'm not sure where I would start to find him. If something pops up, I'll do it, I promise."

"I know. I was just…unclear about what that had all meant. Blame the drugs."

He grinned. "Do you like to sled?"

I never got to answer that because his phone rang. He frowned and stared at it. Most people texted these days. Max answered it. "Michael? What's going on? Okay." He took the phone from his ear and put it on speaker. "She's here. She can hear you."

"I need you two to get out of there. Your location is compromised."

Max blinked, fast. "What? How can that be?"

"Your sister has been posting about Hope on social media. It's been seen by the wrong people. I'm sending the guys from a nearby location to come get you. We'll figure out where to go from there."

"Which fucking sister?" His face was all hard lines now, the easiness of earlier totally gone.

Michael sighed. "Seems like Trina really doesn't like Hope."

No, she didn't. I closed my eyes for just a second. Well, she'd wanted me gone. She might have arranged a permanent solution and not even known it.

"I fucking told her," Max yelled. "We'll be ready." He hung up the phone, and we both stood there for a long moment staring at each other.

This was both the worst and best possible time for me to say what I had to say. We couldn't take a step forward in this world until we did.

"Max, do you love me? If you don't, do you think you ever could?"

He stepped back like I'd struck him and shook his head. "What?"

"You heard me." I wasn't going to move on this or be put off. "Answer, please, because I'm in love with you."

His whole face fell from the angry horror of a second earlier to utter disappointment. "I think I've been very clear about this, Hope."

I held up my hand. "I want you to say it to me, okay? I'm telling you that I'm in love with you. That it came on…not all of a sudden…not like wham, Hope is in love with Max…but like it was just there one day, something that happened when I wasn't paying attention. I'm in love with you. Max, can you love me?"

He visibly swallowed. "No, baby. I'm sorry. I'm not built for love. I'm just not right."

I held up my hand to stop him from saying whatever else he would have said. I wasn't crying. This was too awful for tears. They'd come. Later. When I let them loose. *Now isn't the time.* "You *are* built for love. I've seen it. When you're not guarding yourself. When you're not paying attention or

242

convincing yourself that you're not. All of those very good people who love you? They don't do so in spite of you, they do so because of you. The same reason I love you. You just don't understand yourself, and that...is dreadful." I took a long breath. "But that's neither here nor there. We all get to determine our futures. I'm rambling. Listen, you can't come with me."

He strode toward me so close, he could touch me, but he didn't. "Hope, don't be ridiculous."

"I'm not. Here's how I see this." Oh yes, there was the pain. Deep. All-consuming. Threatening to pull me under. Still, I continued. "You have to go back to your restaurant. If you loved me, if we were in love, then that would be one thing. But you don't. I can't take one more thing from you. There is a line with *friendship*, and I've long crossed over it. It's time for you to go."

"For the love of god, Hope." He shook his head. "I can decide when I need to go back to work."

"I won't be responsible for another restaurant of yours failing. I can't live with it. And okay, I'm also being selfish because I have to stop being in love with you, and I can't do that with you here. Not with you standing there, being you. All the things about you. Your big caring heart. The way you laugh. How it feels to sleep next to you. The way we watch movies together. How you know the names of every plant we pass outside. Seeing you in the kitchen. Even your stupid bad moods. I can't stop loving you if you're there, so you can't go with me."

I looked around for things to grab that I could take with me, but nothing in the house belonged to me. I'd brought nothing but the clothes on my back, and even they had come from the clinic in Germany. Well...that was easy. I'd find a way to get these clothes back to his family. "Listen, I have no right to ask for anything from you. You've done nothing but give and give." I shook my head. "But I need one more favor, okay? I need you to never contact me again. I don't have a phone, so I'll have to get a new one, new number. Don't find it. Never see me again, so that someday, I can live in the world and not think of us, okay?"

The tears I'd held off flooded down my face. Apparently, the gates had opened and there they were. I sucked in my breath. "You can do that for me, can't you, Max? You can stay away." There was a knock on the door. The guards arrived. I looked at Max one last time. He was stiff, unreadable. I had no idea what to make of him. Maybe I never had. "Goodbye. Be safe. I'll...I'll always be rooting for you. Thank you. For everything."

And I ran. Like the coward I was. Away from him.

WHEREVER I WAS, whoever lived here, they lived in a house where the clocks audibly ticked. I didn't know how he could stand it. *Tick. Tick. Tick.*

I got up. It was the first time I'd moved since I'd been brought to this place, and I took the batteries out of the back of the clock in my room. That was better. A knock sounded, and I opened the door. Then my mouth fell open.

Michael?

"I heard you moving," Michael Li explained as he leaned against the doorframe. "Come eat something."

I nodded. "I thought they'd bring me to Layla's."

"We can arrange it if you want to be there. I wouldn't want to be around people and their loving family if I was feeling like you are. That's the last place I'd want to be, no matter how much my sister loved me."

244

He made an interesting point. I wiped at my eyes. "I don't even really remember getting here."

"You cried yourself to sleep on the plane. Barely moved when we got you off. I was getting worried, but then I remembered that you're a survivor, kid."

I laughed. "I'm a coward, and I don't know if I'm a survivor, but thank you."

He'd poured cereal for me, so I sat at the counter by the bowl. Michael came by with coffee and placed it in front of me. It wasn't how I took my coffee, and I wasn't sure what the cereal was. It looked like cornflakes. I was grateful for anything. Except I couldn't help but think about the oatmeal or waffles Max would have made. Tears came again, and I pulled them back from where they threatened. How did I have any left?

"You are. All of you are." He walked to the window and looked outside to where the light shone through the window.

I took a bite of the cereal. "Where am I?"

"Idaho. My house. I'm almost never here, but it's mine." He shook his head. "We have to talk about what to do with you now. Eat your cereal. Drink your coffee, then we'll work it out."

I did as he directed because I needed food. Still, I had barely gotten any down when I just couldn't eat anymore. My stomach twisted in knots. Maybe I'd made a terrible, terrible mistake. Max didn't believe he could love someone because of whatever shit he'd been through that he wouldn't talk about. If I'd just hung on, maybe he would've come around. I groaned. No, that was how people got themselves in trouble —believing in what couldn't be. If someone told you who they were, you were obligated to believe them.

He was an almost forty-year-old man. If he didn't love me, I had to believe he knew what he was talking about.

Michael took my bowl and put it in the sink. "The day I had to leave Layla in France unprotected was the second worst day of my life, and I've had pretty big ones."

I sipped my coffee. "I can wash my own dish."

"Yes. Do that. I'm just leaving it in the sink." He grinned at me. "I'm a little…compulsive when it comes to certain things. Dishes have to go in the sink when they're done. We're lucky if I don't start clearing the table while everyone is still eating."

That was a funny image. It made me grin. "Can I ask what the worst day was? Or is it one of those things you don't talk about?"

He sat in the chair. "The day after Layla left with Zeke for Washington, I told Bridget how I feel about her. Then she left for Hong Kong."

"What?" I practically shouted and almost fell off the stool.

He held up his hand. "I came to suspect you didn't know. The secrets you keep from each other in this family could fill up my whole house. I tell you this because I want you to understand that I feel your pain. Not that I've felt it, but that I feel it. All the time." He tapped his fingers on the counter. "It hasn't yet gotten better for me. It might never. But I've been able to live my life, and my concern is that locking you up to keep you safe is just going to make things so much worse."

I was still trying to digest that A, he had confessed to Bridget and she'd run away, and that B, Michael had been walking around taking care of all of us in this mess in this amount of pain. What in the fuck was the matter with my sister? Who threw away that kind of love? Not to mention, I was downright convinced she'd been in love with him for forever too. I really needed a phone. Being out of touch was getting old.

"Should we throw me to the Russians and be done with it?"

"No." He shook his head. "But I've been considering how we can let you loose, with a discreet guard, and not keep you locked up. So that you can have a life, see a therapist." He threw that one in there, and I supposed I could be upset if he hadn't been absolutely correct in my need for one. His being around since I was sixteen gave him some rights to say things to me. "And find some happiness. Max is a moron. I mean, I really liked him. He had you, and he let you go. Idiot."

I smiled. That was the kind of thing friends said, and right then, for the first time, Michael felt like my friend. We'd gone through gunfire together. Maybe that had opened some kind of door. "Do you have any suggestions?"

"If you could pick any place out of New York, where would you go?"

Good question. Max's words about Portland and how that could have made him close but not too close to his family resonated with me. "I'd like to be able to see Layla. See Noah grow up. Listen to Zeke go on about the wine. I'd prefer to do so without having to live with them, but they are really remote. I need...I need to go back to school. Get some kind of certificate to go with my degree, so that I can do something other than live off my reputation. Maybe raise money for organizations that help people? Not just the very rich amusing themselves. Meet people."

"And that would be where?" He asked the question, raising his eyebrows like he already knew the answer.

"Seattle." It occurred to me that I'd known the answer this whole time. Of course I should go to Seattle. I loved Seattle. It was a really fantastic city.

"That would work, if you're willing to do the hard part."

I swallowed. "What's that?"

"You're too recognizable. Hope Radford is wanted by the Russian mob, so Hope Radford has to disappear. Your middle name is Amelia. That was your great-grandmother." Michael really knew quite a lot about us. "Her maiden name was West. Amelia West. She can go wherever she likes. I'm actually quite good at disappearing people, better at it than I should be. Paperwork can be altered easily, particularly when taking the name of a dead person who already had a social security number."

My mouth fell open. "Wow. I...I guess I could go by Amelia."

He nodded. Michael had really thought the situation through. "You can. There's just one more thing."

"What's that?" My tired brain struggled to keep up with him.

"The red hair. That is why people recognize you. Change your hair, and you can live a more normal life. With security quietly watching. The Russians will be dealt with. Soon. In the meantime, there is this. What do you think?"

I'd always been a redhead. I'd made a living from it. Matched my sisters. Stood out in public because, for some reason, it had garnered so much attention. It was also why I'd gotten stuck. Somehow, it had become my identity. Was it possible to leave Hope Radford in Maine? To leave behind the woman that had one-sidedly loved a man who couldn't feel that way about her? Start over?

"Sure. Let's do it."

Michael touched my shoulder. "I can never get over how brave you are."

"I'm not. I'm pretty much a coward."

He shook his head. "I wish you could see yourself the way the rest of us see you."

There was still just one more thing I had to do as Hope.

One final loose end to tie off. "I need a phone. A new number. Can you register it to the new name?"

"Easily." He patted my shoulder.

Later that afternoon when he handed me the phone, he'd programmed a lot of numbers into it. I scanned through, noting Zeke's was in there. Zeke. Layla. Bridget. But no Max. That was perfect. I'd never learned his digits, just having relied on it being in my phone. This was like a detox. Sort of.

I could be done with Max soon. After I sent Zeke a message. Michael had discussed my name change with Zeke. They all knew who I was going to pretend to be.

Hi, it's Amelia. That was so strange to type. *Can you find out how much Max would need to pay off his investors?*

There was a pause, and he answered me. *Are you sure you want to do this?*

Final step. Sometime in the future, we can talk about what I did to him, but I need to finish this first. And I didn't really particularly feel like I needed to explain it to anyone anymore.

Right before I went to bed, he pinged me with a number. A huge number. More than I currently had in my bank account, but I knew how I could get it.

Michael had gone to bed hours ago, so I shot him a text he could get in the morning. *I need to sell something. Can your guys do it for me?*

～

THREE MONTHS LATER.

I'D THOUGHT it might feel huge, overwhelming. The day that I had the bank anonymously wire the money to Max's investors so they were paid off, I put an end to a time that was feeling further and further away from me. But it actually didn't. Selling my mother's painting hadn't been as monumental as I thought it would be. *September* had belonged to the old Hope. It came to represent a time I was leaving far behind.

Everything about my life was different moving forward. My therapist said the move was probably cathartic. I liked that word. It was a good one. He'd be free to have the life he should have had before I'd come out of nowhere and disrupted it.

The news blasted in the room to give me background noise while I wrote my paper, due at nine in the morning, that I'd just started. I'd forgotten what a procrastinator I was in school.

Done yet? Bridget texted.

Nope. I answered her.

We still hadn't talked about Michael. I'd kept my secrets, so she was entitled to hers, even if I itched to ask her every time we spoke or texted.

You should have been working on it all week.

I rolled my eyes. If I procrastinated, Bridget had always been annoyingly early in getting all of her work done. Her nagging me wasn't helping.

"And in other news," the reporter said. "A sad story today. Shawn Callihan Junior, the son of Senator Shawn Callihan, drowned while out on his boat. Seems the young lobbyist was swimming when he must have gotten a cramp and drowned. His body was recovered earlier today. A spokesperson on behalf of the senator says…"

I couldn't hear any more words. Shawn was dead. The asshole who drugged and raped me was dead. My hands shook so hard, I could hardly hold my phone to text. Tears fell from my eyes. *Relief. Yes, sweet relief.* I should never wish dead on anyone, but I wouldn't have to see him anymore, wouldn't have to face the possibility of watching him run for office or even bump into randomly at any point for the rest of my life.

Shawn's dead. I texted Bridget and Layla at the same time.

I just saw, Layla texted back. *Was just texting you.*

What? Bridget answered a second later. *How are you? Are you okay?*

I'm shocked. I think. That was the best I could do.

At three in the morning, with my paper badly done, I listened to my ceiling fan when my phone dinged again. *Do you think he really drowned?* Bridget asked.

I dialed her number. If she was up and texting, she could talk. "Why wouldn't I think he drowned?"

"I don't know. It just seems...strange. He drowned. After all this time. Was he out on the boat alone? Swimming by himself?"

No one had mentioned a thing about it being strange. "Maybe that's a thing that he did. I mean...people swim."

"Sure. Of course they do. It's just...I don't know. Something feels fishy to me."

I snorted. "Fishy? Great choice of words." I shouldn't be laughing, but sometimes I did have a lot of dark gallows humor inside of me.

I just did.

My therapist said I had to stop being ashamed of the things that made me, me. I was who I was. In a lot of ways, there wasn't a thing wrong with that.

"I'm glad he's dead," she whispered. "I wish I had killed him."

Not able to sleep after that conversation, I texted Layla at nine the next morning. *Do you think someone killed him?*

Zeke says it wasn't Michael or anyone Michael sent. They both wish they had done it.

Darting rain drops, I made my way back to my apartment later after turning in my paper and sent my cousin a text. Michael, my therapist, my cousin from the state department, Zeke, and my sisters were the only ones who knew Amelia was Hope. Otherwise, I had dropped out of the world. *Did someone kill him?*

He would know who I meant. As he'd been unwilling to help me years ago, I knew there was a limit to how far his help would ever go, but still, it was worth asking.

We have no idea. Looks like he really did just drown.

Well…that was that.

~

ONE MONTH later

"HOPE." Michael's voice sounded strange over the phone. I lifted my eyebrows. He'd been calling me Amelia forever now.

"What's wrong?" I sat up in bed, the book I had been reading falling to the side. I had a date that night, but if I needed to cancel it, I would. Had I been found? No one took my picture. I was never online. I had no reason to think I had been caught. No one, to my knowledge, had realized who I was. That didn't mean I hadn't been found.

"It's over." He exhaled. "They've called off the hit on you and Bridget." Layla had always been fine, thanks to Zeke. No one wanted to fuck with him.

"What?" I couldn't believe it. How was that possible? "You did it?"

"Not me. I can't really explain it. It's just over. I wish it had been me. I had things in the pipeline. Meetings coming up. Artyom Lebedev, the leader of the Bratva himself, announced you aren't to be touched. I can't…I can't make sense of it. I'm trying to find out. You are free, Hope. Free to be you if that's what you want. No one will bother you ever again."

The room seemed to spin. "How can this be? What does it mean for my father and Justin?"

"Truthfully? I have no fucking idea. But congratulations, you are free."

I threw myself back on the bed and hung up the phone. I was free. The one person I wanted to call, I couldn't. Every day it felt like this. It had been months, and Max had done just what I wanted him to do—he'd left me alone. Yet I still wanted to tell him about my day, like we'd done in New York. I wanted to watch TV with him when I was up at night. I wanted him to know the mob was gone. Fuck, I wanted him to hold me after we had sex and tell me I was beautiful.

Maybe I was going to be one of those people who never got over their first love.

He probably never thought about me at all.

CHAPTER 20

Six months later

"I don't know if I can go through with it." I sighed. "I know it's time. Fifth date. Jerry is very nice. Patient. Not pressuring me. He's cute enough. Likes me. But he thinks my name is Amelia, and it feels like a terrible way to cross into this part of our relationship. When he says Amelia, it makes me want to cringe."

My therapist crossed her legs in her black pantsuit. It was a great look for her. "You could tell him. You are allowed to be Hope now. Why aren't you?"

That was the million-dollar question, and one she asked me every other week. Why was I still hiding? Why did I still have my hair dyed dark brown? My joke about wanting to look like Snow White hadn't gone over particularly well. The pale skin. The dark hair. Yeah…she hadn't been amused. Avoidance… Not as good a word as when she said cathartic.

"I don't know. Maybe…maybe Hope wasn't someone that did so well with things." I shouldn't talk about myself in the third person. It was still me. "The last time people called me Hope—well, outside of my family, who never stopped—I was destroyed. I'm still destroyed. It's just easier to not think about him all the time when I'm pretending not to be Hope."

She nodded. "Go on."

"All the things I told him about love, about how it was like living without the other person was unbearable? That's how I feel all the time. I'm ready to fill that hole up somehow. I don't know that it's with Jerry, but I need to do something. I'm tired of missing him."

My doctor nodded. "Good."

Why was it good?

I was still contemplating that question when I got dressed to go out with Jerry. We were supposed to have dinner at a trendy place that had okay food. Yes, Max had made me a food snob. I'd already sort of been one, but he'd pushed me over the edge. It was very hard to find anything delicious when I'd been eating food that defined that word every day I'd been with him and knew the difference. And then back to his place. Where I supposed we would be having sex.

The idea did not fill me with joy. I wasn't dreading it. I was sure I could get through the experience. I was consenting to it. But he wasn't Max. Good-looking. Successful. Jerry just didn't make my knees weak.

I threw on a black dress that would accentuate my dark locks and met him at the restaurant.

Every once in a while, I still startled myself when I caught a glimpse of myself in the mirror. The dark hair. The ink on my wrist, the butterfly I'd decided to get there. She meant rebirth to me. Even if everyone and their mother had a butterfly, I still loved it. The ring in my belly button that I supposed Jerry would see tonight.

That thought did not make me hot. I'd touched myself a

lot when I'd first gotten it, picturing Max's hand running over it, his tongue through the center.

Yep…I was obsessed. With a man who had told me a year ago that he didn't and wouldn't ever love me.

I need to visit this weekend, I texted Layla. Whenever I got too lonely, too much in my head about leaving him, I visited them. It was good to remember that people loved me. To hold Noah when he napped. To walk through their vines. They'd sent out their first commercial bottles earlier this year, and I guessed it was going well.

They were happy, and even though I'd been allergic to happy when I'd first gotten to Seattle, it felt comforting now. Like there might be a future where I was, if I could just stop obsessing about Max.

Jerry waited for me by the entrance. He bent over to kiss my cheek, and we chatted about work. My mind couldn't stay on the conversation as I gave him answers to keep him talking so I wouldn't have to speak.

The restaurant, which was also a bar, had televisions on where they usually showed sporting events. Tonight, however, it was the Food Network. Jerry excused himself to use the bathroom, and I shook my head. What was wrong with me? Women were looking for Jerrys everywhere. Good-looking. Successful. Patient. Kind. Fuck my stupid stuck heart.

A voice I'd thought to never hear again caught my attention, and I jolted in my seat, turning around to find where it was coming from. The television screens?

Yes, there was Max. He spoke with Baker Monroe, celebrity chef of the moment. His name was sort of fitting. He liked to laugh about that on late-night programs.

Why was he talking to Max? I jumped off my chair and darted to the bar. It was crazy, but it was like I was dying to see him, like I'd been denied an essential vitamin that I now had to binge.

"Turn it up," I begged the bartender.

He shot me a look as he did it. "I guess you really like food."

The man had no fucking idea.

"We're so excited to have you join the Food Network family." Baker grinned at him. "And before we check out your new digs, I've got to ask you because I'm being assaulted by questions about you on Twitter, are you single?"

My heart fell. First time I was seeing him—and he looked good, albeit slightly skinnier than he had been with me—and I was about to hear he was taken. I'd survive this. I would. Somehow.

"I'm not with anyone," Max answered, running a hand through his hair. "But I'm taken."

Baker scrunched up his face. "What does that mean?"

"It means that I met the love of my life and I lost her. I let her go because I was a big, stupid idiot. I'd use other words, but we're on television. I don't want you to have to edit it out." Baker laughed, Max didn't. "I let her go. And I...I continue to believe that someday, she'll come back to me, that she'll come back home."

I swallowed. It had to be me, right? He had to be talking about me? Dizziness made my head spin. I could hardly breathe. Shallow, unsteady breaths were all I could manage. Unless he met someone else, and he let them go too?

"I think our audience just fell more in love with you, Max. Whoever you are out there, come home to him. He's sorry." Baker laughed again and then stepped backward. "So we're here in Portland. You had a huge hit with Hyperion in New York and then unbelievably sold it and came back here to Maine. Just miss home?"

257

Max winced. "Couldn't stay there. Hard to explain, but it seemed like all the heart left the city. So I came here, where I probably always should have been, to make this restaurant. I've been lucky because people have embraced it ever since."

"They sure have. That's why you're our first guest on *Hometown Pride*. We love when famous chefs bring their talent home, and so do our viewers." This had to be a new show. I'd never heard of it. "Let's take a look inside your place. The camera panned back. And there it was. The name of his new restaurant was Hope.

"Hey." Jerry came out of the bathroom. "What's going on?" He stared at the screen. "I feel like I'm missing something."

No, I was. Or not something. Some*one*. And I was so tired of it.

I DIDN'T TEXT my sisters. Or Michael. I didn't do anything after I left Jerry in the restaurant but sink into my couch and stare at my phone. That was how I stayed for almost twenty-four hours. I'd get up, eat, drink, and then go back to staring at my phone.

Eventually, enough was enough. I knew what I was going to do. How could I not? He'd just gone on national television and said he wanted me to come back. I'd told him to leave me alone, and he'd done that, but he'd named his restaurant after me. And he'd essentially asked me to come back to him.

I grabbed my phone. First, I tried to use the reservation app and found that it was filled. There was no way to get a table at his place. Not surprising. Everyone wanted to eat Max's food. With shaking hands, I called the number on the website. Maybe there was a waitlist I could get onto.

The woman who answered said, "Hello, it's a great day at Hope. How can I help you?"

She was perky, and it was strange to hear her say my name, even though she wasn't, not really. I'd gotten used to hearing people say *I hope,* or *hopeful* over the years. This was different.

"Hi." I cleared my throat. "My name is Am—Hope Radford, and I was... That is…can I please get on your waitlist for a table?"

The woman gasped. "Did you say your name is Hope Radford?"

Yes, and it was the first time I'd said my own name in over a year. Maybe the last time had been introducing myself at Max's family home? "Yes, that's right."

"Oh, Ms. Radford. Hello. Yes. Um. We have a table for you. Every night. It's always open for you. Chef keeps it there for you. Wow. Okay. Do you want to come right now?"

I would have. Right then, if I hadn't been across the country. "I…I'm afraid I'm not in town. I need to come to Portland. I can't do that before, um, Monday." It looked like I was getting a flight the next day and missing work and school. *Fine. That is fine.*

"Great. Monday it is. What time?"

"What time?" I had to be better at this. This woman must think I was nuts. But he saved me a table every night? "How about seven?"

"Great. See you then. Oh, can I get your phone number, so I can confirm your reservation?"

"No, you can't." I hung up. If I changed my mind, or chickened out, I couldn't let Max have that. I'd barely survived him the first time around. Was I really going to do this again?

I was, and I did. As I landed in Portland, I was still

stunned that I was doing it. I almost turned around in the airport and flew back home. I stopped myself. I'd come this far. Worst case scenario, seeing Max would be awful and it would help me get over this lunacy. Best case... *What is the best case?*

I didn't dare to hope for anything.

It took me way too long to get dressed. I'd brought five outfits, and I almost went shopping to buy five more. The truth was that I looked totally different than the last time he'd seen me. He might very well not be attracted to me anymore, and that was a scenario too.

A bad one.

My hotel was down the street from his restaurant, so I walked on leaden feet toward him. Someone held the door open, and I stepped inside. Immediately, the smell was familiar. Someone was cooking the barbecue sauce he'd made for me. I caught my breath and stared at my feet. I could still leave. *Go right now.*

"Can I help you?" The chipper voice from the phone addressed me.

"Hi." I looked up. "I'm Hope Radford."

"Oh." She brightened up. She must be eighteen years old. Cute. Perky. I hoped she got to stay this way. "I'm so excited you're here. I'll take your coat." She did, and then I followed her to a table at the back of the restaurant.

Away from the other tables.

Perky hostess scurried away to be replaced by a nervous waiter. His eyes darted left and right before he spoke to me. "Hi. Welcome to Hope. What can I get you to drink?"

"I... Hello. Thanks. I need a glass of wine. Something red. I don't care what." That was a change too. I drank in public lately. It was one of the first brave things I'd started doing in Seattle. I didn't drink much, but I did have wine at restaurants.

"Be right back with your menu." He scurried off, and I stared at my hands. I'd never eaten alone in a restaurant before. Other than Max's kitchen, and that had hardly been alone.

Like I could sense he was suddenly there, Max's presence moved over me. I lifted my head. He came out of the kitchen and walked over to the bar. He didn't look at me, not once. Instead, he pulled out a bottle of wine, grabbed two glasses, ignored the bartender, and with a quick turn, strode toward my table.

For a second, my heart forgot to beat.

Then it raced to catch up and wouldn't stop. He met my gaze and tilted his head to the side as he took me in, his eyes widening, registering the shock of my new appearance. Yes, it was really fucking different. Did he hate it? Damnit. I shouldn't care, but I did.

He walked over and stopped, setting down the bottle in front of me and then the glasses. "Hope." His voice was low, barely a whisper. "I... That was so brilliant, changing your hair."

Max sank rather than sat in the chair right next to me. Not across. I could immediately smell his warm, sandalwood soap scent. It was heady and didn't help my racing heart. I touched my hair because he'd mentioned it. "Thanks. It seemed…the thing to do. I saw you on television."

He took an audible breath. "Good. That was my," he gave me a wry smile, "hope. That you would. I wasn't sure what else to do. I was going to try magazines next. And then morning shows." He visibly swallowed. "Surely you know that you're safe now. That the mob isn't looking for you. You could go back to your hair color, even, if you wanted to."

I knew that, yes, but how did he know? "It was you? You made them leave us alone."

His nod was fast as he poured two glasses of wine. He set one in front of me and one in front of himself. The waiter appeared, and Max shook his head. "There's a set menu for Hope. She doesn't need that. Just bring out what Anna gives you."

"Yes, Chef." The poor, scared waiter scurried off. I almost felt bad for him, but I had no room for anyone's emotions but my own at the moment.

Anna was there? They came with him when he moved to Portland. That must be wonderful for him. "All you're going to do is nod? You don't want to say more on that subject?"

"I…I didn't listen to you. I tried to find you. Right away. I yelled at my sister for being an asshat, and then I realized what I'd done. That you were gone. That I'd fucked the whole thing up." He cleared his throat. "I don't know that I really understood things yet. How…how much I had destroyed, but I thought I could find you, stop you. You were gone already. Then you weren't in New York." He took a long sip of his wine, and I did the same thing. He watched me drink mine. "I'm glad you can do that now. Have alcohol in public. I worried about you drinking alone, among other things."

I stared at the red liquid and then noticed the bottle. "That's Zeke's brand."

"Yes. We serve it here. He won't talk to me, but I buy his stuff. Michael won't talk to me either. Wouldn't tell me where you were and then blocked me. Then you sold your apartment. I think by then, I understood."

I leaned forward. "Understood what?"

Max touched my wrist. One long swipe of his hand across my butterfly. I caught my breath, my body buzzing from the brief connection. He really was like a drug to me—one I desperately wanted to take.

"That I love you. Deeply. Profoundly. It's different for me than it is for other people, but you were right—I can love. At least, I can love you."

I could hardly form words. "Different?"

"I couldn't find you, not anywhere. You stopped posting online. You vanished. No internet searches. You were just gone. So, I...I became consumed with getting you safe. If I couldn't be with you, I could at least make sure you were safe wherever you were. So yes, among other things, I found the man who owes me favors, even though he is all but findable, and I cashed in."

I took his hand. "Thank you, Max."

There was such warmth in his eyes when he looked at me. "You don't ever need to thank me. Not ever, my Hope."

"No, I need to apologize to you."

He winced. "For what? I think you have that backward."

"For placing you in that position, with the mob coming and no time, demanding answers. It was my way or no way at that moment. Your back was against the wall. It wasn't at all the emotionally appropriate way to do that."

He scooted his chair closer just as the waiter arrived, setting down two bowls of soup. Max couldn't possibly expect me to eat that?

"Hope, I wasn't wrong—I don't love like other people. I...I am more obsessive than I have any right to be, but that is how I need you, how I love you. It's not just a void to be without you, but a total absence of sunlight and anything good."

Was I crying? "Max..."

"You paid off my restaurant. I know it was you. How did

you do that? Even you aren't walking around with that kind of cash."

I wiped at my face with a laugh. "I'm not nearly as rich as I once was, trust me on that." Although both Bridget and Zeke were investing my money, so it was better than it was. "I sold my mother's painting. Remember the sad one? *September*?"

"Fuck." He reared back and closed his eyes. "You didn't have to do that, love, you really didn't. You didn't owe me anything. You didn't fuck up my life. I could have done any number of things I didn't do. I could have hired a PR firm. I could have approached you and asked you to say something publicly. I could have even responded myself. I did nothing but sink. That's on me, not you. Please stop thinking you screwed up my life when you *are* my whole life, and I cannot do without you."

Now it was my turn to scoot closer. "Max, I didn't do it only because I screwed up your life."

"Then why did you do it?" We were just a breath away from each other.

"Because I love you, and you needed it, and it felt like goodbye. Like I could give you something that you could have for the rest of your life. And sure, yes, there was some element of me wanting to fix what I'd broken. Yes, that was there. That's always going to be a part of me. I'm not ashamed of it."

He squeezed my hands in his. "I want to be worthy of you, Hope."

"I don't even know what that means." Worthy of me? I wasn't anything particularly special.

He shook his head. "I need you to let me make up this year I took from us. Can you do that? Can you let me make you so happy every day that you'll eventually forgive me for taking this year from us? Please, baby."

"Max." I ran my hand down the side of his face. "It might have been a good thing. Not that we both suffered without each other, not that we had to hurt, but because the time forced me to get some help I might not have otherwise gotten. To do some things. Figure myself out. Get stronger."

He ran his finger over my tattoo again. "Get inked."

"Yes." I grinned at him. "And other things."

Max tilted his head again in that questioning way that he did. "Other things?"

"I'll tell you if you elaborate. I think you said other things earlier yourself." I forced him to meet his gaze. "What other things did you do?"

"I…" He spoke in a very low voice. "I used my considerable set of abilities to rid the world of someone who didn't deserve to still be here after what he did to you."

He'd killed Shawn. "You could have been hurt."

His mouth fell open. "Hope, I just told you that I did a thing that most people will never do, and that I'm obsessed in how much I love you, and you are concerned that I might have hurt myself?"

I nodded. "I'm glad that you didn't. And…and thank you, Max. Thank you for ridding the world of him." I pressed our foreheads together. "I got my belly button pierced. That is my other thing."

He kissed me. I was so glad he did. It was what I needed more than I did my next breath. Just his mouth against mine. He smoothed his finger down the side of my face as he kissed me again. The waiter arrived with another dish, and Max surged backward in the chair before he dismissed him with his hand. "Tell Anna to hold the food."

"Right." The waiter ran again.

"You terrify him."

He scratched his head. "I've maybe been in a very bad mood for the last year."

"That so?" I wanted him to kiss me again. But we were in public. In his restaurant. I had to behave. Somehow.

"Well, my girl vanished. I couldn't find her. Couldn't make the tears that I made her shed go away. Couldn't beg her for forgiveness. Couldn't know if she were happy or healthy. If she was warm. It's put me off."

I kissed his cheek. "Seattle."

"That's where you've been?" He rubbed his face. "I should have looked there."

"The whole city? Searched the city all around until you found me?" I lifted an eyebrow.

"Whatever it took." His face said he was dead serious.

"I took a page from your book—close to family, but not too close. I went to school. Got a certificate so that I could actually work in fundraising for nonprofits and not just trade on my name and face. Learned some things. Got a job. I'm getting another certificate now. Or I hope I am. I might fail since I skipped out today. Used a fake name. Michael got me set up with paperwork. That's what I've been doing."

He was so quiet, I didn't know what to do. Should I just keep talking? "Hope, I have no right to ask you this. None. But could you please come home to me? Could you please come do all of those things here? Please."

266

CHAPTER 21

"WE HAVEN'T SPENT A DAY TOGETHER IN A YEAR. YOU MIGHT regret asking me that."

He tugged me so close to him that I practically sat on his lap. "I love you. However you've changed. Whatever you have done or will do. You are mine. I can close this place down and come to Seattle if that is what you want. I can do that. You are all I need."

That actually sounded completely wrong. He'd created a life, and all these people had jobs because of him. No, he wasn't going to shut anything down and move for me. That would be just awful to do to these people, even if they were afraid of him because he'd been in a bad mood for an entire year.

"I'll come." I said the words that I knew would change everything for me. "It's going to take me a little bit to get things together and to get Michael to change my life back to my real name. But I'll come."

He pushed back his chair. "Can we get out of here? I know you must be starving. I will feed you tonight. Myself. Please."

I rose. "You don't have to keep saying please to me. Of course, we can get out of here if that's what you want."

He put his arm around me and dragged me against him. "I do."

We left there just like that. I hadn't eaten a bite, but we'd certainly made a scene, even though we'd been quiet. All eyes were on us.

He didn't live far from the restaurant, within walking distance. Once we got into the place, it was just as I would have pictured it—sparsely decorated with no pictures anywhere and just enough furniture to function.

"I didn't have any pictures of us. Not any." He put his arms around me from behind when I stopped in the living room. "Nothing but your old social media to stare at all the time."

I spun around in his embrace and put my arms around his neck. I don't know what I would have said because he kissed me, hard. It was possessive, and it was clear he had no intention of stopping. Max kissed and kissed and kissed me. His tongue slid over my bottom lip, then he bit me. Our tongues danced together, and he moaned. It was like one thing was happening and then the next. I couldn't think or process. All I could do was feel.

Was it possible that my body could have been this lonely for his? It was like he was pooling energy back into me where I had been completely depleted from needing him and not having him. Finally, I pulled back enough to speak to him. "I was so tired from missing you."

"Exhausted. You are life to me. I wish I could have known myself better before you were gone. Then I would have said yes, Hope, I love you. But I'm going to love you in a really fucked up way because I've got a number of screws loose."

"Your brand of fucked up works for me, Max."

He picked me up and carried me to the bedroom. I knew these sheets. They were the same one he'd had at his cabin. He laid me down on the bed, gently, and with the sweetest, easiest movement, he came over me so that his body hovered over mine.

"I really want to be inside of you."

I kissed his chin. "That's what I want too. It is the endgame for what we're doing."

He smiled down at me. This was real. This was happening. I was there. With him. "What I mean is that I want to be inside of you. No condom. Just you. Just me. Nothing between us."

That sounded like heaven. "You can have that."

Max lifted his eyebrows. "You're ready to potentially have a baby? I would love that. Putting a baby inside of you is one of my fantasies. I didn't think you'd want that just yet."

He smelled like mine. "Don't worry about that. I'm on the pill now. Not going to get me pregnant, not yet."

His face fell. Was he that disappointed that he couldn't get me pregnant right this second? We were absolutely not in a place yet where we should be getting pregnant, not that I was opposed to the idea of having his babies. "What's the matter?"

"I...I'm just... I guess I didn't realize you'd be on the pill. I didn't really let myself think that you'd have been with someone else. I couldn't. You were mine, and I let you go. The fact that you were with someone else is my fucking fault. I just want to kill whomever it was. I need a second to reset."

I shook my head. "There hasn't been anyone else. I'm on the pill to take care of my bad periods. The cramps. The doctor in Seattle thought it was ridiculous I wasn't already on it."

Max blinked. For a second, he looked downright befuddled. "Oh, I thought…" He closed his eyes. "Shit."

I smirked at him. "Actually, if you want the honest-to-god truth, I was thinking about having sex with someone else." His eyes flew open. "And then you showed up on television, so I broke up with the guy and came here."

"Thank fuck I filmed that segment." He took a long breath. "Have I spoiled the moment?"

I ground my hips into his. "Not possible."

"Good."

Max went back to kissing me, and I let myself get lost in it. Slowly, we undressed each other. I'd been right when I thought he looked thinner on television. Still gorgeous, but leaner. Apparently, he'd been cooking for others but not eating any of it himself. He smoothed his hand over my belly button with the ring before he smirked at me. A second later, he tongued it.

I moaned. Yes, this was the image I'd had that I'd gotten myself off on so many times. Max had just done it. Exactly like I'd wished he would.

"Oh, you like this." He kissed my stomach. "And I really like this new decoration you gave me to play with on your body."

I grinned at him. "Can I admit that when I got it, I kept thinking of you?"

"Yes, you can admit that. I fucking love it."

I ran my hands over his body, feeling his muscles jump beneath my touch. I couldn't believe I was back in his arms. He loved me. The thought spurred me to kiss his chest. Then his stomach. He groaned. "You do that, and I'm going to be in you very, very fast."

Leaning back, I stared up at him. "What would be wrong with that?"

"Fuck, Hope."

That seemed to really spur him onward. He was all over me like he couldn't stay in one place long before he had to have his mouth someplace else. Both of my thighs. My stomach, my hips, my chin. I could hardly hold on to him, and then he was there.

He placed a finger inside of me and pulled it out to suck on the taste. "You are so wet."

I caught my breath. Wow. That was really hot. "Probably have been since you first walked into the restaurant."

His smile was slow. "Nothing between us."

"Nothing."

I wanted to stroke him, but I never got the chance. Max pushed himself inside of me. Balls to tip, all at once. I cried out. Yes, suddenly I was full where I had been empty. "Stay still." I spoke in a low whisper. "I just want to feel like this for one more second, so I can remember it all the time."

"Hope, open your eyes and look at me." I hadn't realized I'd closed them, but I did just as he asked. I've give him anything right then. "I will stay wherever you want me for as long as you want me, but we are going to have lots of moments like this. You won't have to remember it. We'll be like this forever and ever."

I touched his cheek. "Okay."

"I swear I'm going to make you believe it." He kissed me, the sweetest caress, and I sighed against his lips.

"If you want to move, you can. Thank you for the moment."

He shook his head. "Don't ever thank me for anything."

Then his body took mine. These were the moments I'd craved—the way Max always knew how to move, how to make me respond to him. The way that he just defined sex to me. No one could ever make me feel the way that he did right then. I wrapped my legs around him and held on. Each thrust, each pull, better than the last.

We moaned together, and when I made a particular noise —I didn't even know what it was—his lips met mine, begging me for more, like he wanted to drink me down, ingest whatever it was that I'd done.

He scooted us back until I was up against his headboard. His movements were rough, and I was glad for something to hold on to. I couldn't get enough. There was no such thing as too much right then. Just more. I needed more.

Then I exploded. A years' worth of nothing became something right then. He was inside of me, his skin touching mine, his body claiming mine again. I needed to be owned by him. I wasn't ashamed of it, so I took it as my own because I had him too. He belonged to me.

Max spent inside of me. For the first time, I felt that warmth. It filled me in a new way, and I reveled in it.

He smoothed his thumb over my bottom lip. "I like this grin."

I bit the tip of his thumb, and he grinned. "Forgive me, Hope."

"You're forgiven," I whispered back, and he nodded. Max rose and came back with a washcloth to clean me. He was gentle, almost reverent. Then he tugged me against him in the bed. "Can't get you close enough."

"That's okay." I pressed my head against his chest. "I like being this close."

"I can't spare you my need for you. Can't put it away where I can't touch it. Won't do that. And I haven't figured out how to tame it yet. Soon. When I'm certain I have you with me, I'll be able to push it down, but this is what I never let myself acknowledge. This…need I have for you. Essential."

"Not complaining." I closed my eyes and breathed him deep into my lungs. "I have to get a ticket in a second, have to pull away to book a plane back to Seattle, so that I can pack up my life, quit my job. To come back here."

He loosened his grip. "For that, I'll let go."

I shook my head and made myself move away from him to grab my phone where it had fallen on the ground when we'd undressed. I had a million texts. My sisters had officially seen his show. They didn't know I was there, but their curiosity was going to have to wait until morning. Max was getting all my attention. I used an app and quickly made arrangements to leave the next day. He rolled onto his side to watch me.

"What name were you living under?" He stroked his finger over my thigh.

"Amelia West." Having gotten the arrangements done quickly, I went back to where I'd been, and he rolled onto his back to let me.

Good. I was settled. I was there. He was mine. He loved me. "Say it."

He kissed my hair. "I love you so fucking much, Hope."

I closed my eyes.

I roused just a bit when he tugged me against him. "You moved too far. Sorry, baby. Go back to sleep."

That was perfectly fine. I wanted to be that close too. "So much better."

"It is." I knew he'd understand.

I woke again when his finger slipped inside of me. This time, I smiled. That really was the best way to rouse from a dream.

273

~

THE SUN STREAMING into the window woke me. I still lay smushed against Max, and that made me smile. We hadn't separated during the night, or if we had, he'd put me right back against him. Now, he was sound asleep, even snoring just a little. It was the tilt of his neck. I remembered that sometimes used to happen.

I lifted my head to admire him in the early morning light. He was beautiful. I stared at the clock. I had three hours left before I'd have to get up, go back to my hotel room to collect my things, and leave for the airport.

This whole thing was such a whirlwind. I'd gotten there, and I was going to leave again just to come right back. Crossing the country in bursts of speed to get where I needed to go.

His eyes fluttered open, and he blinked. "You really are here."

"I am." And I was going to be sad not to be when I got home to Seattle tonight. Now that I'd tasted this again, the absence would be even more acute.

"I'm sorry, but I have to come with you." He rolled over and grabbed his phone. "I know. It's too much, but I explained last night. I can't…I can't stop it just yet. I can't have you across the country right now. I have to be with you. I'll help you pack."

My mouth fell open. "That's perfect."

He stopped touching his phone. "Really?"

"I was just thinking that I was going to be wrecked tonight without you. Please come if you can. I have to pack. Quit my job. Unenroll from school. And go see Layla, Zeke, and Noah. They're having another baby."

He leaned on his elbow. "Do you think Zeke will let me in the house?"

I smiled at him. "He'd better."

It was crazy how fast things moved after that. We didn't have seats together, but Max shot a pointed look at the guy next to me while he pretty much demanded—rather than asked—that they switch, and it happened. I rested on his shoulder and watched movies on my phone.

Then he was in my apartment, poking around at my things for a minute before he threw me on the bed and took me first fast and then slowly. Then both again. I woke up tangled in both the sheets and Max the next morning.

Packing sucked, but he was better at it than me, and we were halfway through my apartment in no time. Max did things I hadn't thought about. He called movers, arranged for my car to be transported, and only grumbled a little bit about not coming with me to quit my job. I didn't want him sitting in the car while I was in there for however long. Plus, I had a surprise I wanted to do without him with me.

My hair stylist was thrilled to put my hair back to red. It wasn't my exact color but it was close, and growing it out would be less startling. My boss wasn't thrilled with me. There was nothing I could do. I'd pick Max anytime, I just knew I would. I lived a year of my life without him. I didn't want to anymore. Unenrolling from my certificate program was fast, and I arrived back home to find he'd packed my whole apartment.

Max actually stumbled when he saw me with my red hair before the smile stretched his lips. "There you are, my redhead."

I wanted to be his whatever. His anything.

"Forgive me?" he asked before we went to sleep, still panting from making love once again.

"Yes," I told him again. His nod was the same as it had been in Portland. He wrapped me against him.

For two insomniacs, we were both falling asleep at night, which was such a gift unto itself.

The trip to Layla's was familiar to me by then, and Max chatted with me about the upcoming menu and his signing on with the Food Network. "I wanted to be able to give you the life you deserve. I knew that this would push me over the edge. We'd be able to have whatever you wanted."

I stared at him. He'd insisted on driving. "You know I don't care about that. It's so much less important to me than anything else."

"I do know that, actually. That doesn't mean I didn't want to give you the life you should have. The restaurant is paid off. You sold your mom's painting to give that to me. We should be able to live really well now, not worrying about things the same way I had been."

I sighed. "Max...I think we've both proven we can express our love in dramatic ways. If you want to compare who did what, I think you win in the acts of love game. What you gave me...I still can't fathom what it cost you."

"Nothing. It cost me nothing. He didn't deserve to keep living."

I smiled at him. "I was actually thinking about the Russian mob thing."

Max winced. "Yeah...that cost me nothing new. Those were old costs."

"Thank you for everything you've done, but if you hate filming, don't do it."

He shook his head. "We'll see."

The vineyard was hopping with activity, but inside the house, it was quiet. Zeke shot Max a look when we arrived, but then he extended his hand which, after a poignant pause, Max accepted.

"A year. You could deal with the Russians faster than you could find Hope?" Zeke walked into the kitchen to get some wine.

"You knew?" I practically shouted at Zeke, while Noah ran up for me to pick him up in my arms. He always did that when I came over. Much to Bridget's chagrin, I was his favorite auntie, but what was he supposed to do when he saw her almost never?

Layla leaned against the wall. Her pregnancy was showing now. She cradled her swollen stomach.

Zeke shot me a look. "Who else was it going to be, if it wasn't me or Michael?"

I'd asked Michael to start the process of bringing me back to being me and not Amelia anymore. He was working on it.

"Do you know how many times I called you over the last year?"

Zeke smirked. "Why should I make it easy on you? If you could find the Russians, you should have been able to seek out Hope. Looks like you worked it out. Good job with the Food Network move."

"Thanks." Max took the wine from him. "You know I sell your product at my restaurant."

Zeke grinned. "Thanks for that."

I groaned, and Layla shook her head. "They're working it out. Go sit down. He's out."

It was Noah she motioned toward, and I realized that yes, he'd conked out right on my shoulder. This was the second time he'd done so upon my arrival. Last time, his nap lasted for two hours. I loved his trust, and my heart clenched with my love for this little boy—the cutest boy ever born, I was convinced of it.

I sat down on her couch and realized the room had fallen silent. They all watched me. My gaze met Max's. I really had no idea what he was thinking right then, but it was intense. His gaze was heated. I didn't look away. He was mine, alongside all the intensity that came with him.

"What if we went to Vegas? Right now?" Max asked me while we drove back to Seattle.

"What?" I stared at him. "Why? Are you feeling like you want to go gamble?"

He shook his head. "Never. I'm not a gambler because I know sometimes you can lose. No, I want to marry you. Right now. Tonight. Or tomorrow really early in the morning. Do you want a big wedding? If you want that, we can have that, but that means my family, as you know. I'd love to see you in a dress. Don't get me wrong. I would. However, I'd rather have you be my wife tonight."

I gasped. "Max...um. I think you have to ask me first before you plan the wedding."

His smirk was stupidly adorable. "Yes, there is that. Hope, will you marry me? Will you make me the happiest man there ever was? Will you let me make you happy every day? Will you be my wife? Tonight?"

I dramatically sighed. "So what you're saying is you want to ask me what I want for dinner and discuss vacation plans with me?"

"Hope, I would cook you anything you want, anytime you want it. And I'll go anywhere in the world with you. Please just let me come. Anything you want. Anywhere you want." His expression was serious. "I want all the things that married couples do. I never want to argue with you, but if we do, then I want to make up right then. I want to plan a future. I want to wake up with you. I want to see you holding our baby like you held Noah. Our baby. In your arms. I want to see you get big with that baby. I want to get old with you. You know I'm older than you, so I'm going to go first. I want to look at you at the end, know you're there with me, and—"

"Stop," I said, interrupting him. Tears had hit my eyes. "I can't...I can't think of that. Okay? Not that. Not ever that image. I already live with a ghost. I'm not going to add some sort of future anticipatory grief to that. Don't ever say that again. None of us know what's going to happen. You know that I'm never going to be entirely...normal. I still sometimes have to lock and relock my doors. Things like that. Are you sure you want a wife who does that kind of thing? The mother of your children to do that?"

He let go of the steering wheel to tangle his hand in my hair. "I want you, Hope. Everything that comes with that. I'm fucked up too. I could start listing what that is again if you need. I love you, Hope. Everything about you."

"You don't want to take a breath and get used to having me around again before you commit to this?"

He scrunched my hair harder. "Because you think I might change my mind? I know who you are. This is your self-doubt rearing up. Do you need some time? To decide about me? It's okay if you do. I am going to work every day, married or not, to be worthy of your love. To be at the point where you can say unequivocally, yes, Max, I'll marry you."

"Yes, Max. I'll marry you."

He audibly caught his breath. "Thank you, Hope. Thank you."

"In Vegas. Tonight." I didn't need or want a white wedding. There wasn't a thing about that experience that I wanted.

I just wanted Max.

"Even if the food I asked for was frozen fish sticks?" I'd developed a little bit of a taste for them over the last year.

He made a face. "Maybe I draw the line at that."

When he kissed me that night in a wedding chapel the concierge suggested, and I officially became his wife, I was home.

"Forgive me?" he asked in my ear.

I nodded. "I do, Max."

"Love me?"

I kissed his cheek. "In every way. Love me?"

"Completely."

EPILOGUE

MAX

I HATED traveling because it took me away from home, but I had to do it to film and so I did it. Anna handled the restaurant just fine when I was away. Maybe better, in some ways, since she had no temper. And my beloved Hope was a superstar at home with our babies. Still, it was like hell to be away from her. From them.

As quietly as I could, I opened the door to enter our home and closed it just as quietly. It was midnight. I hoped they were asleep. Of course, if Hope were out cold, I'd have to wake her in one of the ways that she liked.

There were many, many ways.

Only she wasn't asleep. In fact, she was wide awake, on the couch, with both girls attached to her breasts. This was very unusual. Nicole and Chloe had both been sleeping through the night for three months. We'd been really lucky that they were such good sleepers and started doing that at four months old.

Hope lifted her gaze to meet mine, her eyes wounded. I strode toward her, dropping my bags. "What's the matter?"

My heart pounded hard. If something had happened when I was out of town, I was going to freak the fuck out. My daughters' eyes were both closed as they nursed, one on each of my wife's breasts. This was basically sleep feeding. In the dim light, I could still see their red hair starting to form curls.

"They're sick. I'm sick." She winced. "Keep a distance. You don't need this, trust me. They can't get comfortable, and I don't blame them. This…this feels terrible. Bad cold. I took them to the doctor this morning."

I knelt, ignoring her statement to stay away, and placed my hand on her forehead. Luck or genes or whatever it was, I had a really good immune system. I almost never got sick, and if I did, so be it. Hope was hot, and so were the girls.

"Did you take yourself to the doctor? And why didn't you tell me? When did you get sick?"

She shifted slightly. "Yesterday. I didn't want to worry you. What were you going to do from New Orleans?"

"Come home." I sighed. This was the shit that kept me up at night when I was away. Something could happen.

"You had one day of filming left. It's a cold, it sucks, but it's not terrible." She closed her eyes. "Seriously, my love, stay away."

I put a hand on Chloe's back and moved her until she let Hope go. "Give her to me. Both of them." I did the same thing to Nicole, and Hope didn't fight me on it. They were going in their crib, the one we kept in our room for times like this. They didn't wake when I set them down, and I felt their heads again. Not too hot. Warmer than they should be, but not scary.

After they were settled next to each other the way they always wanted to sleep, I took a second just to make sure all was well. I'd been terrified when I heard there were two, because...fuck. Multiples obviously ran in Hope's family, although Layla hadn't had any yet. Two boys, born years apart.

My daughters were perfection, like their mother, and even though people seemed to think that other than the hair color, they looked like my side of the family, I knew it was bullshit. All I could see when I looked at them was their beautiful mother. My Hope, who had, for some reason, decided I was worth taking back into her heart. Her love wasn't something I ever took for granted.

I went back into the living room to find her asleep on the couch. She was a lot hotter than our daughters. I picked her up, and she stirred. "Thanks for taking them. I might have just let them stay there all night. I don't have the wherewithal to move."

She was way too hot for my liking. "Did you take something for your temperature?"

My life, who I held in my arms, shook her head. "Can't."

"Why can't you?"

Her sigh moved through me. "I'm pregnant. Surprise!"

"What?" I stopped abruptly. "When? What?"

Her smile was fast and then gone as she closed her eyes, pressing her head against me. "I'm pregnant. Surprise."

Well...so much for breastfeeding acting as birth control. My heart swelled. *Another baby*. They were going to be so close in age to our twins. *Fuck*. It could be twins again. Or triplets. I couldn't go there in my head right then. Whatever we were facing, we were facing it together. I did all the filming so we could get help if we needed it. Hope never wanted it, but if there were more than one again, I would insist.

"Thank you, my love." I kissed her cheek. "Thank you for this family."

I meant it in every fiber of my being. I'd never thought I could have our life or even thought I wanted it. This was everything.

I laid her down on the bed. "You can take something. I know you don't want to when you're pregnant." I remembered it from the last round. "But you're going to right now because I don't like how hot you are. The baby will be fine."

She was basically unmoving while I took off her socks until she spoke again. "This is Trina's fault."

Well, that wasn't surprising somehow. Hope had spent part of the week at my mother's so that she could have company and my family could fawn over the babies. I liked that she'd been with them. Most of her work was virtual, so she could do it anywhere. "What did my sister do?"

"She brought her sick kids to your mother's house. Who brings sick kids to babies? Who does that?" She groaned.

Things were never going to be peaches and cream between Trina and Hope. Trina had a lot to make up for, and she knew it. Hope was kind to her, but damn if there were tense undercurrents, and I was on my wife's side. Trina could earn back Hope's trust or not.

I wasn't sure I would ever really believe in her again. I handed her some pills that were okay for her to take, and she swallowed them down with the water next to the bed.

I climbed in next to her and turned off the light. Our daughters snored in the corner in their crib. Hope rolled toward me. "I'm going to get you sick. Go in the other room."

"No." I ran my hands through her hair. This was my happy place. My love.

My phone dinged, and I picked it up to look. Hope officially snored against my side. I kissed her forehead, looking at my phone.

Going to Russia to get Bridget.

It was from Michael. What? Why was Bridget in Russia? "Baby?" I said, but Hope didn't budge. I stroked her back. "Hope?"

She slept comfortably next to me. Tonight would be one of those times I didn't sleep. That was fine. I was used to it. The girls needed me, Hope might, and now I had to worry about her sister.

Why is she in Russia?

I waited for the answer.

I'll text more later. This is Justin's fault. Tell Hope not to worry, I'll bring her sister home.

That wasn't likely. Hope was going to worry, so I wasn't going to tell her until her fever went away. She was mine to take care of. Period. End of story.

I texted Zeke.

How freaked out are you?

It took him a moment to answer. *How do we convince them they don't want to go to Russia?*

Fuck if I knew. I'd figure it out. I held my wife. My everything. Nothing was coming near my family. Not ever.

THANK you so much for reading Redheaded Redemption (Redheads #2). If you have a moment and could leave a review for this book, I'd be so grateful. Be on the lookout for Real Men Love Redheads, Michael and Bridget's story coming soon!

· · ·

AND PLEASE TURN the page for a complete list of my books.

Please Turn the page for a complete list of my books

ABOUT THE AUTHOR

As a teenager, I would hide in my room to read my favorite romance novels when I was supposed to be doing my homework.

I am the mother of three adorable boys and I am fortunate to be married to my best friend. I live in Austin Texas where I am determined to eat all the barbecue in town.

I am in love with science fiction, fantasy, and the paranormal and try to use all of these elements in my writing. I've been told I'm a little bloodthirsty so I hope that when you read my work you'll enjoy the action packed ride that always ends in romance. I love to write series because I love to see characters develop over time and it always makes me happy to see my favorite characters make guest appearances in other books.

In my world anything is possible, anything can happen, and you should suspect that it will.

I'd love to hear from you! Please visit my website at www.rebeccaroyce.com to sign up for my newsletter and learn about my books!

Here's where you can find me online:

Rebecca's Randomness Reading Group https://www. facebook.com/groups/RebeccasRandomness/

https://www.rebeccaroyce.com

https://www.facebook.com/authorrebeccaroyce/

www.twitter.com/rebeccaroyce

Instagram: rebeccaroyce79

Cheers!!

Rebecca

OTHER BOOKS BY REBECCA ROYCE...

Contemporary Romance

Redheads:

Redhead on the Run

Redheaded Redemption

Real Men Love Redheads (coming soon)

Reverse Harem Story (completed series)

Unconventional

Unexpected

Undeniable

Kiss Her Goodbye (completed series)

Hard Truths

Dark Truths

Deadly Truths

Stupid Boys (writing with C.R. Jane)

Stupid Boys

Dumb Girl

Crazy Love (coming soon)

Science Fiction Romance:

Wings of Artemis (completed series)

Kidnapped By Her Husbands

Rescued by Their Wife

Crashing Into Destiny

Meeting Them

Reclaiming Their Love

Loving Them

Ship Called Malice

Saving Them

Dark Demise

Light Unfolding

Still Waters

Rising Tides

Lost Star

Pointed Arrow

Illicit Minds

Illicit Senses

Illicit Connections

Illicit Alliance (coming soon)

Shifter World

Planet Bear

Planet Cat

Planet Wolf (coming soon)

Heart of the Nebula (writing with Heather Long) completed series

Queenmaker

Deal Breaker

Throne Taker

Stranded Hearts (writing with Vivien Jackson)

The Girl Who Fell From The Sky

The Girl Who Crossed The Stars (coming soon)

Through the Gates (writing with Skye MacKinnon)

Purgatory City

Infernal Land (coming soon)

Paranormal Romance:

Last Hope (completed series)

Tradition Be Damned

Past Be Damned

Destiny Be Damned

Compassion Be Damned

Future Be Damned

Dragon Wars (completed series)

Forever

Eternal

Always

Evermore

Endless

Wards and Wands (completed series)

Hexed and Vexed

Curse Reversed

Meow, Baby (novella, co-written with Ripley Proserpina)

Tragic Magic

Alpha's Sacrifice

Alpha's Truth

Alpha Enticing

Hidden Alpha (coming soon)

Cascade (completed series)

Haunted Redemption

Phoenix Everlasting

Fragility Unearthed

Persuasion Enraptured

The Swamp (completed series)

Hidden

Pursued

Caught

The Coveted (writing with Ripley Proserpina)

Eyes in the Darkness

Voices in the Darkness

Return to the Darkness

Prison Princess (part of the Prison Princess world, writing with CoraLee June)

Young Adult/New Adult Urban Fantasy/Post-Apocalyptic:

The Warrior (completed series)

Initiation

Driven

Subversive

Redemption

Justice

Warrior World (spin off of The Warrior, completed series)

Deacon

Micah

Jason

Fantasy Romance:

The Outsiders

Love Beyond Time

Love Beyond Sanity

Love Beyond Loyalty

Love Beyond Sight

Love Beyond Expectations

Love Beyond Oceans

Love Beyond Flames

Love Beyond Lies

Love Beyond Death (coming soon)

The Storm (writing with Ripley Proserpina) completed series.

Lightning Strikes

Thunder Rolling

The Deluge

Stand Alone Titles

Under The Lights

No Quitting Allowed